The Wo the Cabin

Also by Becca Day

The Girl Beyond the Gate
All Her Little Lies
The Secrets We Buried

The Woman in the Cabin

Becca Day

embla books

First published in Great Britain in 2024 by

Bonnier Books UK Limited
4th Floor, Victoria House, Bloomsbury Square, London, WC1B 4DA
Owned by Bonnier Books
Sveavägen 56, Stockholm, Sweden

A CIP catalogue record for this book is available from the British Library.

1

ISBN: 9781471416439

This book is typeset using Atomik ePublisher.

Printed and bound in Great Britain by Clays Ltd, Elcograf S.p.A.

Embla Books is an imprint of Bonnier Books UK.
www.bonnierbooks.co.uk

To Mum . . .
. . . who let me watch my first horror movie when I was nine.
It's no wonder my books are dark AF.

Prologue

Gemma

2016

I'm probably going to die tonight.

I grip the pen in my trembling hand so hard its plastic shell is starting to splinter and crack under the force. The tip has hovered over my sheet of paper so many times while I've tried to think of the best way to phrase what I want to say. How I'm going to be able to get all this across in so few words and so little time.

I haven't got long to write this letter. It's not the first I've written. Writing letters has been my way of staying sane, my way of holding onto a tiny shred of hope. Some to my Mum. Some to my sister. Some to myself. None will ever be sent. They'll live under the floorboard, where I keep them safe, hidden, and probably never see the light of day. But it gets the words out of my head, which is the main thing.

To be honest, I should probably be doing something else with my final hours. I'm sure most people spend their last day on Earth surrounded by loved ones, reminiscing about the good old days, flicking through family photo albums or scrolling through camera rolls.

Not me.

I don't think I've ever held a responsibility quite like this one. I've never done anything so important in all my life. My life that's about to be cut short.

Of course, I might not die tonight. There are two other options. A happily ever after, or a fate much, much worse than death. I'm not scared to die but I'm terrified of the potential alternative. And I'm so tired of being terrified.

Swallowing all that fear down, I press the nib of the pen to the page and start to write. Whether I die tonight or not, this letter will be my legacy. Potentially someone's saviour.

My final act of rebellion.

Part One

Part One

Chapter One

Mary

2024

He works long days. We're so far from anyone or anything out here he has to drive miles before he even hits the road, and then once he reaches his destination the work waiting for him varies. Sometimes, when he just has a few front garden rowan trees to prune and tidy, he'll be home just after lunch. I have to make sure I look nice, touching up my hair and makeup throughout the day, just in case he does return early. Most days, the days when he's removing branches from the tops of towering Scottish pines and firs, balanced in the thicket with his chainsaw, he'll be home late.

Today is one of those days.

I often find myself thinking about what he's doing. It seems so dangerous. There's a recurring vision that pops into my head every few weeks or so that one day I'll place dinner on the table and he just won't show up. That something awful will have happened to him at work and no one would know to contact me. What would I do? How would I feel?

I set the table, opting for our set of blue china today, paired with the lace place mats I sewed last week. Blue goes nicely with lace. It looks refined. Cal likes things to look refined. I lay out two plates, two sets of cutlery, two wine glasses and two water glasses, and pause, just like I do every day, to imagine what it would be like to set the table for a large, bustling, happy family. This is a lonely place. Just me and him.

There's something missing from the table. Flowers, I realise. I pick up my basket and a pair of scissors and step out into the garden, breathing in the fresh scent of my roses and peonies. The garden is really thriving this year, both the flowers and the vegetables. The chickens cluck in their enclosure at the bottom of the hill on which our cabin is perched, the only sound beyond the light whistling of the wind passing over the surrounding heather moorland. I select a particularly vivid bunch of pink roses and snip their stems, depositing them into the basket before carrying them back to the house and arranging them in a pot in the centre of the table. I pair them with a candle and admire my work, casting my eye around the small open-plan living area of the cabin to check for stray mess. The cabin smells of sawdust but the scent of the candle and flowers is starting to drown it out. Everything is exactly how he likes it to be when he returns home.

Cal will often bring things like the candles or the pot home with him. Gifts to make amends for leaving me alone for so much of the time. He says it's his way of giving me my very own slice of the world he disappears to each day. New thread for my sewing projects, paints in an array of beautiful gem tones, a puzzle perhaps, to help while away the hours. No television. They're just vessels for spouting the devil's agenda, according to Cal. Though, in all honesty, I have enough to be getting on with here that even if we did have a TV, it would probably end up just becoming another thing to dust. Sitting down to work on the latest puzzle or paint a canvas to brighten up the wooden walls is a rare treat. Procrastination and passivity are not an option, not if I want our cabin to continue to run smoothly, as Cal makes clear is my duty as his wife, the homemaker. Luckily Cal handles the slaughtering and preparing of the meat – as an animal lover, it makes my stomach churn just thinking about it – but I'm responsible for the rest of our food. Plucking endless weeds from the garden, foraging, collecting eggs, dehydrating fruit, kneading dough. Then there's the splitting and stacking of the firewood, fixing yet another leak in the roof, scrubbing the latest grass stains from Cal's utility trousers. By the time I've found the time to rest my bones beside the fire, all I usually want to do is fall asleep.

I wonder, momentarily, if Cal will bring anything home with

him today, though I wouldn't dare ask and risk his judgement, because, as he has told me often, greed is a sin. Cal always claims it's his life's work to ensure I have everything I could ever want or need. On the face of it, I do. I have a roof over my head. Clean clothes. An abundance of food. I've spent many an hour thinking about what I used to find value in, what I considered a necessity that I couldn't live without, back before I met Cal. My phone. God. If I ever found myself without it, it was like I was missing a limb. I once tore my bedroom apart looking for it. Now, all these years later, things like that seem so ridiculous. Material objects aren't what matters. Not really.

I'm standing at the stove, stirring the pot of beef stew so that the rich, mouth-watering aroma fills the tiny cabin, when I hear his truck rumbling up the dirt path. I crane my neck to look out of the window. The truck, though it's close enough for me to make out his outline behind the steering wheel, looks little more than an ant crawling towards me against the vast backdrop of our rugged environment. I often stare up at the towering mountains that surround us, cloaked in mist and perpetually shrouded in grey, at the slopes carpeted with ancient pines, their twisted branches reaching out like gnarled fingers, and wonder just how far he has to drive before he reaches any kind of civilisation.

I suppose it's one of life's ironies. When I was a little girl I used to draw pictures of cottages with white picket fences and flower-filled window boxes. It all felt very princessy to me. Somewhere straight out of a storybook. In the city we lived in when I was growing up I was never allowed out to play on my own. Too many scary men waiting to snatch up little girls. I always thought it would be nice to live somewhere quieter, away from all the crowds, where you don't feel the need to have three separate locks on your front door. I've now been here, living in the middle of nowhere, for . . . what? Ten years? I've lost count.

By the time the front door opens, bringing with it a sharp gust of wind, I've already plated up our dinner, given my hair a quick once-over with the brush, poured him a glass of wine and am stood waiting, red-lipped smile plastered on my face. It's part of the rules for how to be a good wife, snipped from a yellowing 1950s textbook and framed up on the kitchen wall.

> *Have dinner ready – This is a way of letting him know that you have been thinking about him and are concerned about his needs.*
> *Clear away the clutter – Your husband will feel that he has reached his haven of rest and order. Doing this for him will give you a lift also.*
> *Prepare yourself – Touch up your makeup, put a ribbon in your hair and be fresh looking.*
> *Minimise all noise – You've had plenty of time to do things during the day. Don't do them now. Be happy to see your husband and greet him with a warm smile.*

He shakes his jacket off his shoulders and hangs it on the hook beside the door. His eyes lift to meet mine and his face shifts. The strain of the day swapped for the satisfaction of being home and greeted, as ever, by a hot meal.

'Smells good, Mary,' he says in his thick Scottish accent.

I know it does. I'm a wonderful cook, having practised tirelessly over the years.

'Thank you.' I smile nicely. 'I've missed you.'

It's not true and he knows it, but he likes to hear it all the same.

He kicks off his boots before moving to slump into the dining chair, his legs stretched out under the table, head tilted back, eyes closed. He always looks exhausted when he gets back from a long day.

'Don't let it get cold.'

His eyes flick back open and he smiles. 'Couldnae let a meal like this go te waste.' With that, he picks up his fork and digs in, his appetite from a day of manual labour kicking in. I follow suit. It isn't until the tender meat lands on my tongue that I realise how hungry I am. When Cal works late like today it's often nearly dark before I'm able to eat dinner.

'How was your day?' I ask after a few minutes of uninterrupted feasting.

'Good. I had someone helping me out today. Young laddie. Max. D'ye remember him?'

I don't remember him. I've never met him. But I remember Cal talking about him, and I can imagine him. In my mind I picture Max with bright red hair that sticks up at all angles. 'The one just out of school?'

'Aye. Taken him on as a bit of an apprentice. Hard worker, he is. I'll make a brilliant tree surgeon out of him yet.'

I smile and return to my food, wondering if I'll ever get to meet Max. Maybe, if Cal brings him to the cabin one day, though I doubt it.

My fingers tap on the handle of my fork. Things have been good for a really long time now. I've done everything that's been expected of me. I don't remember the last time he was displeased. Very few arguments. Hardly any disagreements. I've become an expert in Cal. What he likes. What he doesn't like. What to say to make him feel better. What to absolutely not say under any circumstances. All these years I've kept him happy. I've become so used to my role as his wife, his perfect wife, that I know how to do it to a tee. I think it's about time he rewarded me.

'I was wondering . . . it was only a thought . . .' I lick my lips, wishing I had planned out what I was going to say properly before blurting anything out. 'It's just that I'm always here, at the cabin. I haven't really ever seen beyond the loch. I thought . . . and maybe it's a silly idea . . . but I thought maybe we could go away together? It doesn't have to be far or for very long. Just camping somewhere maybe.'

He stops eating.

'We cannae,' he says, not looking at me.

My heart sinks. I thought it might be an idea he'd like. Taking a holiday together is a typical husband and wife activity, after all. A fleeting thought, a longing for something different, something beyond the confines of our cabin.

'I don't understand. Why?'

He lets out a heavy sigh and leans back in his chair.

'I'd love to but it just wouldnae work. There's too much to do here, isn't there? Who will fix the ceiling if it starts to leak again and we're gone? Who will tend to the plants? Who will feed the chickens?'

Of course he's right. He's always right. Has always thought things through before I even reach the point of asking. It was stupid of me to even have suggested it.

'I'm sorry,' I say.

His face softens and he reaches forward, clasping my hand in his across the table. His thumb strokes the top of my hand.

'I know it cannae be easy for you, being alone here so often. But this is where you belong. You know that, aye?'

I nod.

He releases my hand and leans back in his chair. 'I'll get ye some more paints tomorrow, how does that sound? Once you've got a good painting on the go, you'll feel much better.'

'Thank you.' I smile, though I'm acutely aware that it hasn't quite reached my eyes.

When we finish dinner, we both let out satisfied sighs. I've eaten too much and I'm bloated, but I am careful to suck my stomach in as I stand to clear the table. I always end up using far more pans than necessary to cook meals and the post-dinner clean-up always takes hours. Sometimes I'm still cleaning by the time he finishes his crosswords and goes to bed. Tonight though, I can sense his desire for me to hurry up and as I'm scrubbing the last of the sauce from the pan I feel him close in behind me, his hands moving round to my front. He kisses my cheek softly as I empty and rinse the sink. As soon as I'm finished his strong hands turn me to face him. My eyes roam his face, sweeping across his defined jawline, his slightly scruffy head of thick dark hair, his intense gaze, but it's mere seconds before he nestles into my neck and his lips dot kisses along my skin.

When I first met Cal I knew if it wasn't love at first sight, it was the next closest thing. When you're twenty-one and you've been dragged on holiday to Scotland with your parents simply for the fact that it's tradition, even though you'd much rather be hanging out with your friends, spotting someone like Cal across the other side of a bar is always going to leave an impression. He's the kind of handsome you see in movies or read about in books. I didn't realise people like him actually existed.

The first night I went to that cute little pub I admired him from afar. The second night I actually worked up the nerve to talk to him and the rest, as they say, is history. We spent the entire evening together. I was sort of captivated by him. He seemed so different to anyone I had ever met. Brooding and thoughtful, mysterious. Mature. Not like the guys back in my uni who still thought fart jokes were hilarious. He was a gentleman too. Didn't even try to kiss me at the end of the evening. Just said he hoped we'd see each other again soon. Mum and Dad were furious when I got home so late but I didn't really care. I was already smitten, even if I wasn't ready to admit it to myself. If only I knew then what I know now.

It takes a few seconds for me to register that he's stopped kissing my neck and his eyes are now back on me. His brown irises look almost black. At first I think he's staring at me with the same primal hunger I've seen on his face so many times, but it's a different look than the one he usually gives me.

'Have ye been using that cream I got you?'

Something uncoils in my stomach.

'Yes. Every day.'

He raises his hand and traces the lines on my face, pausing at the tiny wrinkles that have formed beside my eyes. I noticed them the other day but didn't think they were prominent enough for him to spot them. It had been one of many moments of dread I've been experiencing these past few months. It is edging closer and closer to my birthday. thirty-one years old. The wrong side of thirty. I can slather my face with all the expensive creams he brings me home, but is it really possible to pause ageing in its tracks? I know he wishes it was. He prefers me to look young, flawless. A picture-perfect wife.

He's still staring at me and I wish I could shrink back into the counter behind me.

'I'll start using it twice a day.' I hold my breath, searching his expression for reassurance, for any sign that a few lines are not enough to dilute the love he feels for me.

There's a beat, and then his face relaxes into a smile. He slides his arms around my shoulders and pulls me close so that my face is pushed into his chest.

'You're such a good wife,' he says.

Chapter Two

The sex last night was intense and afterwards I lay exhausted and sweaty in his arms. I could tell by the way he immediately sprawled out, one arm flopped over his head and his other hand stroking my shoulder in lazy, rhythmic sweeps, that he was going to fall immediately to sleep. He usually does after we have sex. Work, eat, clean up, have sex, sleep, eat, and repeat. Our routine.

I rise early, as I always do. My body is conditioned to it, my eyes flickering open at the first hint of daylight, though the crusty residue lining my lids reminds me just how long I lay awake last night, staring at the ceiling. Blinking the tiredness away, I slide out from beside him, careful not to disturb his sleep, and make my way to the kitchen. The cabin is cloaked in a dim, early-morning haze as I set about getting the fire started. Sun-bleached photographs balance on top of the mantel. Pictures of our lives together, here in the solitude of the Highlands. One of the photos was from our anniversary picnic last year. We balanced the camera on a rock and sat together amongst the heather. I think that's the happiest I've ever seen him.

I move on to collecting the eggs and ensuring breakfast is ready and waiting for him on the table by the time he wakes. Did I dream last night? If I did, I don't remember it. Occasionally when I've woken I've remembered my dream, remembered the delicious, defiant feeling of hiding in the boot of his truck during one of his trips to town so that I could catch a glimpse, however brief, of the world he gets to see when he goes to work.

'Good morning,' I say in my most soothing voice as I gently shake his shoulder, cup of steaming coffee clasped in my other hand. He flinches, eyes snapping open. There are only a few seconds of displeasure though before he smiles and stretches.

'Mornin', beautiful.' He shuffles back in the bed so that he's sat up, and takes the coffee from me.

'Breakfast is on the table.'

'I'm so lucky to have you,' he says through a stifled yawn. Luck has nothing to do with it but I don't say that.

Breakfast is a silent affair, punctuated only by the clinking of cutlery against plates. Even though he seemed his usual self when I woke him, I'm still acutely aware that there is a tinge of annoyance about him. Is he angry about the question I asked last night? Or about the eye cream? I tell myself I'm imagining it, though make a mental note to ensure I'm doing everything I can to make it up to him today.

After we've eaten, I clear away the plates while he disappears into the bathroom. I watch him out of the corner of my eye through the half-open door as he splashes his face with water.

Those hands were on me last night. Running across my body, fingers tangled in my hair.

He pulls the medicine box down from its high shelf, retrieves the key from his pocket and stands there, a commanding figure, meticulously organising the contents. His movements are deliberate, each item carefully counted and arranged, as if seeking a sense of control in this small act.

'Here ye go.' He places my single white pill in my outstretched palm as I join him in the bathroom, the culmination of his careful selection from the box. I go to place it on my tongue, but am stopped by an awareness that he is staring at me, his gaze piercing and expectant. 'What d'ye say?'

'Thank you,' I'm quick to respond.

The pill slips down my throat. This, like everything else in our life, is part of the routine. Next step; the scales. I step gingerly onto them, feeling Cal's gaze lingering on my body, scrutinising its curves and contours.

The dial on the scales rotates and his expression softens, satisfaction dancing in his eyes as he reads the numbers. 'Lookin' good,' he murmurs, his voice laced with pride.

He digs his hand into his pocket. I realise what it is before he fully pulls it out, have already caught sight of the patterned paper and the end of what looks like a tiny satin bow. My birthday present.

A smile flickers across my lips and I wait for him to hand it to me. He takes his time. The present is small, fitting comfortably into the palm of my hand, and I allow myself a moment to imagine what could be inside. A bar of Galaxy chocolate, perhaps. He sometimes brings those home with him and he knows they're my favourite.

I unwrap the gift with practised grace, knowing that any reaction too excitable is not fit for a lady. It's a delicate necklace with a bird pendant, its silver chain glinting under the soft morning light. This has been carefully chosen, I can tell. He knows how much I love the birds.

'I saw it and thought of you.'

'It's beautiful,' I say. 'Thank you so much.'

He turns me on the spot so that he can place the pendant around my neck. 'A beautiful piece of jewellery for a beautiful wife.'

As the front door clicks shut behind him and the truck grumbles away, leaving me alone again, the weight of his presence still lingers in the air. The isolation gets more and more suffocating every day, a constant reminder of my dependence on him for both physical and emotional sustenance. The hours drag here, even with so much to be getting on with.

The one chore I do genuinely love is tending to the garden. The second I step out into the sunshine it's like a pressure has been lifted off my chest. This is my happy place. I dig and I prune and I water. I pick a few strawberries, probably the last of the season's harvest, and drop them into my basket, sneaking one into my mouth and revelling in the sweetness. I think I'll make strawberry jam tonight. That way it'll keep.

I feel less alone out here. The robins jump from fence post to fence post as if they can tell how in need of companionship I am. Sometimes I talk to them, pretending I'm a real-life Snow White. Aside from the various Bible editions stacked neatly in rows, we have a few other books on our shelves. Nothing that could corrupt or damage my soul. Cal would probably die if he knew I used to keep a well-read copy of *Fifty Shades of Grey* tucked under my pillow in my dorm at university.

Of the books in our collection, *Little House on the Prairie* is my favourite, so much so that I have it memorised, but I do love *Snow White* too. She was like me, lonely, with only the birds for company, until her prince came and set her free. Of course, I already live with a man and there's no evil stepmother out for my blood as far as I know, but the similarities are still there.

As I drop the last strawberry into my basket I spot him, my favourite robin, the one with the vivid red chest, sitting on a branch mere inches from me, chortling. I haven't seen him since last year, when he and his little family all left for the winter. Cal doesn't believe me when I say that during the spring and summer months the same bird visits me each day, says there's no way to tell one from the other, but I know. There's a certain glisten in his eyes. He has a particular way of cocking his head to the side as if appraising me. My lips quirk up and I hold out the smallest strawberry, hoping today might be the day he plucks up the courage to flutter onto my hand.

He doesn't. Instead, as usual, he watches me for a few seconds, then ruffles his feathers and takes off, flapping, making me startle. Disappointed, I watch him as his wings carry him off into the distance, soaring over the tips of the pines. It always strikes me just how quickly he can get to where he's going despite his size. Where is he going? The loch? The town? Another country? Maybe a different place every day. I would if I had his wings and his freedom to go where he pleases. I'd explore every tiny nook and cranny of this world.

As I watch him flutter away into the thicket of trees, I'm overcome by the desire to follow him. I could. There's nothing physically stopping me from venturing past the perimeter of our land. I've done it before.

For our fifth wedding anniversary Cal treated me to a picnic by the loch. We packed up smoked salmon, crumbly oatcakes, artisanal cheeses, juicy fruits and mouthwatering confectionery from town, far more than we could realistically eat, and made the long trek to the water's edge. It was a perfectly still day. The air seemed to hold its breath, in awe of the untamed beauty that lay before us as we sought out the perfect spot, a grassy knoll that offered an uninterrupted view of the glistening surface, and laid out our blanket. Cal has often commented how he always enjoys us being together but that that day was something special, and I have to agree.

I could go there again. Perhaps I could even take my paints and a canvas. If there's ever a good landscape to paint, it's the loch. But I know it's not an option. Not really. The glinting in the trees reminds me of that on a daily basis.

It's then that I hear it, the rumble of Cal's truck. Frowning, I crane my neck to see where it's coming from. He's been gone maybe half an hour. He's never come home this quickly before. Not without reason.

I retreat back to the strawberries, the other few times I've left the confines of the cabin circling in my head, a highlight reel on replay. As the truck approaches I pick up my basket and take it back inside, where I spread the berries out on the chopping board and start cutting off the stalks. By the time Cal comes through the front door I've already got the jam simmering in a pot on the stove.

'Is everything OK?' I ask, moving to give him a hug and a kiss, even though he's been gone for such a short time I can practically still feel his goodbye kiss on my cheek.

'Yeah,' he says, though the slight trailing off of the word reduces the conviction in his voice. 'I just . . . I didnae want to work today. I want te be here. With you.'

My eyebrows flick up.

'You blew off work for me?'

'Aye. Called in sick. Can't hurt once in a while, eh?'

His arms snake back around my waist and he pulls me closer to him. I nuzzle my head into his chest, wondering what's brought this on.

'What do you want to do today then?' I say as we separate, calculating in my head how many hours we have together. 'We could go and have a picnic like we did for our anniversary?'

Cal's forehead crinkles. 'I think you've got enough to be gettin' on with here.'

His eyes roam the cabin, landing on the bubbling jam, the surfaces I have yet to dust, the pile of clothes that need scrubbing and wringing and hanging out on the line. My eyes follow his and disappointment drops like a stone into the pit of my stomach. Why did he come home to spend the day with me if I'm just going to be doing all my usual chores?

I'm about to ask the question when Cal squeezes my shoulder. 'I'm gon' go skin them deer hangin' up in the barn. I fancy venison pie for lunch. Make sure that jam's done in time, aye?'

And with that he trudges out into the garden, down the long dirt path to the skinning barn, and I am alone again.

Chapter Three

I can tell something is wrong even before I open my eyes. Usually, when I wake, especially at this time of year, light has only just started filtering into our room. But from behind closed lids I'm sure I can see the bright glow of the sun peeping through our window. My hand shimmies across the mattress to where I can usually feel Cal, still snoring and dead to the world. But he's not there. The bed is cold where he lies.

I sit upright in bed with a jolt. Where is he? What time is it? My head spins, still half asleep, as I try to make out the numbers on the clock on my bedside table. Three of each number dance across the clock face, blurred and distorted. I blink a few times to clear my vision.

7.20 a.m.

I've overslept.

The duvet gets tangled around my legs in my hurry to stand up. I don't even remember the last time I slept in. My head feels groggy, not at all refreshed from the extra couple of hours of slumber. There's something else too, something tugging at my insides and making my chest tighten.

Cal will have already gone to work. Would he have had to fix his own breakfast, or would he have gone without? My question is answered as I emerge, bleary eyed and shell-shocked, out of the bedroom. The kitchen looks as if a bomb has gone off. There's a dirty frying pan on the burner, egg whites burned to the edges. Oil is spattered across the walls and counters. The loaf of bread I made a couple of days ago has been hacked at with the wrong sort of knife, and greasy plates have been left on the table alongside his Bible.

An eggshell crunches under my foot as I approach the sink, wondering where to start, wondering what he's going to say. Surely, if he'd been annoyed at me for neglecting to make him breakfast, he'd have woken me. Perhaps he wanted to give me a lie-in. A nice gesture. Thoughtful. No. This doesn't feel thoughtful. Not leaving the house in this state of destruction for me to wake up to. This feels angry. Calculated. Like he wanted to send me a message.

I swallow the annoyance down and make a start at cleaning up. Twice I make matters worse by spilling yet more oil down the cupboard doors and I consider giving up and leaving it, curses playing on my tongue. I know full well though, no matter what I want to do, I won't leave it. Imagine what he'd say if he got home from work and the cabin still looked like this. It isn't his duty to care for the home. It's mine.

By the time I've got the kitchen back to its usual state the morning has slipped through my fingers and I have to rush through my usual chores, prioritising the chickens and the dinner prep, since they'll make the most difference if they're not done. I choose to forego watering the plants – one day won't kill them and Cal will be none the wiser – and instead opt to bake some shortbread biscuits. A goodwill gesture to make up for the fact that Cal had to fend for himself this morning. Once they're in the oven I collapse into the armchair by the wood burner. Flour is dusting my eyebrows and making my hair look grey in patches but I don't care. I need to not move for a moment.

I wonder what time Cal will be home and reel off the things left to do in my head. I must bathe before he gets home. I can't let him see me sitting here, a bedraggled heap in the corner. Part of me wishes he had a normal job where he starts and finishes at the same time every day, but apparently there's no jobs like that around here. For that to even be a possibility we'd have to move closer to the city.

I asked Cal once why he prefers life out here so much to life amongst the hustle and bustle, even though I know the answer. The news stories he told me and the detail with which he did it made me wish I'd never asked. The attacks. The rapes. The murders. 'The city is an evil place,' he said, 'and while we can never be truly safe, not even out here, we're in the safest place we can be.' I think he actually likes the unpredictable hours as a way to keep me on my toes.

I feel much better once I'm out of the bath. The water wasn't as hot as I usually like it thanks to the delay in getting the wood burner going, but it eased my aching muscles nonetheless. I pull the shortbread out of the oven and arrange them on a rack to cool, fix myself a spot of lunch, and then pause to consider what I should do for the rest of the afternoon while I await Cal's return. The voice at the back of my head is telling me I know what I should do this afternoon. I should do the chores I missed this morning, or start on the other pressing jobs that need addressing. The bath and toilet could both do with a good scrub. I silence that voice, not able to face my body hurting again like it did this morning, and turn my attention to my easel instead.

It's been a while since I last had time to paint, and I'm nearly out of a few colours. Cal did mention getting me some more, though I imagine after my performance this morning that won't be top of his list today. I crack open the green and blue and brown tubes, flakes of dried paint fluttering onto the floor, and squeeze the colours out onto my palette.

I'm never quite sure what to paint when I'm faced with a big blank canvas. Usually I start with the sky, since I almost always prefer to do landscapes, and then the rest just comes to me. I don't even usually make a conscious decision. I just allow the brush to move and the picture sort of comes to life before my eyes. The otherwise drab walls of our cabin are covered in my colourful attempts at capturing the mist rolling over the hills, or the sun glinting across the loch's surface. Only this time the creative process doesn't seem quite as free flowing as it usually is.

I pause once the base of the sky is done and my brush hovers for a moment. There aren't a whole lot of scenes I have yet to paint. I could try painting my little robin friend? No. I'm terrible at animals close up. Whenever I choose to include them in my painting they're always at a distance so that I don't have to go into too much detail.

My eyes drift to the window. I peer across the landscape, at the vast emptiness that stretches as far as I can see. I wonder where Cal is right now.

The tip of my brush dips into the brown and without allowing myself to think too much about it, I start to paint something I've never even considered painting before. My lips press together as I swipe in boxy, rectangular motions, depicting a row of brick houses. I mix up a sort of grey colour and dab it along the bottom of the canvas; the roads I'm picturing are not dusty tracks like ours but of a man-made substance that I can't quite remember the name of. Of course it's been years since I last saw any of this, but as I close my eyes I think I can picture the scene. Whether it's accurate or not, it has come together quite nicely, easily in fact, considering I only ever paint from reference. As a finishing touch I squeeze the last of my white paint onto my palette and use it to create a sign at the end of the road. Then, using my finest brush dipped in black, I add a few tiny letters.

Shore Road.

I pause. A few tiny drops of black paint drip from the end of the brush and splatter onto my dress.

Shore Road.

The scene stares back at me, the old road I grew up on. It's been so, so long since I saw it and yet looking at my attempt at capturing it in acrylic and brushstrokes, it's like it was only yesterday.

The sound of the front door opening makes me jump so violently I drop the brush and it misses the fabric I had laid down to protect the floor. It bounces across the wood, leaving three little black blotches on the grain. Pressing my lips together, I snatch it up and replace it on the easel. I then grab a new, blank canvas and place it carefully over the one I've just painted, covering the still-wet scene, before turning to face the door. I must have been so wrapped up in what I was doing I didn't even hear Cal returning.

Hands behind my back, I step gingerly over to him as he shakes off his jacket and hangs it on the hook. Worry gnaws at me, as if I've been caught out doing something I shouldn't, but I know he didn't see anything. If he had, the arguments would have already started.

Then I remember this morning and the state of the kitchen and realise where the worry is coming from.

'I'm so sorry I slept in this morning,' I say, my voice cracking as I speak.

To begin with, I think he hasn't heard me. He continues with what he's doing as if I've not said a word, bending down and unlacing his boots, tugging them off and placing them on the shoe rack. It's only after he's brushed a little dirt off his knees and stood back up straight that he looks at me.

'Did you enjoy the extra sleep?'

I frown. I can't honestly say that I did. It made me groggy and the shock with which I awoke was certainly not the ideal way to start the day. But from the tone in his voice I can't quite tell what answer he wants to hear.

In the end, I avoid the question completely. 'It was lovely of you to let me have a lie-in. I hope breakfast turned out OK?'

'Not like when you do it.'

I smile, though it's an effort. The compliment would suggest he's not annoyed at me, but his voice says otherwise. It's like he's night and day, warm and cold, Jekyll and Hyde, right in front of me.

'You've been paintin'.' His eyes fall to the droplets on my dress. I brush away at them pointlessly. It'll need to be soaked for the black to come out.

'I was going to,' I say, unsure whether this change of subject is for the better or the worse, 'but it didn't turn out right. I'll need to start over.'

His eyes flick over to my easel and I'm quick to move over to the shortbread, hoping his gaze will follow. I pluck one of the biscuits, still slightly warm, from the plate and hold it out to him.

'Here, to tide you over until dinner.'

I glance from the biscuit to Cal and back again, wishing he would prise his eyes away from that goddamned easel. Silent words escape my lips. *Take the biscuit. Take it. Take the fucking biscuit.*

He doesn't take the biscuit. He leaves my arm hovering stupidly in the air and makes his way over to the easel. As he pulls the blank canvas away to reveal my picture underneath, I close my eyes, waiting for it.

'Where'd you get the idea for that?'

My eyes flick back open and I chance a peek over at him. He's not looking at me. He's focused on the lower half of the canvas, eyebrows pulled together. He nods in the direction of the road name. I drop my arm, the biscuit hanging by my side.

'Oh. I'm not sure.'

It's a ridiculous lie. He knows full well what it is. He just wants to hear me say it. Wants to drag it out of me. He continues to stare at the painting. I can't bear the silence so I say more stupid things.

'It must be our road name?'

Stupid.

Cal shakes his head. 'We dinnae have a road name. We live out in the middle of nowhere.'

'Oh.'

I drop my gaze and take a bite out of the biscuit. It crumbles in my mouth. A particularly large crumb lodges in my throat and I cough and splutter but still Cal doesn't remove his eyes from that sodding painting, face stony.

'Perhaps I read it somewhere,' I suggest. 'Yes, that must be it. It'll be in one of our books somewhere.'

I don't even know why I'm trying to pretend. Only an imbecile would fall for these half-baked reasonings. Even so, after what seems like an eternity his eyes drop to the floor, to where the brush fell when I jumped.

'You'd better make a start at cleaning this mess up if you want to get dinner on the stove. Or am I doing that tonight an' all?'

Cal's mood improves as the evening goes on. Once some good food is in his belly he seems pretty much back to normal, and I realise his attitude was probably down to having not had a proper meal today. As he always says, I need to make sure he's nourished each day otherwise of course he's not going to be his usual self.

As I clear away the dishes and he begins his evening devotional, my eye is involuntarily drawn back to the painting, to the road name. Tomorrow I'll get rid of that canvas. He's in a decent mood today but who knows how he'll react to it after a night's sleep. As this thought enters my mind a stabbing sensation pulses behind my eye. I press my palm up to my socket, squeezing my lids shut.

'Cal? Could you grab me a painkiller please?'

The sound of his chair scraping back against the wood goes right through me and only increases the shooting pains.

'What's up?'

'Just a headache. It came on really suddenly.'

I hear him move to the bathroom and pull down the pill box, hear the rustling of the packets inside. A moment later he is beside me. I hold out my hand and he drops a single red and yellow capsule into my palm. I peek out at it with my good eye and look up at him questioningly. Usually, if I need a painkiller for my headache, he gives me two.

As if reading my mind he says, 'Just have one for now.'

Not wanting to question him, I gulp the pill down.

'And you never had your other one this morning, what with you sleeping in and all.'

He hands me another pill, this time my usual tiny white one. I obediently swallow that one too.

'No wonder you had a headache. That's what happens, see? When you don't look after yourself. We've got our routine for a reason. It works.'

I nod. He's looking at me as if he wants me to say something but I'm not entirely sure what. The pain in my head is still pulsing behind my eye but I try not to let it show.

He wraps his arm around the back of my neck and pulls me into him. I press my head against his chest, glad to be able to close my eyes against my headache.

'We'll go back to normal tomorrow, aye? Breakfast on the table, aye?'

I say nothing. Despite the headache and Cal talking to me, all I can think about is the painting.

Chapter Four

The next morning I do not sleep in. I'm up and busying myself with the chores before the sun has even started to peek over the hills. I prepare a hearty breakfast with double helpings, resulting in a chuckled, 'You dinnae have to make it up to me, you know. Your normal would have been plenty good enough,' from Cal, and wave him off to work with the smile of the perfect wife I've moulded myself into.

Only I am not going to be the perfect wife today.

Though the garden work calls to me and I know I'm neglecting my duty by not answering the call, my mind is elsewhere. I push the armchair right up against the window so that I can keep one eye on any sign of Cal returning home early, plump a cushion to make it extra comfortable and set about brewing a cup of tea. Painting that sign yesterday was silly. Careless. A large canvas is difficult to hide. But there's something gnawing at me and if I can't paint it out of my system I'm going to need another outlet. I'm becoming too comfortable, too set in my ways, and if I'm not careful I'm going to end up losing myself. I need a way to force myself to remember who I really am.

An hour later my tea is on the windowsill only half drunk but stone cold, and I've written four pages into a notebook. This notebook will have to be where I keep these thoughts, these memories. Almost like a journal. A notebook is much easier to keep to myself than a painting.

My eyes flick across my handwriting and I let out a heavy sigh, shutting the book with a little too much force and trapping my fingers in it. This exercise, while needed, has made me feel claustrophobic in this tiny cabin. Just as I consider going out to do some gardening, if only for the sake of getting a little fresh air, my ears prick up. The cabin has fallen silent. The cabin is never silent. There's always the sound of the generator rumbling quietly in the background, providing just enough electricity for Cal's select few gadgets. But the rumbling has stopped.

Frowning, I uncross my legs and take my notebook into the bedroom, where I slide it under the mattress on my side of the bed. Then I move over to the front door, slip on my boots and leave the cabin, rounding the corner to the cupboard fixed to the outside wall. When I open the doors it's clear the generator isn't working. I have no idea what could have happened to it or how I would even start to go about fixing it, but neither of those things matter right now.

I peer at the dirt track. Assuming it's one of Cal's normal work days and he hasn't decided to head home early again, he should still be out for a good three or four hours. I could take a wander, see what I can see beyond my usual view of the Highlands, how far I could get, and be back in time to sort the garden out before he's home.

My heart batters against my ribcage as I take a few tentative steps. The two sides of my brain battle it out as I edge further and further away from the cabin. One side, the logical side, tells me that I'm not doing anything wrong, not really. That all I'm doing is taking a little walk, something I've done many a time with Cal by my side. There's nothing hugely different between this and those other outings.

But the other side of my brain knows what he'd say if he saw what I was doing. Cal would be furious if he knew I was heading out without him to accompany me. He always insists on us walking together. 'So's I can protect you,' he says whenever we go anywhere. 'So's I can help ye if ye get hurt.' The more I deliberate, the more time I waste. I've made up my mind. I won't make it far, but I need to be away from the cabin for a little while before I go crazy.

Gripping onto sheer determination, I pass the skinning barn and shudder. I'll never set foot in that barn. After Cal's hunting sessions he can spend hours in there and I have to force myself not to think about it. Each time I focus on the prepared meat he brings to the kitchen that I can cook up into a delicious pie or roast dinner, choosing to forget entirely where it has come from. One time I caught a glimpse of Cal carrying a deer from his truck to the barn and I spent a good half an hour sobbing while folding laundry. I never want to go in there. I never even want to go near it.

I give the barn a wide berth as I reach the circle of trees that surround our little clearing, and close my eyes while I strain to remember the way we went before. We followed the dirt path to the perimeter of our land and then turned right. I think.

Sure enough, after some time I spot a laminated sign up ahead, nailed to a tree and flapping in the wind. I approach it and run my fingers along the text.

PRIVATE LAND. KEEP OUT. NO TRESPASSING.

Even though I know it's ridiculous and there's nothing about this flimsy sign actually protecting me, for some reason there seems to be a massive difference between staying within this boundary and stepping beyond it. An invisible line is flashing on the floor in my mind's eye, and I feel as if the second I cross it someone will jump me from behind.

Once I've passed the sign, things become less familiar. I glance over my shoulder back at the way I came, wanting to imprint reference points on my memory for my return journey – a rock, a plant, a mound of dirt. I had felt sure I knew where I was going, but one tree starts to look the same as the next, and before I know it I'm positive I'm wandering around in circles. How long have I been out here? Half an hour? An hour? I have no way of knowing. Cal always has a watch attached to his wrist when he's heading out to work but I don't even own one. I've never needed one. I'm never out of the house beyond tending to the garden.

Panic starts to gurgle in my stomach and despite myself I wish Cal was with me. I wouldn't get lost if I'd waited to come out here with him. He knows the Highlands like the back of his hand. As this thought crosses my mind and I emerge at the brow of a hill, the breath is snatched away from me.

I'm at the loch. Whether it's the one I came to with Cal or another I cannot be sure. If it is the same I've come at it from another angle. I stand and stare, awestruck. It's a study of contrasts. On the one hand, the world around me hums with life; lush greenery and flying insects buzzing around the wildflowers. On the other hand, there is an eerie stillness hanging over the loch, the grey sky mirrored in its waters. There's nothing for miles and miles. How far does Cal have to drive each day before he reaches civilisation?

Frozen still, I peer up at the sky and try to ascertain where the sun is compared to when I left, but it's hidden behind angry clouds that threaten rain. I certainly don't want to get caught out in a storm. Perhaps if I just retrace my steps I'll find my way. I turn on the spot and peer at the ground beneath my feet, searching for footprints, evidence of the route I've taken. My sense of direction isn't great, having rarely been used or practised, but as I trudge back through the thicket of trees I think I can see the *No Trespassing* sign flapping in the distance.

My pace quickens. I'm suddenly aware of how tired my legs have become, how hungry I am, how desperate I am to be back. By the time the cabin appears in the distance, barely visible through the thin layer of fog that's settled over the area, I'm practically running.

The relief that washes over me as I cross the threshold is short-lived. My eyes carry over to the clock on the wall. My stomach constricts.

It's late. Really late. I've been out for hours and I didn't even realise it. Lunchtime is long gone and I should have had dinner cooking for at least half an hour by now, not to mention all the chores I should have done. I chew on my lip as I contemplate my to-do list. If only I could know what time Cal will be home. I must prioritise. I can't let him down on the meal front two days running, so my first port of call is to begin chopping meat. I'll do another stew. That way I can leave it simmering while I get on with the housework. Hopefully he won't mind having it twice in one week. Once that's going, I tackle the big wins. Picking up any items that aren't in their home, running the duster over the surfaces, mopping the floors. The areas he'll notice.

As I plump cushions and position them on the sofa the smell of burning filters into my nostrils. I drop the cushion, curse, and hurry over to the stove. I haven't been stirring the stew enough. There is a thick layer resting at the top of the pan and it's started to congeal and blacken at the sides. I grab the ladle and try my best to spoon the lumps out, dropping them into the bin below the counter. Nerves creep through me like spiders. I've been a bad wife these past couple of days. I'm allowing temptation and fixation to detract my attention from my duties.

I do my best to save the stew and there's at least an edible dinner on the table by the time Cal returns home. I watch him as he eyes the food, then sweeps his gaze over the house.

'You OK?' he says.

'Me? Yes, fine. Why?'

He can tell something is off, I'm sure of it.

'Generator's down.'

'Is it?'

'Aye. Looks like the battery's knackered. Cannae you hear how quiet it is?'

'I suppose I didn't notice. What are you going to do?'

'There's a spare in the barn. I'll fix it up in the mornin' before I go te work.'

'OK, that's good.'

His eyes narrow but he doesn't say anything else. After slipping his jacket off, he comes to sit at the table. I do the same. It's a good five minutes before he leans back in his chair, scrutinising the stew as if it's been laced with poison.

'What's wrong with it?'

'What do you mean?'

'It doesnae taste right. What's wrong with it?'

A lump forms in my throat. 'It burned a little. I'm sorry. I thought I'd managed to rescue it.'

Forehead creasing, he returns to surveying the cabin. I instinctively copy, searching for areas I might have missed in my haste to get the place ready for his return home.

'Not as clean as it usually is either.'

I redden. 'No. No it's not. I'm sorry.'

'What about the leak in the bathroom? Sealed that up yet?'

The lump in my throat is so large the only response I can muster is a small shake of the head.

'So what have you been doin' all day?'

'I . . .' My attempt at words is fruitless. I'm not sure what to say. Part of me wants to be honest and tell him I went out for a walk, that

I got lost and struggled to find my way home. That's what a good wife would do. But I know better.

'I got caught up reading. The day sort of ran away with me,' I say eventually.

A horrid, metallic taste gathers in my mouth at the lie.

His eyes shrink to slits and he shakes his head. 'Do you not care about me?'

'What?' The word comes out a half-laugh. 'Of course I do! How could you say that?'

The sneer he gives me is so out of character, so unlike him, I shrink back in my seat and lower my gaze. Speaking into my lap, I try to keep my voice steady, not wanting to betray the tears that are threatening to burst out. 'I'm so sorry, Cal. I've just not felt myself these past couple of days. I've been so tired. I promise I'll do better tomorrow.'

I sound like a child apologising for making a mess with my toys.

There's no response, so after a minute or so I dare to peek up at him through my eyelashes. His face, his gorgeous face that swept me off my feet all those years ago, is contorted into a grimace.

After a long, long while his expression finally softens.

'Perhaps you're just under the weather.'

I let out a breath. 'Yes. Yes, that's probably it.'

He nods, almost imperceptibly, then pushes his barely touched dinner away from him and stands. I watch as he heads to the bathroom and retrieves two white pills from the medicine box.

'Here,' he says as he drops them on the table. 'Take these. I'll sort the washing up tonight. Go and get some sleep, get yourself better, so that you're back to yourself tomorrow, aye?'

The last thing I want to do is leave the washing up to him but I nod obediently and swallow the pills. As I shuffle past him towards the bedroom he just sits there, still and silent, until I'm in our bedroom and I've pushed the door closed, and I hate myself for wishing for his approval.

In the privacy of the bedroom, I allow the tears to fall. They dribble down my cheeks, gathering in the corners of my nose. I sit on the edge of the bed and stare at my reflection in the mirror above our dresser. The room is bathed in the warm glow of the sunset. I'm plunged into a silhouette and my features are barely distinguishable in the reflection, but I can still make out the hurt on my face.

My hand reaches for the notebook. It's difficult to find it under the mattress. Just as I'd hoped. I pull it out with a tug and lie back against my pillow with it, reading and rereading everything I wrote earlier today.

I won't do it.

I won't forget.

I won't allow myself to forget.

Chapter Five

He woke me up when he got into bed last night and we had sex. It wasn't like it normally is though. Usually I can feel his adoration for me coming off him, even when he's caught up in the most animalistic of desires for me. Last night it was impersonal, angry, and today I feel bruised and sore, though it's partly because I've been on my hands and knees most of the morning. I've scrubbed and I've washed and I've fixed and I've scrubbed some more. There is an apple pie in the oven and the ingredients are prepped ready to start cooking dinner in a couple of hours. The garden has been tended to and the animals cared for. I've fitted about three days' work into one morning and it's nearly killed me.

Exhausted, I've resigned myself to needing a rest. A bath. A bath would be good. Not only will it help to ease my aching limbs, I could use one of the flowery fizzers Cal sometimes brings back from town and make myself smell divine. That would make him happy.

I run it as hot as I can stand while still leaving enough hot water to last the few chores I have left. It burns my skin as I step into the water but I sink into it, lying back and resting my head on the edge of the bath. The tension doesn't immediately drift away as I'd hoped it would. On the contrary, the water seems to only make me more aware of just how sore I am.

I wonder, as I lie staring up at the ceiling, what he got out of last night. Did it feel good for him? Did he enjoy holding me like that, manhandling me like that?

The sudden banging makes me jump so wildly, water sploshes over the side of the bath as I slip, bashing the back of my head on the enamel. My initial thought is one of horror as I realise how angry Cal would be if he knew what was going through my head. He'd tell me lust is a sin. I'm becoming a lazy, forgetful, lustful sinner. These wrongful desires and obsessions are turning me into a crap wife.

Then, I realise what it was that snapped me out of my reverie and made me jump in the first place.

The door.

Someone knocked at the door.

But it can't be. No one has ever knocked at our door. We live in the middle of nowhere. There isn't a soul living anywhere near us.

I clamber awkwardly out of the bath and edge towards the bathroom door, gripping its wooden edge tight, peering around it as droplets fall from my naked body onto the floor and a puddle forms at my feet. My eyes narrow as I focus on the window beside the door.

There's no one there. I was imagining things. Maybe I fell asleep and dreamt it. It was probably my conscience knocking, a figment of my imagination telling me to stop being such a bad wife.

The knocking comes again and this time a figure appears at the window. Large, dark, hulking, pressing his terrible face against the glass, hands cupped over his evil eyes and peering in at me.

I yelp and spring back from the door, hiding myself once more in the privacy of the bathroom. My heart thuds against my chest, *thud, thud, thud*, and I hear it echoing in my head. Possibilities whirl in my head. Cal warned me years ago. He told me what would happen if ever someone trespassed on our land. He'd be entitled to do whatever was necessary to protect me from the people out there, the men who would hurt me, who are only interested in one thing. That's why we live where we do, in seclusion and safety. That's why he put the warning signs up around the perimeter of our land. To keep everyone out.

And to keep me in.

He's shown me photographs of poor girls who thought themselves immune to the dangers of the world. Young mothers who have been cut up into tiny pieces and turned into furniture. Best friends whose innocent night out on the town turned to being tied up and mutilated for months until they begged for death.

'This is what people do,' Cal had said to me. 'This is what I have to protect you from. The world is evil. People are walkin' around with the devil inside 'em.'

We've gone so long, so many years, without seeing a single living soul anywhere near us I've allowed myself to think no one would ever come here, and now look. There's someone at the door.

Another knock comes and then, 'Hello?'

I suck in a breath and hold it, as if he'll be able to hear the sound of my chest rising and falling.

'Hello? Is anyone there? I'm lost. I wondered if you could help me?'

My brow furrows. He doesn't sound like he's here to brutally murder me.

'I know someone's in there. I can see the candles lit. Please, I've been wandering around for hours. I've run out of water. Look, I won't take up much of your time. If you can just give me directions I'll be on my way.'

I believe him. The Highlands can be perilous to someone who doesn't know them. The more you wander the more lost you can become. Even I found myself unsure of the way home yesterday. I know Cal would say this man is here to kill me but I don't think so. I think he's a very unlucky soul who needs help. Two sides of my mind battle against each other. I know what I want to do. No. I know what I'm desperate to do. So desperate I feel as if I might split in two. But is it worth the risk? No. Not with the generator up and running again.

A shuffling sound comes from outside and I peek once more around the corner of the door. He's turned his back to the window and is leant up against it, his shoulders slumped, the outline of a defeated man.

A shiver runs down my spine and I realise I'm still naked. My eyes flit across the room and land on my dirty clothes, still bundled in a pile on the floor. I hastily snatch them up, minus the underwear, grimacing as I pull the jumper over my head and catch a whiff of the stale sweat from my day's hard work. Holding my breath, I edge out of the bathroom. My hands tremble by my sides. As I pass the wood burner I peer up at the mantel. I wonder how long it will be until Cal comes home.

The man doesn't turn around as I approach the door. He doesn't know I'm here. It's not too late. I could run back to the bedroom and bury myself under the covers until he goes away.

'Let me see your hands,' I call through the door with as much confidence as I can muster.

The man starts, his body flinching against the glass. When he turns to face me I realise I was mistaken; he's not got an evil face at all. He's got a tired, weary face, and kind, if a little surprised, eyes. He's what I would imagine Pa in *Little House on the Prairie* to look like. Still, I know better than to let appearances fool me.

'My what?' the man says.

'Your hands. Let me see them.'

He frowns for a moment but does as I ask, lifting both hands high so that I can see them through the window. No weapons. It's as I suspected. He's just a poor, lost soul.

'I'm not going to hurt you,' he says, as if reading my thoughts. 'Please, if you could just point me in the direction of the main road I'll get out of your hair.'

I purse my lips. Now that I've revealed myself to him I might as well give him directions, if only for the sake of getting him away from this cabin, but should I say anything else to him?

'You have to go that way.' I nod in the direction I see Cal drive every morning. 'See those tyre tracks? You can follow them. They should lead you out.'

The man glances down at the ground and gives a little laugh.

'What a numpty. I hadn't seen them. Thank you! Thank you so much. I really appreciate it.'

He makes a move to walk away and relief flutters in my stomach, but then he stops and looks back at me.

'I don't suppose I could have a drink, could I?'

My eyes shrink to slits.

'If it's not too much trouble,' he says.

He chugs the water as if he's never had a drink in his life, and within seconds the glass is empty. I take it from him and fill it again, my eyes continuously flitting to the window where I'm sure I'll see Cal appear at any moment. I wonder what he'd say if he came home to see a stranger in his chair at the dining table?

As I pass the glass back to him I settle myself in the chair opposite.

I've decided now that this man is definitely not here to kill me. If he was, he'd have done it by now. All he had to do was wait until I'd unlocked the door and he could have done whatever he liked. I'd have been more or less powerless to stop him. But no, he's sat and he's gulped down glasses of water and he's thanked me endlessly for my generosity. I'm glad I let him in. I'm like the good Samaritan helping someone in need. I just need to figure out what else to do in this situation.

'How long have you lived out here then?' he asks after his third glass of water. He's not Scottish, like Cal. If anything, he sounds more like me.

'About a decade.'

'Do your parents live here too then?'

'Oh no.' I shake my head, trying not to let on how bizarre it is to be sat talking to someone other than Cal. I can't stop staring at him, drinking him in, every wrinkle, every patch of stubble. A new face. 'I'm from just outside London.'

'Small world. Me too. I'm Croydon. You?'

'Well, I went to university in central but I grew up in . . .' My words trail off as my mind strains. 'I can't actually remember the name of it.'

'You can't remember where you grew up?' The man raises his eyebrows and I feel myself blush.

'I guess I haven't really thought about it in a while,' I say eventually.

'You've not been back home?'

I shake my head slowly. 'Not since I came to live here.'

Tell him. Do it.

'Ah, that's a sad thing. I was just the same with my dad. Never got a chance to make amends before he passed.'

I press my lips together, unsure of what to say and wondering whether it's normal for people to give intimate details of their life so freely in conversations with strangers. I suppose I wouldn't know.

'So is it just you and your man here, then? All alone, all the way out here?'

I nod, still unable to tear my eyes away from him.

'Must get lonely, eh?'

Before I can even think about responding, that sound rumbles through the air once more. Cal's truck. He's coming home.

I stand up so quickly I hit my stomach against the table and the glass topples, smashing into pieces on the floor.

'Easy now,' the man says, reaching down to pick up the shards. 'Where's the fire?'

'My husband. He's coming home. You need to go.'

My voice is panicked and the man picks up on it. He stops picking up the fragments of glass and looks at me, brow furrowed.

'Surely he wouldn't mind you giving me a glass of water?'

I don't respond, just rush to the under-sink cupboard to grab the dustpan and brush, eyeing the approaching truck as I do so. Thank God I didn't tell this man.

When I turn back to start sweeping up the broken glass, he's still standing there.

'You can go out the back door,' I say, gesturing towards the garden, a sense of urgency in my tone.

'I'm not sure I should.' The man crosses his arms and my stomach clenches. 'You seem awful rattled at the thought of your husband coming home and seeing me. Is he a dangerous man? Are you afraid of him?'

'No!' The word comes out as a sort of strangled screech. 'Nothing like that, I just know he wouldn't like . . .'

But the words are snatched from me at the sound of the front door opening. I wince and turn around.

I'm not quite sure how to describe the look on Cal's face. Confusion mostly, the corners of his brows drawn together, eyes narrowed. But there's something else there. It's gone before I can identify it, replaced with a broad smile.

'Hello,' he says, stepping across the kitchen towards the man and holding out his hand. 'Cal Douglas. It's nay often we get visitors, I can tell ye that.'

The man glances at me before taking Cal's hand and shaking it.

'Yeah, I . . . Sorry. I was lost and your lady here was kind enough to give me a glass of water.'

Cal's eyes drop to the smashed glass on the floor, but he doesn't mention it. The smile remains fixed on his face.

'Ah, it's nay hard to get lost in these parts. If you want, I can drive you down to the main road? You look mighty knackered.'

The man darts another look at me. I wish he'd stop doing that.

'Thank you. I know which direction to go in now though. I'll be all right.'

'It'll take you hours, lad. That's assuming you dinnae get lost again. Up to you, of course. I'm just trying to help.'

'Hours, you say?' The man peers out of the window at the direction I pointed him in, at the dense thicket of trees and sprawling hills separating us from the rest of the world. 'I don't want to put you out.'

'Eh, it's no bother. Looks like my dinner still has a way to go before it'll be ready anyway.'

This time, Cal's eyes meet mine, and ice trickles down my spine.

'Well, all right then, if you're sure. Mind if I use the bathroom real quick?'

''Course. Just through there.' Cal gestures towards the bathroom and the man obediently shuffles towards it. I'm expecting Cal to say something when the bathroom door shuts, but he doesn't. He just stands there, leaning against the kitchen counter, eyes roaming the cabin. I want to say something to him, to break the unbearable silence, but my throat has constricted, vice-like. I don't understand how he's being. Cold and friendly all at once, anger and kindness seeping off him simultaneously.

After what feels like an eternity the toilet flushes and soon the man is emerging back into the kitchen.

'After you,' Cal says, holding open the front door.

The man shoots one last look in my direction. 'Thank you for your hospitality,' he says.

It's all I can do to force a nod in response.

And then the two of them are gone.

As soon as the truck starts trundling once more up the dirt track I'm moving, flitting from room to room, unsure what to do first. The pans clatter as I pull them out of the cupboard, dumping them on the hob and scooping the carefully chopped ingredients I prepared earlier into the biggest. It seems like days, weeks ago that I stood slicing them, proud of all I'd accomplished in a short morning, deciding that it wouldn't hurt to take a bath.

The bathroom. Food now cooking, I hurry into the little room and yank the plug out of the tub. The water swirls and glugs away as I take in the mess I left on the floor in my panic, the dirty underwear, the puddles of water. Part of me is mortified that the man saw the bathroom in such a state, but I don't allow myself to focus on that now. I fall to my hands and knees and mop up as much of the water as I can, before snatching up the underwear and stuffing it into the wash pile in the bedroom. I remember how much I must stink, wearing my old clothes, so I shimmy out of them and put on a fresh dress; the red one with the daisy print. One of Cal's favourites. I'm itching to grab the hairbrush and to start trying to tame the half-wet, frizzy mess that's the result of an interrupted bath, but I don't have time for that. I move back to the kitchen and pull out the apple pie. At least that isn't burnt.

Cal's back. I'm surprised. It doesn't feel like he's been gone for that long, though I have no idea how long it takes to drive to the main road versus walking. I busy myself stirring the vegetables and wait.

His footsteps are slow and deliberate when he comes into the cabin. He hasn't taken off his shoes, so they sound that much louder, thumping through me. I tilt my head towards him.

'That was kind of you,' I force out. 'Taking him to the main road.'

For a moment, Cal doesn't say anything. Then he grabs my arms and spins me around so fast my ears ring.

'Did you not listen to me? Were my warnings not enough?'

His fingers are digging into my muscles, making my eyes water. 'Cal, you're . . . you're hurting me.'

'I'm protecting you!' he spits. 'Or at least, that's what I've been trying to do all these years. I told you what would happen if you let someone in. I warned you what these people want to do to you!'

'I know. I'm sorry. He just seemed . . .'

'What? What did he seem? Nice? Of course he seemed fucking nice! It was all part of the act!'

He pushes me away as if I'm filth. Relief floods through my upper arms as pain simultaneously shoots up my spine where it had impacted with the counter.

'If I hadn't come home when I did . . .' he mutters. His words are no longer directed at me. It's as if he's talking to himself, running scenarios through his head.

'I'm sorry.' My chin trembles and I suck in a breath to try and stop it. His eyes flick back to mine and I wish I hadn't said anything.

'He was going to hurt you, you know that, right? If I hadn't shown up he would have tied you up and raped you and tortured you. He'd have taken this knife and removed your fingernails one by one.' He grabs the knife from the counter and places it at the tips of my fingers. The thought of it makes me want to vomit. He steps forward, his face inches from mine.

'He'd have sliced bits of your skin off like an animal and enjoyed watching you scream. And then, when you couldnae take any more, he'd have killed you.'

Tears spill down my cheeks and his eyes glint.

'Not all . . . p-people are evil.' The words come out in hiccoughing gasps.

He retracts his head slightly so that he can look at me properly, take in my red, blotchy face. His lip turns up.

'You've changed,' he says, disgust dripping off his words. 'Look at the state of you.'

And with that he drops the knife back onto the counter and heads to the bedroom, slamming the door behind him so that the wooden walls rattle.

Chapter Six

Today has gone by in a sort of haze. I've gone through the motions, preparing the meals, making myself and the house look presentable, getting my work done, all while Cal pretty much ignored me. The realisation hit me just after I woke up, when I checked another box off the calendar. My period is late. By a couple of weeks. I feel like I should be reacting more than I am. There should be tears or elation or fear or . . . something. But there isn't anything.

Once Cal left for work I curled up in the armchair with *Pride and Prejudice*, one of my favourites, and I haven't moved since. I want to lose myself in the world of Elizabeth Bennet. Despite having read this novel countless times, I still get an excited flutter when she meets Mr Darcy. True, enduring love. But even the words of Jane Austen are not enough to captivate me today. My mind has turned into a void.

I wonder what kind of book I would write, should I try my hand at it. Probably daring escapades in far-off countries, meeting people from all walks of life. It's mad, when I sit and really think about it, that the hiker yesterday was the first person I've actually seen aside from Cal since I came here.

I place my finger on the page so as not to lose my place. There's that urge again. That yearning to document who I was before. To force myself to remember the places I went, the things I did, the people I met. My parents. What would they say if they could see me now? If they knew what I have become?

My eyes squeeze shut as I try to picture their faces, but it's like trying to look at someone through a thick fog. They're there but they're not. Blurry figures. I told the man I couldn't remember much about my life before the Highlands because I haven't been home in so long, but it's worse than that. I'm starting to forget my parents' faces. I'm starting to lose the sound of their voices.

I think about the collection of cells inside me, rapidly dividing and multiplying. I wish I could call my mum. It's crazy when I think about how long it's been since I last spoke to her. I spent most of my time crying about it when I first came here. Cal always tried to assure me that I was better off, that he knew what toxic relationships with parents could do to a person. He never elaborated, but I assume his relationship with his parents was strained. I didn't ask.

I always thought I'd be a good mum. The type whose children would always come and talk to when they had a problem. Yet here I am, sitting in this chair, unable to even think of the life inside me as a baby. Worse. I'm sitting here thinking if there's any possible way for me to get rid of it without Cal finding out.

I can feel a headache coming on again, the words of *Pride and Prejudice* swirling before my eyes. I haven't been sleeping properly these past few days and fatigue is starting to overwhelm me.

I wake with a start as the book thuds on the rug, landing upside down and open with its pages crushed. Shaking myself, I run the back of my hand along my mouth, mopping up the saliva that's pooled there. My limbs are heavy. How long have I been asleep? My head jerks towards the shadows cast by the sun pouring through the window. It's OK. They'd be at a different angle if it was too late in the day.

The headache is still there, thumping away in the background, so I heave myself forward and rub my temples, all too aware that the painkillers are too high for me to reach. I need to distract myself, rid my brain of the embryo inside me and the hiker and my parents and Cal. Stretching my arms out as wide as I can manage, I stand and begin my fitness routine. Sometimes I don't bother with it. The work I do at the cabin is often more than enough to get my muscles burning. But Cal likes me to work out when I have spare time. Says it helps to keep me fit and healthy.

By the time I'm ten minutes in, sweat is pouring down my forehead and stinging my eyes but I keep going, enjoying the burn, enjoying the fact that I can't think of anything else. I run on the spot and I lunge and I push up until I fear I might pass out. Only then do I crumple back into the armchair, huffing and puffing, unable to move, and immediately the thoughts return to me.

I'm getting out of the bath when Cal returns home. Two baths in two days – a luxury – but I needed it. Body odour wafting from my general direction was not the way I wanted to greet him. Dinner is nearly ready, which I notice he's pleased to see when he shakes off his coat and flicks his eyes towards the fireplace. I don't say anything, I'm still not sure what to say, but dutifully set the table while I rake back through the day in my mind, trying to remember if I've done anything stupid again that might make him angry. I don't think I have.

As I place the last fork down on the table he steps towards me and I flinch. The involuntary jerk causes a pained expression to flash over his face. He places a hand on my shoulder and pulls me towards him. Then his other arm wraps around my back and he's holding me close, my face pressed up against his chest.

'I'm sorry,' he whispers against my hair, making the roots at my scalp stand on end, and I close my eyes. 'I shouldn't have gone off on you like that. You know I'm just trying to keep you safe. I dinnae know what I'd do without you.'

My eyes flick open.

Ordinarily his apologies give me relief like a fuzzy blanket being draped over my shoulders and I pull them tighter to me. But things are different now. They have been since I looked at that calendar and realised what must have happened.

'Would you mind if I lie down for ten minutes? Dinner just needs a little more time on the stove.'

I can see he's considering protesting, but he doesn't. He nods and I shuffle towards the bedroom. Once the door is closed behind me I drop to my knees next to the bed and slide my hand under the mattress. My notebook rests under my palm. I won't risk writing in it. I don't need to. Just touching it is offering me the morsel of reassurance that I need.

Feeling a little better, I lean with my back to the wall, legs stretched out in front of me so that my toes disappear under the bed. I stare at the space between our mattress and the floorboards, at the layer of dust that's built up in the very centre where my broom clearly doesn't reach.

My eyes narrow. There's a small lift in the corner of one of the floorboards.

I lean forward on my hands and duck my head low to get a better look. My stomach gets in the way so I have to lie awkwardly on my side and shimmy forward, peering into the dark space beneath the bed. Brushing away some of the dust and debris with my hand, I run my fingers along the edges. There's a small gap between this board and the ones around it.

My heart begins to race as I realise this board is loose. I can't believe I've never seen this before. I dig my nails in and prise it up. It comes free with a soft creak, revealing a small hidden compartment underneath.

Cobwebs coat my hand as I reach in and a small shudder works its way down my spine. I grit my teeth and hope I'm not about to have a giant spider scuttling up my arm.

My breath hitches as my fingers brush along something. I twist my arm, reaching further into the cavity, until I finally retrieve the object. My back clicks furiously as I sit up. In my hands is a pile of letters. Old letters by the looks of things, bound together with a flimsy elastic band that's seen better days. Left undisturbed under that floorboard for goodness knows how long.

The elastic band snaps as I go to remove it and the letters spill out over the floor. The pages are yellowed with age, scribbled in handwriting I don't recognise. There's something about these letters. Some sense of danger here, like the pages themselves are telling me that once I look at them there will be no going back. Holding my breath, I pick up the closest one and begin to read.

Chapter Seven

Cal coming into the bedroom to let me know that dinner is boiling over shatters me from my daze. There's a moment where everything is still and silent. Him from the shock of seeing me sat here with letters penned in another woman's handwriting strewn around me, and me from the shock of finding out I'm not the first wife that's lived in this cabin.

That's who the letters were written by. Cal's first wife. A woman he's never mentioned or shown any trace of in all the years I've been with him. And I don't have to tell Cal that because by the look on his face as he picks one of them up I know he recognises the handwriting.

'Where'd you get them?'

My lip twitches. 'I found them. Tied to the underside of my drawer.'

I don't know why I just lied about where I found them. Something is telling me not to mention the space under the floorboard.

'Mary—'

'Who's Gemma?' I interrupt. That's bold. I know better than to interrupt Cal. But in this instance it looks like he might allow me to get away with it. It's a pointless question really because these letters tell me exactly who Gemma is, but I feel the need to ask the question anyway. I want to understand how she fits into Cal's life. I need to understand what happened before I came to this cabin.

Cal hesitates for a moment. I don't think I've ever seen him look unsure of himself, but he does right now. Eventually he moves further into the bedroom and settles himself on the floor beside me. His head tilts back and rests on the wall.

'She was me wife.'

My eyebrows flick up. I had been sure he was going to lie.

'So there was someone else before me.'

'Aye, but Mary, believe me when I say—' he grips my hand and stares me dead in the eye '—I love you wholeheartedly. Whatever there was before with Gemma and me it wasnae a touch on what we've got. What we've got is special.'

It's all I can do not to allow my lip to curl.

'I thought the Bible told us to devote ourselves to one partner only.'

That's a risky thing to say – to quote his precious Bible – but the revelation that there was another wife here in this cabin is more than I can bear and I want to see him squirm. And squirm he does. I've touched a nerve.

'Lots o' great men of the Bible had multiple wives. Abraham, Samson, David, Solomon. Ain't nothin' wrong with it.'

He sounds like he's trying to convince himself more than me. Before I can say anything else he's dropped my hand and is leaning forward, scooping the letters up in his arms, the paper crumpling and tearing as he does so. I know I'll never see those letters again but it's OK because the last letter, the one Gemma wrote for me, is safely tucked away in my back pocket. He hasn't seen that one. Doesn't even know it exists. And he never will.

The letters burn in the fireplace while we sit down to dinner. Things are back to the way they used to be. As we talk it's as if the letters and the hiker and the arguments never even happened. After dinner, he lays his cutlery on his plate and leans forward and says, 'What do you want to do?'

'Pardon?'

'This evening. Your choice. We can go for a walk together or play a board game or . . . whatever you want.'

I press my lips together, thinking for a moment. This is an unusual turn of events. Usually after dinner Cal decides how we spend our evening and I've never really thought to suggest an activity. Possibilities pop in and out of my head like little fireworks. God help me, a plan has started to form. Something that came to me, a moment of brilliance, as I read Gemma's letters and realised I wasn't the first. It's an awful, horrific plan. But it's a means to an end. I've always wanted to leave Cal. Of course I have. But now it's not just a desire. It's a need. A desperation. Now there's not just me to think about.

My eyes roam the room, landing on my easel. The plan turns over in my head.

'We could paint together?' I suggest, and Cal unsuccessfully tries to hold back a laugh.

'I'm not much of a painter.'

'I could teach you.'

He thinks for a moment, then nods. 'All right, you're on.'

Ten minutes later I've washed up the dishes as quickly as possible and am laying extra blankets across the floor. We create a makeshift second easel by pulling the console table over and placing a canvas on it, leaning it up against the wall. I then squeeze a few primary colours onto one of the palettes and hand it to him along with a brush. He flourishes the palette above his shoulder, making the paints slide dangerously close to the edge, and pastes a ridiculous, over-animated half-smile onto his face.

'Mademoiselle,' he says in a strange accent, wiggling his eyebrows up and down. ''Ello, allow me to introduce myself. I am Monsieur Alphonze LeBlanc, artiste extraordinaire.'

The voice and his facial expressions at least settle my nerves somewhat.

'What are you doing?' I laugh.

He leans over and whispers urgently in my ear in his usual Scottish drawl, 'This is my persona. I'm a French painter,' before springing back to his alter ego. French. That was the accent he was trying to mimic. Other than the hiker, it's been a long time since I've heard anything other than a Scottish accent.

'Oh, I see. Well . . . Monsieur LeBlanc, I believe you are here for an art lesson?'

'Lesson? Oh no, no, no. *Mon dieu!* I am a genius, known for my childlike scribbles. Talent like mine cannot be taught.'

He keeps up his French persona throughout our painting session, and the more over the top he acts the more I second-guess what I'm about to do. I spend most of my time trying to get him in exactly this mood. Happy. Content. Do I really want to ruin that?

When I try to show him how to paint a reflection in the water, his attempt looks more like a dead body floating in it, and when I point this out to him he dramatically declares that he was going for that effect all along, before dabbing his paintbrush against my nose and leaving a splotch of greeny brown on the tip.

And then it happens.

He sees it.

He freezes, stock-still, staring at my painting, at the little white sign near the water's edge. Shore Road. Last time I painted it he was lenient. Surely he won't be twice.

I brace myself, readying myself for the inevitable shouting. But he doesn't. He looks at me with an odd expression on his face that I can't quite read. His eyes are shining as if he's about to cry. He forces a smile as he raises his thumb and wipes the paint off my nose.

'Is there something you want to talk to me about?' he says.

Yes. There are so many things. So much I'd kill to say to him right now. But I can't just blurt it all out. If this plan is going to work I need to bide my time. It needs to be gradual. Calculated.

'I wondered . . . I've just been thinking about . . .' The words are tangling in my mouth, an incoherent mess of jumbled thoughts that I've not had time to string into a proper sentence. I take a moment to collect myself, my throat straining to swallow.

'It's so lonely here,' I say eventually.

Cal's brows pull together. 'What do you mean?'

'You work a lot, Cal.'

'I have to. Do you know what's going on out there? The price of everything has gone up. We're just lucky we're mostly self-reliant.'

'I know. That's not what I mean.'

Cal stares at me for a moment, and I try desperately to figure out what he's thinking. Nerves flutter in my stomach. Letting out a deep breath, he places his hands on his thighs and leans back against the arm of the sofa.

'What do you mean then?'

I shrug. 'The hiker yesterday made me think it might be nice to have someone else around here.'

Cal's eyes narrow. 'Someone else?'

'Maybe. For company when you're not here. And it would be good to have an extra pair of hands. If I didn't have so much to do around the cabin I could put more effort into doing nice things for you.'

'Ah, I see. You want te slack off, eh?'

'Not at all. I just . . .' I exhale through my nose and close my eyes. 'I just thought it might be nice. That's all.'

Without another word, he stands and heads to the bedroom, and I know our painting session is finished. I purse my lips as I pack away the supplies, glancing at the painted road sign. My hand drops to my stomach and I stand for a second, letting it rise and fall with the rhythmic flow of my breath. There's a spark of life beginning inside me. I should feel something. There should be some kind of emotional response.

'A good wife shouldnae keep her husband waiting,' Cal calls from the bedroom.

Chapter Eight

We're in the middle of it when it happens.

I'm lying on the bed while he's huffing and grunting, my plan turning over and over in my mind. Part of me hating myself. Most of me convinced that it's just something that has to be done. The thought is clawing its way up from my stomach now, scratching at my oesophagus, spilling into my mouth. Except it's not just a thought.

I clasp my hand around my mouth as I lurch sideways, practically throwing him off me. He lets out a cry. I'm not sure if he's hurt himself or is just frustrated to have been interrupted, but I don't care. The vomit misses the toilet by inches. I hunch over in a shuddering ball and retch and shake. By the time I'm done I feel wrecked. Completely wiped out. I reach out feebly for the toilet paper and start mopping up the mess.

'Are you OK?' Cal's voice behind me makes me start, and the bathroom is suddenly bright as he lights a lantern. I turn my face away so that he can't see the state of me.

'Yes. Sorry, I don't know what came over me.'

As I resume clearing the floor, I feel his eyes boring into me. He's watching. Why is he watching? The sense of it is making me feel claustrophobic, as if the walls are shrinking around me. I risk a glance back in his direction. His face is like stone.

'Are you ill? Is it something you ate?'

I shake my head. 'I don't think so.' The reason for this sudden bout of sickness is, of course, clear in my mind, but I can't bring myself to say it.

He sweeps past me, expertly avoiding any remaining splashes of sick, and reaches up to the medicine box. I wonder what he's going to give me. Is there a pill you can take when you're not even sure what's wrong with you? But he doesn't retrieve a pill from the box like he usually does. This time he pulls out a long, thin foil package. He rips it open and hands me the contents. I frown at the plastic stick.

'What is it?' I say stupidly. I know exactly what it is.

'You need to piss on it.'

He says it in such a simple manner I find myself wanting to laugh. Pressing my lips together, I take it and move to the toilet. My hands hover at my underwear.

'Can you go into the bedroom while I do it?'

No response.

My cheeks burn bright red as I realise he's not going to leave the room. He's going to continue to watch me while I pee. The shame, the indecency of it, makes my stomach gurgle again. Please no. No more. I swallow hard to stop myself from throwing up again and focus on the task at hand.

Trying to force pee out, especially when being watched, is an experience I never want to repeat. Eventually I manage and awkwardly hold the stick under me. Once I'm done I hold it between my thumb and forefinger, distinctly aware of how disgusting this feels.

'Now what?'

'We wait.'

And so we do. I'm not sure how long for exactly, I can't remember how long these things are supposed to take, but it seems to stretch on and on. He's no longer staring at me but at the test, his gaze laser-focused on the little window in the middle which now displays a flashing sand-timer. Nerves rattle around inside me even though I already know what it's going to tell me. There's a small part of me that thinks perhaps it will flash up negative. That my period is just bizarrely late and that the symptoms I've been experiencing have all been in my head. That would be for the better, wouldn't it?

Eventually, after what feels like years, the sand-timer disappears and is replaced by one word.

One single word.

Pregnant.

I stare at the word, saying it over and over in my head, double and triple checking that I haven't somehow misread it. The positive result is unmistakable. I look up at Cal.

He is not smiling.

He steps forward, snatches the stick out of my hand and squints at it, so close to his face it's a wonder the word isn't blurring before his eyes. Then he looks at me instead and slaps me.

Hard.

My head whips to the side. I'm momentarily stunned, the breath knocked from my lungs. Tears stream down my face. If I looked bad before, I dread to think how I must look now. My cheek is hot and it's like I can still feel his handprint burning into my skin. His head droops backwards and he drags his hand through his hair. I want to scream at him. But there are no more words. Nothing to say. All I can do is watch as he turns his back on me and stalks off to the living room.

I suck in a shaky breath and rest my hand on my stomach.

No matter how much guilt I feel over my plan, it has to be done. It has to.

Chapter Nine

To my astonishment, Cal ventures out once more. At first I thought he was going to go to the barn like he normally does when he's angry, but he doesn't. The door slams shut, echoing louder than usual, quickly followed by the low rumble of his truck's engine. I watch from the window as he disappears into the distance, leaving me alone.

Except I'm not alone. Not really.

Time passes, and I remain where I am, sitting watching through the window, waiting for his return, hoping it never happens but knowing that it has to or I'm screwed. My cheek still throbs, the lingering evidence of his reaction. But it only comprises a tiny percentage of the agony I'm feeling. My throat constricts at the recollection of my time in this cabin. Within me, a turbulent blend of anger and sadness battle.

I hadn't wanted him to find out about the pregnancy. I had hoped my plan would come into play before that, that I'd be free of him and this place before he realised. What, I wonder, will he be like when he returns, once he's had a chance to clear his head? Will it be like it was before? I grimace at the thought.

Cal is out for hours. I drift in and out of sleep and it's getting light when I hear the truck. I look around me. My initial instinct when I hear him coming home is to wonder whether I've done enough, whether the house is tidy enough, and even though it's the early hours of the morning that initial panic is still there. I push it away, though, because it's all part of it. No longer striving to look my best. No longer keeping this place immaculate. No longer attempting to be the perfect wife just so that he doesn't turn on me. If this is going to work, I need to deal with the fact that he's not going to be happy Cal when he walks through that door.

I'm fully prepared to stand my ground and argue with him, but his face makes me stop in my tracks. When he sees me standing waiting for him a flicker of what looks like relief flashes across it.

'I wasnae sure you'd still be here when I got back,' he says, his voice gruff. I hesitate, caught off guard. Where did he think I'd go?

For a moment we stand quietly facing each other, a kind of awkward stand-off while each of us waits to see who will speak first. It's not going to be me.

As if reading my mind he bows his head and runs his palm over his beard.

'I'm so sorry.' His voice cracks as he says it. 'I don't know what came over me. It was just . . . a wee shock, you know?'

My eyebrows rise. 'A shock?' I repeat. 'You hit me.'

'I didnae hit you. Bloody hell, Mary. That makes it sound like I pummelled you. It were a slap.'

I'm about to start indignantly ranting about semantics, but he's obviously realised this isn't the way to apologise because he's quick to add, 'Not that it matters. I shouldnae have laid a hand on you at all.'

I want to laugh, remind him of everything that happened all those years ago, but I don't. He takes a step towards me and though my immediate reaction is to move away I'm rooted to the spot.

'I swear, it'll never happen again. I will never, ever hurt you again.'

Tears gather in my eyes but I'm quick to blink them away.

'How do I know you won't?'

'Because o' that wee bairn in that belly o' yours.' He takes another step forward so that he's close enough to place a hand on my stomach. A tingle crosses my skin at his touch. My lips are so dry they're close to cracking. I lick them, my resolve weakening.

'None of it's an excuse,' he continues. 'All I can do is ask for your forgiveness and promise you it'll never happen again.'

He's still stroking my stomach. The feel of it makes me want to throw up again.

'OK,' I whisper, and the corners of his lips pull up.

For the remainder of the morning, and actually the rest of the day too, Cal looks after me like he's never done before. He insists on me putting my feet up with a cup of tea while he cleans around me, even going so far as to don my hand-embroidered floral apron and prance around on his tiptoes with the feather duster in a feeble attempt to make me laugh. My cushions are plumped, lunch is brought to me on a tray, and even when I tell him my back is starting to stiffen from sitting down all day he still won't let me start the dinner prep.

'Today is your day,' he says. 'Leave the housework to me.'

Despite my urge to protest, I allow him to chop the carrots and potatoes. If he wants to wait on me for a change, who am I to argue?

Dinner isn't great – Cal's cooking skills leave something to be desired – but I eat it up eagerly nonetheless. I've found myself becoming ravenous these past few days. That old wives' tale about eating for two circles my mind but I'm pretty sure I'm just using the pregnancy as an excuse.

'I've been thinking,' Cal says through a mouthful of mash. 'Maybe we could take a holiday after all.'

My mouth hangs open slightly as I lower my fork. 'Really?'

'Mmm, people do that, don't they? What do they call it? A babymoon. Like a trip you take before little'un comes.'

I nod, though I've never actually heard of a 'babymoon'. The sensible voice in my head is telling me to leap at the suggestion, to take full advantage of his good mood and get exactly what I asked for. But there's another voice. One that feels like Cal might be overcompensating just a little too much.

'Cal,' I venture, despite the first sensible voice screaming at me not to. 'Is anything the matter?'

Cal's forehead creases. 'What do you mean?'

'I don't know.' I shrug, not wanting to let on what's really on my mind. What I want to ask him is if he's started to do what I hope he's started doing. 'Just I want us to always be honest with each other. Especially with this baby coming. I don't want there to be any secrets between us.'

'Agreed. No secrets.'

I smile and return to my food, but with less gusto than before. No more is said for the remainder of dinner, and I can tell my question has spoiled Cal's good mood. Contrary to his insistence that I put my feet up and do nothing today, once we finish eating I'm left to do the dishes while he retreats to his armchair, and his quietness continues until bedtime. Still, when I slide into bed beside him, he wraps his arms around me and buries his face into my neck. His hand slides across my abdomen.

'Goodnight, little'un,' he says.

A shiver runs down my spine.

Chapter Ten

I try to tell myself, when I wake the next morning, that I need to stay strong. That any lingering doubts I might have about my plan are uncalled for, probably a result of the pregnancy and all the worries and anticipation that come along with that. It's not like I know what to expect from carrying a child. It's no wonder my mind is hurrying to every worst-case scenario.

At breakfast I listlessly pick at my bacon as Cal sits across from me at the table, in his usual place. He's said he's going to bring a present home for me today, which, relatively speaking, should be something to look forward to, but I'm struggling to feel excited about it.

Cal seems to be in an even better mood today than he was yesterday. I mention the lack of knowledge about what to expect with this pregnancy and he promises that the present he'll bring me home today will be a book on pregnancy, and he keeps his promise. It's a heavy tome of a book, detailing everything from the creation of an embryo to the various issues that can arise during birth. I try not to focus too much on that bit. The birth is a long, long way away, and I'd rather not get myself worked up over all the things that could go wrong. But the rest of it I drink up, revelling in every ounce of information I can absorb to try to get a better understanding of what's going on inside me. And the more I learn, the more I start to think of this life inside me as more than just a collection of cells.

Over the next few weeks I learn that my heightened anxiety is probably down to the rapid change in hormones. I learn that my baby is the size of a bell pepper. Every time I experience something, some twinge that I'm not sure about, some ache that has me concerned that something is wrong, I'm back buried in the book, my fingers darting across the index to find the symptom and delving into a mass of medical jargon. Sometimes it helps. More often than not it only increases my concerns.

The more I worry, the more frustrated Cal seems to get with me. His caring, couldn't-do-more-for-me attitude from the night we found out I was expecting has dwindled, replaced by the distinct sense that I'm being a pain when I bring anything to do with the baby up. He hasn't even mentioned the babymoon again.

'I think we should go to see a doctor, just to make sure everything is OK,' I say over dinner one night. Silly – I already know what the answer will be – but worth a try, nonetheless.

He scoffs, knife scraping noisily across his plate. 'A doctor won't tell you anything that book cannae tell you.'

Textbook Cal.

'But what about the birth? We'll need someone here for that.'

'I said no. Stop being so bloody argumentative, woman.'

I bite back the overwhelming urge to retaliate. Times like this I sort of want to go back to how it was before, with me doing everything in my power to please him, if only to make life a little bit more bearable. But I'm well past that.

He proceeds to give me the silent treatment for the rest of dinner, not saying a single word to me until he gets up and puts his plate in the sink, which actually makes a pleasant change. His eyes flick to the pile of washing, still to be folded in a basket on the counter.

'You're slacking on the housework,' he says.

I know I am. I'm doing it on purpose.

'Sorry, Cal.'

That's probably the tenth time I've apologised to him in the past fortnight. I'm always apologising for something or other these days. He can tell my apology is half-hearted, because his lip curls and he looks at me with disgust before putting his boots on again and disappearing back down the hill, to the barn. He does that a lot. Most days in fact. How long he'll be down there, I have no idea. Sometimes he's there for ten minutes. Sometimes hours. Is he doing what I think he's doing down there?

Something stirs inside me. A flicker of annoyance. Driven by reckless impulse and a need to understand why he is the way he is, I dash into the bedroom. My hands shake as I yank open his bedside table drawer and begin rifling through it. I'm not supposed to go through his things. I can clean and tidy every area of this house except for those parts that are his domain. Once, back when I was desperate to do anything I could possibly do to keep him happy, I tried to surprise him by sorting out his wardrobe for when he returned from work. I took everything out and laid it on the bed, before carefully loading it back onto the rail in colour-coordinated order. He hated that. Immediately ripped everything out and yelled at me to put it all back the way it had been. I haven't touched his things since that day.

This thought curdles in my brain as I continue to flick through the knick-knacks in his drawer. Receipts. A pack of tissues. Deodorant. My eyes occasionally flick up to the window, to the barn, to ensure he's not on his way back. I know deep down what I'm doing is against his wishes but my desire to figure him out, to understand him, supersedes any warnings my body is trying to give me. A ruthless determination has settled itself inside my core.

There's nothing interesting in his drawer, so I move instead to the wardrobe, picking through his jackets and jeans and plunging my hands into his pockets. A couple of times I'm hit with a jolt of excitement as my fingers skim a piece of paper or cause something to rustle, but it's just parking tickets and sweet wrappers. His work jacket then. I hurry back to the hallway and start rummaging through it. This jacket has lots of pockets, five on the outside and four on the inside, to hold all of his tree surgeon bits and bobs. A nail stabs my finger and I snatch it back. A bubble of blood swells on the tip. Wincing, I suck on the wound and proceed more carefully with my uninjured hand. In the third inside pocket I find his wallet and I pull it out, letting it flop open in my palm.

At first, I don't see anything unusual, but as I'm about to put it back I spot the corner of something sticking out from behind his driving licence. I give it a tug. A small, cracked photo slides out.

I stop breathing. I've never seen this photo before. It shows a beautiful young woman with gently curled hair pulled back with a ribbon, cradling a baby in her arms and smiling broadly. Standing next to her and not smiling is a man, and at first I think it's Cal. He has the same dark hair and beard, the same piercing eyes. On second look, however, I can see the differences. This man has a scar on his eyebrow that Cal does not have, and his lips are a different shape. I realise that this must be a picture of Cal's parents. I've never seen a picture of them before. And that baby, wrapped up in what looks to be a hand-knitted blanket, must be Cal.

My stomach flutters as I take in the tiny, chubby fingers and the button nose. Is that what my baby will look like?

The sound of gravel crunching interrupts my train of thought. Cal is returning to the cabin. I slide the photo back into its slot behind his driving licence and shove the wallet back into his pocket. My palms sweat as I scramble into the kitchen and start the washing up, hoping that I can make it look like this is what I've been doing for the past ten minutes. When Cal comes through the front door it occurs to me that I didn't have time to check if I'd put everything back in the bedroom the way it was, but it's too late now.

'Have you not finished that yet?' he says as he shakes his boots off once more.

'I'm nearly done,' I respond, even though the majority of the pots and pans are still buried under the bubbles. He grunts and heads into the bathroom to clean up.

He takes his time in the bathroom, and the kitchen is put away by the time he returns. He flops down in his armchair and I place a glass of Scotch by his side. I go to sit in my usual spot on the sofa, but his hand on my wrist stops me. A jolt of panic shoots through me as I wonder what I've done wrong now, but his touch is soft.

'Come sit here,' he says, patting his knee. I obediently move to perch there. His hands snake around my waist and he buries his face into my shoulder.

'I've been thinkin'. What you said about the birth. We could perhaps get a doctor here.'

My stomach clenches.

'I'll ask around,' he continues. 'See if I can find a good option.'

Relief floods through me so rapidly I come over light-headed. 'Thank you. Thank you so much.'

'I love you so much, you know that, right?'

I nod, a lump catching in my throat. 'I love you too.'

61

As Cal cuddles me I find myself once again wondering if I'd be better off opting for the easy route, the one I've been opting for all these years.

'You remind me of me mam, you know.'

I stiffen, thinking back to the photo, and chew on my lip. 'Do I?'

'Aye, she was a good mam.'

'You've never really spoken about her.'

At first I don't think he's going to respond, but after a few seconds he pulls away from me so that he can see my face.

'What do you want to know?'

I shrug. I'd love to ask him what caused him to view women the way he does. Why he's so insistent on wives being wives and doting on their husbands like there's nothing else worth doing in life. Somehow I don't think that question will go down well.

He sighs, clearly annoyed by my lack of enthusiasm for the subject. 'I was a right little scoundrel growing up. Always getting myself into trouble, that I was. Eventually I had to grow up, o' course. Had to start looking after me mam.'

'What about your dad?'

Without warning, he shifts away from me and stands up.

'You need to get an early night tonight. You always look bloody rough these days.'

I feel as though I've been slapped. What was it he said to me that day? 'Have you been using that cream I got you?' He'd been looking at my wrinkles, at the lines etched into my skin, betraying my age like rings on a tree stump.

It's all part of the plan, I have to remind myself.

The rest of the evening is surprisingly pleasant. The Highlands are edging towards summer enough now that we don't have to have the fire on. We play Scrabble and do a devotional and by the time the skies outside are darkening I'm more than ready to turn in for the night. When I go into the bathroom to brush my teeth I discreetly step on the scales, toothbrush hanging out of my mouth, eager to see the dial on the scales crank up an extra notch. All the years I've spent making sure I eat right and exercise enough to ensure it never goes higher than expected and now look at me. I'm excited for my body to start reflecting the life growing inside of me. I've not just accepted this pregnancy now. I'm actually beginning to look forward to all that's to come.

'Mary?'

I spit in the sink. 'Mmm?'

'Come here a sec.'

Quickly washing my mouth out and then the sink, I return to the bedroom.

My stomach flips.

He's sat on the edge of the bed, craning over his open bedside table. From my position I can't see into the drawer to figure out if the contents has been noticeably disturbed.

'Yes?' My voice is hoarse, as if I've been screaming.

'Have you been in here?'

I hesitate. I could lie. I probably should lie. It's the smart thing to do. It's never clear which Cal I'm going to get. Kind, loving, considerate; or angry and hurtful. But then if I lie and he knows it, it'll be worse.

'Yes,' I say.

He surveys me for a moment, absorbing my confession.

'You went through my things?'

'I just wanted to know more about you.' I hate how small my voice is, a pathetic little whisper.

I'm not sure if he didn't hear me or if he's just ignoring me. My hands clench and unclench as I wait for him to react.

Finally, just as I think I cannot take the silence any longer, he stands up. His fingers dance across the edge of the drawer. Then, without warning, he swipes his arm across the surface. The bedside lamp goes flying, smashing against the wall, the lampshade crumpling. The wall pressing against my back tells me I've backed right away from him as he continues to grab and throw things. The clothes basket, the curtain ripped off its rail, the box in which I keep the little bracelets and trinkets he sometimes brings home for me.

'Please, stop . . .'

But Cal isn't listening. Sobs erupt from me as I watch the chaos unfold. I want to run but I'm frozen to the spot. My eyes widen and I'm suddenly afraid that destroying our room isn't going to be enough, that it's going to be me next. My body being flung around. My face being smashed in.

When he's done and every surface is cleared and the floor is littered with broken possessions, he turns his attention to me. He stands inches away from me. I try to recoil but I'm already pressed against the wall. There's nowhere for me to go. I can feel his hot, heavy breaths on my face. His whole body is shaking, as is mine.

'Don't you *ever* go through my shit again.' Each word is punctuated like a knife. My stomach knots and I realise this is the first time in years I've felt truly scared of him.

There's a moment of silence and then his mouth twists. I stare at him, wide-eyed. He's smiling. He's actually smiling. He's enjoying the fact that I'm so scared.

For a good ten seconds he keeps me hostage like this, him with that awful smirk on his face, me trying desperately to put a few more millimetres of space between us. Finally, he steps away and heads back to the living room, slamming the door in my face.

Chapter Eleven

I sit on the bed and stare at the wall, waiting for him to return to bed, wishing he wouldn't. He doesn't return. I don't know if he's fallen asleep in the armchair or if he's still awake like me, but I daren't open the bedroom door to find out.

I turn over images of him destroying our room in my aching head. The evidence still lies scattered across the floor. It's been so long since I've seen him like that. It was pure, animalistic rage. I wonder if that's something his father used to do. It would make sense, why he doesn't want to talk about him. Maybe that's where it came from, a tiny spark of his dad that resides within him that he usually keeps suppressed. I shudder at the thought, picturing small, toddler Cal cowering in a corner and his mother begging his father to stop.

My hand inadvertently moves to my stomach. The question I've been avoiding, the doubt that's been niggling away at the back of my mind since I found out I was pregnant, is working its way to the fore.

Is my plan going to work in time? Am I going to be able to leave Cal before this baby arrives?

So far I've tried to focus on the good. I've pictured the moments that await me. The first smile. The first giggle. The first steps. But life here in the cabin is not one in which to raise a child. I'm now used to all this. But it's not just about me anymore, and this life is one I cannot allow my child to get used to. Here, they are doomed to loneliness. They won't go to school, won't make friends, won't one day find a husband or wife of their own. Can a child truly thrive when they have no human interactions beyond their mother? And what would Cal even be like with this poor kid? This isn't a house of love. It's a cabin of fear.

At some point I must have fallen asleep with these thoughts, because I start awake to the sound of the front door slamming and the truck disappearing down the dirt road. I fell asleep at an awkward angle, slumped over sideways with my legs still hanging off the edge of the bed, so as I sit up I'm plagued with pins and needles stabbing my left side. Rubbing my neck to ease the aching of my muscles, I glance around me. The bed is still made. Cal never came back.

And now he's gone to work.

I ease myself off the bed and eye a safe-ish route through the largest shards of broken lamp. Barefoot, I step gingerly through the mess. My bones crack as I get to the kitchen to make myself a cup of coffee. I'm relieved he's gone. The tension in the air seems to have disappeared up the road right along with him. I can finally breathe.

Clasping my coffee in my hands, I wander out into the garden, wondering what I should do with myself today. My instinct is to busy myself with work around the cabin as a distraction, but the aches and pains in my body are telling me otherwise. Instead, I circle the cabin aimlessly, peering out through the window at our bleak surroundings, watching the birds fluttering over the treetops, allowing myself to imagine what people might be doing beyond the Highlands.

Without really becoming aware of it, I find myself staring at the barn. He disappears to that barn so often these days it's a wonder I see him at all. There's always that question lingering in my mind, wondering if it's happened yet.

I hesitate and take a large gulp of coffee. A shudder works its way through me and I glance at the dirt track. No truck to be seen. I'm fully aware that if I go to the barn he'll know. It'll cause more rows, more anger on his part. Things could become so much worse. But the question of whether or not my plan has worked has been well and truly planted in my brain, growing and spreading like weeds.

I have no choice. I'm not even sure I care that much what he will do when he realises what I'm doing. I pull my coat tight around my shoulders and slip my feet into my boots before trudging outside. The barn glares at me like something out of a horror film. As I walk, my fingers interlace and my eyes drift up to the sky.

If there's a God up there, what would he do? Would he allow my plan to work? Or will I go to hell for being such a shitty person?

The cabin beckons me back and I bite my lip anxiously, forcing myself to continue towards the barn. My eyes flick towards the dirt road. I don't even know if he's gone to work or if he's just nipped to the shop. Maybe he's hunting. He could be just beyond those trees for all I know. I have no idea how long he'll be or how long it will take him to realise what I'm doing. I picture his face as he destroyed our room, then I pick up my pace, urgency and the desire to know propelling me forward.

There is a padlock on the barn door. I hesitate, wondering what I should do.

'Hello?' I call, despite myself.

No answer. Of course there isn't.

I raise my voice a little. 'Is anyone in there?'

I'm met with resolute silence. Feebly, I pull at the padlock and give the door a little shake. It holds fast. I'm not sure what I expected to happen. There's nothing else I can do here. I don't know if this is better or worse than bursting into the barn and seeing what I'm picturing in my head. At least if that had been the case I would know.

Frustration eating at me, I make my way back to the cabin.

It's probably a good thing I didn't manage to snoop around in the barn, because he's not gone for long. Half an hour later he's back and I can already sense the dread creeping into the kitchen.

Though I don't really feel in the mood to welcome him home with a cup of coffee, I do it anyway, plucking the cast-iron kettle from the fire and pouring it into his mug. Usually I'd do this first thing in the morning. It feels backwards to be doing it on his return instead. Everything is backwards at the moment.

When he comes inside he's got two large cans, handles looped over his elbow, swinging as he moves, and a book tucked under his other armpit. He dumps the cans on the dining table with a clatter. I peer at them.

'Paint,' he says matter-of-factly. 'Thought we could turn the cupboard in the bedroom into a baby room. Didnae know if it were a wee lad or lass so went for yellow.'

I don't say anything. Clearly he doesn't know I went to the barn. He'd have said something straightaway if he did. He actually seems rather chipper. It's like he's forgotten last night entirely. Like he's unaware that he slept in the living room.

I think my silence has stung him, there's a flash of a pained expression on his face, but he quickly rids himself of it and produces the book from under his armpit. He places it on the table next to the paint cans. There's a picture of a pregnant woman on the cover and the words *Birth and You – Your Guide to Bringing Baby into the World*.

This time, I do acknowledge him.

'I think it's a little early to be worrying too much about that.'

Even as I say it, I want to laugh. Yes, it's still early, but nine months is short.

'Better we learn everything we need to now just in case little'un comes early. Between this book and the other one we'll be just fine.'

My forehead creases. 'We're still going to get a doctor to come here though, right?'

'There isnae a need. We'll make do on our own just like we do with everything else.'

Anger and panic curdle inside me. Images of the cabin awash with blood seep into my mind. When I speak, my voice is strangled.

'What if something goes wrong?'

'Are you questioning my decision?'

I press my lips tight shut. That threat is back in his voice. My eyes sting from holding back the tears. He surveys me, lip twitching, then grabs one of the paint cans and heads towards the bedroom.

'If you're good I'll think about it,' he calls back over his shoulder, before disappearing into the bedroom.

I stay rooted to the spot, mixed emotions still raging, angry thoughts battling for space in my mind. Any normal expectant mother wouldn't even need a doctor to come to the house for a birth. They'd be able to go to the hospital. That's what I want. I want machines and medicines and the knowledge that if something were to happen, I have a whole team of professionals around me with the proper equipment to do something about it. Why won't he let them come?

But of course, I know the reason.

He won't let them come because then there will be medical records needed. There'll be questions asked. And Cal can't be having questions asked.

* * *

It's dark when my eyes flutter open. I can't see the clock to make out what time it is, but I'm guessing it must be dead in the middle of the night. I can always tell when it's edging towards the early hours of the morning because a mist tends to fall over the rolling hills as the sun rises. There's no grey tinge to the world outside our bedroom window now though. It's pitch-black.

I tilt my head to check if Cal is still asleep, but all that's there is bedsheets. He isn't here.

I sit up, disorientated.

'Cal?' My voice echoes in the darkness and I'm met with nothing but silence.

The floor is ice-cold against my feet as I lower my legs from the bed. I peer around the bathroom door, squinting against the darkness to see if he's in there, but it's empty. So is the kitchen and living room.

'Cal?'

I'm about to reach for a candle when a movement from outside catches my attention. My eyes roam to the garden and beyond, to the slaughter barn. At first I dismiss the movement as that of a deer, but no.

I step closer to the window, arching my neck to get a better look. My heart hammers in my chest. My mouth is so dry it feels like sandpaper.

It can't be.

There, walking towards the barn, lit only by the glow of the moon, is Cal.

And he's not alone.

There's a woman with him.

My plan has worked.

Part Two

Chapter Twelve

Amy

I've forgotten what love is.

That's what I'm thinking as I stand at my sink mindlessly running the sponge in the same circle over and over and over again. This plate is so fucking clean I could have the royal family to tea. The bubbles gather on the surface of the water around my wrists, just a few inches below the bruises. The most recent ones, anyway.

I've forgotten what love is, but it sure as hell isn't this.

The poor plate has undergone ten more minutes of scrubbing when a knock comes at the window and I jump so wildly said plate flies, bubbles and all, across the kitchen and smashes into four jagged, albeit very clean, parts. I swear under my breath and peer out of the window. The knocker has disappeared, but I think I can see the edge of a coat over by the door.

Who in their right mind knocks at a window?

I don't hide my annoyance when I open the door. The man on the other side of the threshold smiles at me but I simply raise my eyebrows indignantly, waiting for him to speak.

'Hey, I er . . . I tried ringing—' he gestures at the doorbell to the side of me '—but it wasnae workin', and I dinnae think ye heard me knocking. I hope I didnae scare you. Seemed to be in your own world, there.'

I glance at the doorbell and close my eyes, mortified. It's been broken for weeks. And it's not a far stretch to say I didn't realise someone was at the door.

'Sorry, I was miles away.'

I try to force a smile onto my face. He returns it and we share an awkward moment where we're just stood smiling at each other.

73

Thankfully, he's the first to break the silence.

'I'm the tree surgeon. Here about your rowan?'

God. The embarrassment just isn't going to end today, is it?

I jump back, swinging the door wide. 'Oh, Jesus, yes! I'm so sorry! Come in. Come in.'

Amusement flickers over his face. It's only now that I realise he's not bad to look at. Pretty good looking, actually. The fleeting moment of guilt I have for thinking about a man other than my husband in a physical sense is gone so quickly I get whiplash. Fuck him. After what he did to me last night, I can think about this tree surgeon whatever which way I want. If I want to imagine him chopping that rowan stark naked I bloody well will.

The man moves into the kitchen and eyes the broken plate on the floor. I lurch down and sweep up the pieces in my bare hands before he can comment, flinging the shards into the bin. He raises an eyebrow at me but doesn't say anything.

'So, um . . . tea?'

How very British. I'm so flustered I'm not even sure if there's a real reason for him to be in the house. The tree is, funnily enough, outside. But my mum always used to offer tea to handymen when I lived with her back in Gloucestershire. I've not had anyone do any work for me since I moved in with Rich two years ago, packing up my life in the process, but I assume it's the same here in Scotland.

'Aye, please.' He flashes a smile – a real one this time, not the awkward one he gave me out on the doorstep – and the flip in my stomach confirms that this man is, indeed, hot. I'm going to rather enjoy watching him working up a sweat in my garden. I turn to the kettle to hide my blushing cheeks and busy myself with the tea. I'm particularly careful when I remove the cup from the high shelf. One crockery breakage is more than enough for an afternoon.

'So, what's your name?'

'Cal.'

'Nice to meet you, Cal,' I say as I pass him the cup. 'I'm Amy.'

I realise too late that he already knows my name since I'm the one who booked his services, but he graciously chooses to not point that out.

'Well, I suppose I better get to work, eh?'

'Yes, of course. It's that one there.' I point at the only tree in my entire garden and want to die.

I blame Rich for this. He's turned me into a blubbering, jumbled mess with his emotional manipulation and gaslighting. That was before he laid a hand on me the first time. The time he told me it would never happen again. Until it did last night. I know if anyone was on the outside looking in they'd ask why I don't leave him. Honestly? I'm not sure I have an answer.

It's as this thought churns in my head that I notice him staring at them. The bruises. I throw my arms behind my back and squeeze my hands together so hard the circulation in my fingers stops.

'Let me know if you need anything, won't you?'

He gives me an odd look then that I can't quite put my finger on. It's as if he's surveying me. Like he's staring straight into my soul with those dark eyes. I meet them for several long, dragging seconds. And then he disappears into the garden.

Chapter Thirteen

I thought it was Rich coming back because he'd forgotten his keys. After he beat seven shades of shit out of me he headed to the pub, as he always does. As if the alcohol flooding his system already isn't enough. I've packed and unpacked my bags during those post-beating hours so many times over the past few months, since the abuse first shifted from emotional to physical, I've lost count.

It always comes down to fear.

Fear that he'll catch me leaving.

Fear that even if he doesn't, he'll track me down, wherever I go.

Fear that, no matter how bad he is right now, if I ever try to leave him it will get unimaginably worse.

So when a tapping at the door sounded just as I was dropping some undies and socks into a suitcase, my heart understandably stopped dead. I threw the suitcase back into the wardrobe with such hurried force I'm pretty sure I dented it. However, it's not Rich looking in at me through the window at the side of the front door.

It's that tree surgeon.

'Um, hi?' I say as I open the door a crack, making sure to keep all evidence of cuts and bruises out of his line of sight.

'Hey. I hope you dinnae mind me stopping by. Can I come in?'

'I don't think that's a good idea.'

That's an understatement. If Rich were to come back and see another guy in our house at this time of night I don't know which of us he'd kill first, even if we weren't doing anything other than drinking a cup of tea. Also, and this is possibly an even stronger reason, this is weird. It's late. Really late. Far too late for a tree surgeon to still be working. Not to mention he's pretty much done with our garden.

'Aye. Sorry. I know it's a bit suss, me turnin' up like this.'

I shake my head as if he's silly to even suggest it, even though it's like he's just read my mind.

'I'll go,' he continues, stepping backwards, away from my door. 'I just wanted you to know I'm in the area. And ye've got my number. Y'know. If you ever need someone to help you.'

I shake my head. 'Thanks. We don't have any other trees, but I'm sure it'll need pruning again next year.'

'I dinnae mean the tree.'

My eyebrows flick up involuntarily. 'What do you mean then?'

'You didnae pull your sleeves down enough earlier. And your man just turned up in the pub with bloody knuckles.'

Heat creeps up my neck and my face begins to burn. My instinct is to deny it. After all, the tree surgeon has never even met Rich.

'How do you know it's my husband?'

'Recognised him from your photos.' His gaze flicks to the framed picture perched on the radiator cover next to me. I stare at it. It's a happy photo of Rich and me. We were happy once.

Despite myself, tears spring to my eyes.

'He wasn't always like this,' I say in a whisper. And even though I know it's a really, really bad idea, I open the door wider and step to the side.

My instinct, when we moved into the kitchen, was to offer him a cup of tea, so I was shocked when he swept over to the kettle and started filling it completely unprompted.

'How d'ye take it?' he says, pulling two cups from the cupboard.

'Milk, no sugar, please.'

I watch, feeling as if I've stepped into some backwards twilight zone where I'm the guest and this near stranger is the homeowner. He makes himself a cup too, his with two spoonfuls of sugar, and hands me mine. We sit at the kitchen table and it would be almost comical, if it weren't for the very real threat that Rich might arrive home at any second. Unlikely, sure. Once he goes to the pub it's rare for me to see him again until the early hours of the morning. But enough of a risk to make what we're doing, as innocuous as it is, feel stupid and reckless.

His eyes drop to the blue fingerprints on my arms. 'D'ye want to talk about what happened? You dinnae have to. We can talk about somethin' else. Take your mind off it.'

My face flushes again. I'd almost forgotten that's why he's here. Because he knows what a scumbag I've managed to get myself tethered to.

I fix my gaze on the grain of the kitchen table. 'You probably think I'm really stupid to stay.'

'Not in the slightest,' he says, his voice completely sincere. 'Me mam were wi' someone like that for a long time. It's a lot easier to say you're gon' te leave than te actually do it.'

I nod slowly, unsure what to say to that. This is not the sort of conversation two people who met just yesterday should be having. So instead I say, 'Are you married?'

I know he is. I clocked the wedding ring when he was up in my tree. But it's something to say.

'Aye. That I am. Name's Mary.'

'Any kids?'

He pauses at this question and for a moment I think I've been incredibly rude. Perhaps he and his wife are one of those couples who have been trying for years and never managed to conceive. Normally, I'd be more tactful. I hate how frazzled I've become.

'I just found out the wife's expectin'. Actually, I found out about an hour ago.'

I desperately want to pry. He doesn't seem particularly thrilled about the news that there's a baby on the way. But of course I don't.

'You should get her something,' I say instead.

He regards me, head tilted. 'Like what?'

'I don't know. Something to tell her you're there for her. A baby vest or something.'

'Mmm.' He sips his tea and I'm pretty sure I can actually see the cogs whirring around in his brain. I sip mine too and we sit for some time in that awkward silence you get from being in a room with someone you don't actually know all that well.

'You probably shouldn't be here when he gets back,' I say eventually, glancing at the clock on the wall. He looks at it too.

'Sorry, I didnae mean to intrude.'

'No, not at all. You didn't.' And it's true. While it was a little odd having him just turn up at my door out of the blue, having someone tell me they understand what I'm going through and that they're there on the end of a phone call if I need help has been a reassurance I didn't realise I needed. 'Thank you for checking on me.'

'I meant it, you know.' He looks me dead in the eye. It's intense. 'Call me if you need to. Day or night.'

I smile gratefully. He seems to genuinely want to help. I've been dealing with Rich for so long I suppose I've forgotten that men can actually be kind.

'Thank you. I will.'

And even though I've said it just to placate him, I think I actually mean it.

Chapter Fourteen

Cal and I have been chatting for weeks now. It was never meant to be more than that one time where we sat at the kitchen table drinking tea. I was never supposed to see him again.

But I did.

First it was a text a few days later, then it was a phone call after Rich had gone to the pub, and finally it was stolen moments in the park while he was at work. I've tried not to think about his pregnant wife. I've tried to tell myself we weren't doing anything to be ashamed of. And we're not. It's nothing sexual. Not outside of my fantasies, anyway. He's a gentleman. Has never so much as attempted to kiss me, even though I definitely wouldn't say no if he did. From my perspective, Cal is a reprieve from everything I was dealing with. The total opposite of Rich. Someone who cares about my happiness and well-being, who listens when I need someone to talk to, who actually makes me feel safe.

With Cal, I can let my guard down. I don't have to pretend everything is fine or hide the bruises Rich leaves behind. Cal sees right through me, straight to my core. He knows what demons plague me, the dark thoughts that keep me up at night. But he never judges me for my faults or weaknesses. Cal makes me feel accepted, even cherished, for exactly who I am. I can breathe again.

I know it's dangerous, this pull I feel towards him. If Rich ever finds out, there will be hell to pay. But I can't stay away. Cal is like a drug, an addiction I don't want to beat. And on the one-month anniversary of our meeting I do it.

I take a deep breath to steady my nerves as I tap through the contacts in my phone. The ringing seems to go on forever, but when he answers I can picture him. Standing there with his phone pressed to his ear, surprise flickering across his face before his mouth curves into a smile.

'Amy,' he says. 'Is everything OK?'

I swallow hard. 'I'm leaving him.'

The line goes quiet, a thousand unspoken words passing between us. Then he clears his throat.

'Are you sure?'

I hesitate at the question. I had been sure. When I picked up the phone to call Cal I've never been more sure of anything in my life. Now though, a million thoughts race through my mind. Where will I go? What will I do? It's not like I can run off into the sunset with Cal. He's married with a baby on the way. Despite Cal's assurances, I'm all alone in this.

'Amy? You there?' His voice is gentle, concerned. Not judging. Not rushing.

'I'm here,' I reply. 'And yes. I'm sure. I can't keep living in this house for a day longer.'

Cal lets out a long exhale. 'OK. Pack a bag with only what ye need. I'll come get ye tonight after Richard leaves. You can stay with me for a bit until you've figured out what you're gon' te do next.'

My heart thumps in my chest, a relentless drumbeat of anticipation, as I reach for the desk drawer. I sift through the clutter to find my passport, birth certificate, driver's licence. Carefully, I slide them into my bag, ensuring they're snug enough that they won't fall out. I then fill the gap in the drawer with my phone. I can't take it with me. I don't know for sure that Rich has put a tracker on my phone but I'd put money on it. Speaking of money . . .

Moving to the computer, I log into my online banking – a shared account that Rich and I have bound our fiscal lives with. My eyes dart to the door, half expecting him to walk in, but the house remains silent.

I type with purpose, fingers flying over keys. The amount is significant enough to sustain me but not so much that it'll raise immediate red flags. It's a calculated risk. A balancing act. The screen blinks back at me as I confirm the transaction, the numbers now syphoned off into a new account only I know exists. A small victory. I log out, my heart pounding double time now. It's done. The first tangible step towards a life where I make the rules. I lean back, allowing myself a moment to feel the enormity of it all. The air feels different already. Lighter.

I tiptoe from room to room, even though he's not here, my movements shadow-like. I collect pieces of the life I'm about to leave behind. Clothes, toiletries, the basics. My hands hover over a drawer, fingers grazing the fabric of a dress I once loved. It's not practical, too conspicuous for a runaway, but it's laced with memories of laughter, before it all turned sour. With a sigh, I leave it behind, choosing instead the nondescript jeans, the jumpers that don't catch the eye.

Once everything I can think of is packed I zip the bag closed. It's heavy with the weight of what I'm about to do. I'm ready. This is the furthest I've ever got. The closest I've ever found myself to actually leaving. Now all I have to do is wait for Cal to get here.

Needing something to distract me while I wait, I slide into the chair at my desk, the cool leather a contrast to my feverish skin. The computer still hums softly and I realise I've left it on the internet banking screen. I shut the tab down quickly and clear the history. Mustn't make stupid mistakes that will make it easier for him to realise what I've done. I lean forward and open up a new Incognito tab.

'Loch Treig,' I type, whispering each syllable. The screen floods with images of rugged beauty. Cal said he lives not far from Loch Treig, but that didn't really mean much to me. I've lived in Fort William now for four years, but I've never been to that part of the Highlands. It really is in the middle of nowhere.

Maps sprawl across the monitor, a digital patchwork of contours and lines. Hills and valleys, places where the earth reaches for the sky, unapologetic in their wildness. I shift in my chair, the leather creaking softly beneath me, and lean closer to the glow of the computer screen. My eyes flit across descriptions plastered across travel blogs. *Lochs mirroring the sky, endless*, one writes, and I can almost feel the chill of the water, the hush of the Highland breeze against my skin. I scroll through pictures and my eyes devour it all. I wonder where on these maps Cal's cabin is, how long it must take him to drive all the way out here.

My question is answered as headlights illuminate the room and I peer out of the window to see Cal's truck pulling up on the driveway. A smile tugs at my lips.

As I open the front door he's standing outside his truck waiting for me, eyes flitting around, on lookout. This is the difference between tonight and all the other times I've attempted to leave. This time, I'm not doing it alone. I hurry towards him and he takes my bag, lobbing it into the footwell of the passenger seat. My gaze pans to the house next door, dark with all lights off.

'Maybe I should at least tell Mrs Henderson where I'm going,' I say, thinking about my elderly neighbour who has been the closest thing I've had to a friend since I left London. 'She'll worry.'

'We dinnae have time. If he comes back and sees what you're doin' . . .'

He doesn't finish his sentence. Doesn't need to. We both know what that would be like. Cal's right. I can't risk being spotted. Can't risk Rich having the opportunity to dig his claws in deeper.

'OK,' I whisper.

'Let's go then.' There's a note of urgency in his voice. I don't need to be told twice. I clamber into the seat of his truck and he closes the door after me, before hurrying round to his side and positioning himself in front of the wheel. The car is cold inside. I can't help but feel like we're fleeing the scene of a crime. My heart races as we pull away from the drive, the rear-view mirror reflecting a sliver of the life I'm leaving behind.

I glance over at Cal and my heart swells at his immediate willingness to protect me. Tears pool in my eyes as I take a shuddering breath. Fear still gnaws at my gut.

'What if he comes looking for me?'

'It doesnae matter even if he does,' Cal says. 'Where I live, it's out in the middle of nowhere. Trust me. No one will be able to find you out there.'

Chapter Fifteen

I take a deep, steadying breath, feeling the truck's vibrations beneath me as Cal drives. We slip through the town like ghosts, unnoticed, the landscape gradually shifting from concrete to greenery. The further we get, the lighter I feel, as if shedding invisible chains with each mile.

'Look at that!' I lean forward in my seat, pointing to the horizon where hills rise like slumbering giants, their peaks shrouded in mist. It's different out here, wild and untamed.

'Beautiful,' Cal murmurs, but he's looking at me, not the view. My stomach flutters and he returns his eyes to the road.

He's married, I remind myself. *That's not what this is. He's just helping me.*

The truck hugs the curves of the road and I lean into the turns, embracing the motion, the sense of going somewhere. Anywhere. My eyes trace the outline of the mountains on the horizon, jagged against the sky. Cal's fingers tap against the steering wheel in time with the song playing on the radio. I don't know the song, it's not what I'd normally listen to, but the chorus is repetitive and rhythmic and I find myself warbling along, stumbling over lyrics but enjoying myself too much to care.

'Top of the charts,' Cal teases.

'Only if you're tone-deaf.'

He then joins in, our voices mingling. We're a mess of off-key notes and missed beats, but it's perfect in its imperfection. I never laughed with Rich. With Cal, I do.

As the song fades into an ad for a local business, the static crackles and the radio dies. We're too far out now to get a signal. The sudden quiet feels heavy.

'You hungry?' Cal says after a while.

'No,' I respond on autopilot, but the question makes me realise that actually I'm starving. 'Well, maybe a bit.'

I think maybe Cal will take me to some remote cafe that sits on the edge of the Highlands, but there's no sign of buildings or life anywhere. Instead, he pulls up at the side of the road, which is more like a dirt track at this point, and kills the engine. He reaches into the glove compartment and retrieves a bag, before opening his door and getting out of the truck. Confused, I stay where I am for a moment, but when he doesn't return I assume he wants me to get out too. I do, stretching my limbs as I stand. I don't know exactly how long we've been driving but I'm stiff as anything.

Cal is sitting in the cargo bed at the back of the truck, munching on a sandwich. He hands me one as I clamber up to join him. When I turn to face the same direction as Cal my breath is snatched from me.

Before us is a vast body of water so clear it's like there's two moons, one up in the sky and another shimmering on the ground. Mountains and trees rise in the distance. I can't remember the last time I saw something so untouched. I want to sink into it, let it wash over me until I forget everything but this moment. Cal's arm snakes around my shoulders.

'It feels like a different world,' I breathe.

Cal nods. 'A better world.'

I peer at him out of the corner of my eye. He must notice me surveying him because he smiles and says, 'It's a crazy world out there. Full of lost, weak men who cannae properly support their families. Who don't know how to run a household. Full of overburdened women having to worry about things like payin' a mortgage and workin' a job instead of lookin' after the home because their husbands are pathetic excuses for the male species.'

I pause, taken aback by his words. 'What do you mean?'

'I mean, a woman's place is in the home. A man should provide while his wife takes care of the bairns and the household. Tha's the natural order o' things. Dinnae you agree?'

A chill runs through me at his words. They don't sit right with me. I hesitate. 'I don't know.'

'C'mon, Amy, you know it's true. After everything you've been through wi' Richard, you must see that a household needs a strong male leader.'

Richard's face flashes into my mind and I shudder.

'Rich wasn't strong,' I say quietly. 'He was controlling. Abusive.'

Cal shakes his head. 'He just didnae know how to be a proper man.'

I fall quiet, mind reeling. Cal's arm still rests heavily on my shoulders. Red flags. Blazing, fiery red flags. If I were at home this would be my cue to politely but firmly say it's getting late and that he should probably get going before locking the door behind him. But I'm not at home.

My eyes flick across the horizon once more. A few minutes ago it was freedom. Now it's showing me just how far out into the middle of nowhere we are.

I swallow hard. I'm being stupid. I don't need to be afraid of Cal. He saved me from Rich. Cal's a good man. He's just got some outdated views, is all. I just won't marry the guy. Not that that was even an option in the first place. Some other lucky lady already gets to play the part of the fifties housewife and carry his 'bairns'. I'm blowing this all out of proportion.

I force a smile and take another bite of my sandwich, chewing slowly as I gather my thoughts, though I've totally lost my appetite. Cal seems oblivious to my unease as he polishes off the last of his food.

'We should get going,' he says, crumpling up the sandwich wrapper and shoving it in the bag. I nod, sliding down from the truck bed. The gravel crunches under my feet. Cal hops down beside me and brushes crumbs from his jeans.

'Do you want me to drive for a bit?' I offer. 'You must be exhausted.'

He smiles and climbs into the driver's seat. 'Nah, lass. I'm all good.'

Chapter Sixteen

'Almost there.' His words should give me comfort. They don't.

I have to remind myself that differences of opinion don't equate to danger. Cal believes in traditional gender roles. I don't. We're different, sure, but that doesn't mean he's a threat.

We pass a 'no trespassing' sign and the cabin is soon visible in the distance. As we draw closer, I can't shake the feeling that something isn't right. Maybe it's the way the dark sky presses down, oppressive, or how the wilderness seems too silent, holding its breath.

'Beautiful, aye?' Cal says, nodding at the cabin.

Beautiful isn't exactly the word I'd choose. The loch, now that was beautiful. The cabin on the other hand looks old and rickety, somewhat cobbled together over the years. I can imagine the draughts coming through those walls.

'Sure is.' My voice sounds hollow, even to my own ears.

'Wait until ye see inside. You'll love it.' There's a promise in his words and I tilt my head towards him.

'I really appreciate you letting me stay here for a few days while I sort out a long-term plan.' He doesn't respond to that. Unease prickles at my skin.

The cabin is just a stone's throw away but Cal veers off the path. He parks up outside a separate building, a barn by the looks of things, and gets out of the truck. I do too, my shoes sinking into the unkempt grass as I do. I frown as Cal heads towards the door of the barn.

'Are we not going to the cabin?' I ask, my voice almost drowned by the wind.

'There's time for tha'. I want te show you somethin' first.'

I hesitate, watching the distance grow between us, though what can I actually do? He's got the keys to the truck in his pocket, and even if I managed to get hold of them and jump back in the truck I've got no idea where to go. I'd get lost before I even made it back to the loch. The reality of what I've done, running off with someone I've only known for weeks, suddenly weighs on me and I realise how stupid I've been. The moment he told me not to bother letting Mrs Henderson know where I was going replays in my mind.

'Come on,' he beckons, now a shadow against the barn's entrance.

I move towards him, wrapping my arms around myself. Why the barn? What's in there that couldn't wait until the morning?

Cal steps aside, gesturing me into the dim interior with a sweep of his arm. Dust dances in the shafts of moonlight that pierce through the cracks in the aged wood, casting elongated shadows on the dirt floor. Animal carcasses are strung up to the left. I recoil and knock straight into Cal. His hands fly out to steady me, gripping onto the tops of my arms.

'Easy there, lass. You's a bit uptight, aren't ye?'

I shake myself free from his grip.

'Sorry. I wasn't expecting the . . .' My words are snatched from me as my gaze falls on an object draped over the side of an old tractor. A dress. Its fabric is a splash of pastel amidst the greys and browns.

Cal sees me looking and picks it up. It unfolds like a flag from a bygone era. Cinched waist, flared skirt, patterned with tiny flowers. 'Thought you could slip into this. A little more fitting for being a guest, aye?'

'I'm OK with what I'm wearing, thank you.' The words stick in my throat. I want to be direct, assertive, but the air feels too thick to breathe.

His eyes meet mine, and they're not the warm pools from before. They're colder now. Harder.

'It's just a bit o' fun. You'll look right.'

'Right?' The word tastes bitter. 'I didn't realise there was a wrong way to dress for leaving your abusive husband.'

He steps closer and I inadvertently take a step away from him. 'You're a guest in my home. It's a simple request. A dress. To show respect.'

I swallow hard, the fabric of my own clothes suddenly suffocating. This is nothing to do with respect. He wants me to play dress-up for his twisted fantasy.

'Cal, you're scaring me.'

He chuckles, the sound ricocheting around the hollow space, bouncing off the rusted tools and cobwebbed corners. 'Scaring you? I saved you.'

His words crawl up my skin like spiders. Is Cal just as bad as Rich? Have I escaped from one hell straight into another?

'Are ye not going to put it on, then?' he asks.

A frigid draught sweeps through the barn and I pull my cardigan tighter around myself. My eyes dart towards the open door. But then, with a flicker of shadow Cal moves. The moonlight is snuffed out as the door swings shut, old hinges groaning.

'Cal, please,' I whisper. But he doesn't hear me. Or maybe he doesn't want to.

Chapter Seventeen

I'm trapped. When my eyes flickered open I thought I was in my bed. It took a moment for me to reconcile the pain in my head, the aching of my limbs, the awkward angle at which I'm lying, with what happened. But as I blink, I realise it doesn't make any difference. I'm in the pitch black.

My heart begins to race. Bile collects in my mouth and I clasp my hand to my mouth. The last thing I remember is refusing to put on that dress. Cal had done something then. Come at me with a piece of fabric. I remember smelling something sweet and then . . .

Nothing.

And now I'm trapped.

The vomit I was trying to hold back splashes off the wall. At least, I assume it's a wall. I don't think I've ever experienced darkness like this. It's like it's pressing in on me, suffocating me. I try to steady my breathing, pulling air in through my nose and letting it whistle slowly through pursed lips. I always thought that if this ever happened to me, if I was ever one of those girls who went missing, I'd be able to handle myself. I'd put up a fight and my attacker wouldn't stand a chance. Yet here I am descending into a puddle of panic and fear.

I shake my head, willing my brain to cooperate. Before anything else, I need to at least figure out where I am.

I reach my hands gingerly in front of me, attempting to avoid the sick. Images from horror movies flash through my mind and I imagine my hand landing on a decaying corpse. When I do touch something I'm so sure it's cold skin I recoil instantly. But it's not. I reach out again and my fingers slide along a smooth curved surface. A rail. In fact, one of many. There's another rail a few inches above, and above that, and again above that. With my other hand I investigate the other sides, then above me. The same cold rails meet me wherever I feel. Heart hammering in my ears, I wrap my hands around two of the ones above me and push. Finally, the sinking realisation comes.

I'm locked in some kind of cage.

The screams that escape me are guttural, raw, terrified, like nothing I've ever heard. I don't know if I'm screaming for help or just screaming because it's all there is to do. I keep going until my throat is raw and my fists are bruised from pummelling the top of the cage.

I don't know how long I've been in here. Minutes. Hours. Maybe even days. Time has warped and twisted in my mind. All there is is blackness.

I've lost my voice. Or perhaps I simply have no screams left in me. Occasionally I sob. Most of the time I think. I think about home. I wonder if anyone realises I'm gone yet. Will a missing persons report have been filed? Will police be at my house? I think about my life, how anything and everything I've done up to this point all becomes rather pointless if I die in here. I think about Mrs Henderson, expecting me to come round for a cup of tea on Saturday. But I'm not going to be there because I'll be dead.

I sob some more and contemplate how awful it's going to be to die here. The hunger is already gnawing at my stomach, but it's the thirst that will get me. My mouth is like sandpaper from all the screaming. My lips are cracked and bleeding. Perhaps I should try to slam my head against the side of the cage as hard as I can. If it doesn't kill me at least it will knock me out so I don't have to feel the dehydration as it kills me.

I don't want to die.

There's someone outside. Outside my cage. There's a shuffling noise, like boots on dusty concrete. I freeze, not that there's much room to move in here anyway. Fear curdles inside me. For a long time I wanted nothing more than for someone to come, to lift the lid and let me out of this prison. But now I'm not so sure. It's probably Cal. Do I want him to let me out? Is what he has planned for me worse than withering away inside this cage?

I brace myself, curl my hand into a fist. There's not much energy left in me to fight with, and if the person outside is Cal I probably won't stand a chance against his tree surgeon's strength, but I'll never forgive myself if I don't at least try. There's another sound, some kind of metal clanking and clicking, and then pain as light streams into the cage. I clamp my eyes shut and a whimper escapes my lips. There's no way I'm going to be able to fight anyone off with my eyes shut, but I can't face opening them. After however long I've been in here in the dark, that little sliver of light is like staring straight into the burning sun. I hug my arm around my eyes, blocking the light out as much as I can, and wait to be dragged out of the cage to whatever horrid fate awaits me.

But nothing happens. There is stillness and silence.

I frown from beneath my arm. Has whoever it was gone away? No. I can sense someone near me, can feel their presence. What are they waiting for?

Cautiously, I peek out from under my elbow with one eye. It still hurts, and I blink rapidly in an attempt to clear my vision. Eventually, ever so slowly, a figure emerges from the light. A dark shadow against the brightness. It is Cal. And now I see properly for the first time where I am. I'm still in the barn, but right over in the corner of it. There's the tractor a couple of metres away from me. The dress is gone now. It is a cage that I'm trapped in but now I see what kind. It's the sort that goes on the back of a trailer. The sort you'd put animals in to transport them to a slaughterhouse.

The light that hurt my eyes so badly is coming from a torch in Cal's hand. I peer up at the cracks in the ceiling where I saw the moonlight filtering in when I first came here. There's nothing. The moon must be shrouded in cloud. That's why it was so dark in here. Does that mean it's not the same night?

'Cal, please,' I sob, the words coming out a husky whisper. 'Please let me out.'

He still doesn't say anything. I crawl forward on all fours and grip the bars in front of me, pressing my face between the narrow gap.

'Why are you doing this to me?' I screech.

'What is your name?' That familiar deep Scottish accent makes me flinch.

'What?'

'What is your name?'

I shake my head, confusion and terror mingling in my core. He knows my name. Has he completely lost his mind?

'Cal, I don't understand. Please, just let me out of here and we can talk.'

'Here.'

Something cold is pressed against my lips, making me flinch, but it only takes me a second to realise it's a glass. Water. Amazing, wonderful, life-giving water. I gulp it back noisily, too quickly, causing me to choke and splutter, but still I drink. Then a bag is dropped through the bars. I peer down at its contents: a selection of vegetables, boiled by the looks of them, not particularly appetising, but I devour them even so.

'Thank you,' I pant as I shovel the last carrot into my mouth.

'Where are your parents?' the man says.

'My parents?' My mind is racing. I don't understand where these questions are going or what he's trying to accomplish. 'They're probably out looking for me. I always call them every day without fail and they'll realise something's wrong.' That's a lie. My parents are probably sunbathing in the South of France right now. I haven't heard from them since they said they'd cut me off if I ran away to Gretna Green with Rich to get married at sixteen and I was dumb enough to do it. But he doesn't know that. It was either a smart thing to say, or an incredibly stupid one. Either the thought of people looking for me will make him let me go because he's scared of getting caught, or he'll kill me because he's scared of getting caught.

'What's your husband's name?'

'What? Richard. You know that. What the fuck is going on?'

There's another drawn-out silence, like when he came into the barn.

'No,' the man says after what feels like forever.

'What?'

'That's not true. Your name is Mary. Your parents are dead. I'm your husband.'

And with that, he backs out of the barn and shuts the door again, and there's that metal clicking sound again as he locks it.

Part Three

Chapter Eighteen

Mary

I've sat awake most of the night. I don't know what to do. My mind has gone to a dark place so quickly I've surprised myself, and it feels like it's going to explode. Every scenario is coursing through it, hammering against my skull.

My plan worked.

But I've changed my mind.

It's what I wanted.

No. There's got to be another way.

I keep pacing up and down the bedroom, wondering if I should slip my boots on and go and investigate. I could burst into the barn, theatrical in my demand to know what's going on, the hurt wife accusing her husband of cheating. Except he's not cheating on me. Not really. Cheating would imply we're in a real marriage. That's what he likes to call it. A marriage. Husband and wife. But that's not what this is. What this is is sick and twisted.

He thinks he's broken me. He thinks everything he did to me – the cage, the punishments each time I've tried to escape, the control he's had over me these past ten years – has rewired my brain somehow. He thinks I don't remember, that now I really am his good little wife.

But I remember everything. That's why I write it all down in my notebook. So that I never, ever forget who I am or what he did to me.

I remember the way I felt as if someone was watching me in the shop, while Mum and Dad paid for the food that we were to take back to the Airbnb we were staying at and I perused the make-up stand.

I remember slipping on my running shoes the day after spending that night with Cal in the bar and assuring Mum that I'd be fine, that

I'd be back in time from my morning jog to tuck into the breakfast she was cooking up on the grill.

I remember being blown away by the breathtaking views of the Scottish Highlands, thinking how incredibly lucky I was to be running in such a beautiful place, wishing our holiday never had to end and dreading returning to university and coursework and deadlines.

I remember hearing a rustle behind me. And then pain. And then blackness.

I don't know how long he kept me locked up in that cage like an animal. Months. Perhaps even years. Long enough that eventually, after begging him to stop and screaming at him that I'd never give up, I did just that. I gave up. It was always the same routine. Days would go by with me locked in the dark, cold, hungry, thirsty, withering away, and then every now and again the lid would open and I'd get water and food. Then the same questions came. Every time the same three questions. 'What is your name? Where are your parents? What is your husband's name?' And every time I answered in a way that displeased him, the lid was closed again. An endless, vicious cycle. I fought a lot of the times. I have vague recollections of kicking and screaming and biting and thrashing whenever he got close enough for me to reach him through the bars. But he left me locked up for too long each time, so that by the time he came to let me out of the cage I was too weak to escape.

I wonder how long it actually took. How many times I got locked away before I finally relented and told him what he wanted to hear. That my name was Mary. That I never wanted to see my parents again. And that he was my husband; my husband Cal. How long did it take for me to alter myself to suit his narrative? I can't be certain.

I tried to escape, of course. Five, maybe six times. It took me far too long to figure out the reason he always seemed to know exactly when I was trying to get away, why he'd cut me off in his truck every single time. The glinting in the trees – they're cameras. Cameras that link to a phone that is never, ever off his person. One time I tried to get away while he slept. I only got to just beyond the barn and an alarm went off to let him know what I was up to. That time was the belt. The last time I tried to escape, now a good nine years ago, I attempted to kill him. Went at him with the carving knife as I served up our Sunday roast. That time I got the iron fresh off the fire pressed to my skin while he reminded me that if I kill him I'll die here right along with him, because I'll never find my way out. Now I have a lovely triangular scar to remind me what will happen if I ever try to leave.

And for a long time I accepted that this was my new life. It's not so bad. As long as I keep him happy my existence here is OK. Boring. Lonely. Mind numbing. But I have food and a roof over my head and Cal actually treats me OK as long as I don't sprout any grey hairs and I don't put on weight and I don't gain another wrinkle.

But things are different now.

I place my hand on my stomach and think about the baby, think about you, the tiny helpless life that relies on me entirely. I cannot, will not, let you be born here.

You are my reason, why I came up with this horrendous plan in the first place. All the time I'm Cal's focus, I'll never have the chance to get free. But if he has someone else to direct his efforts at, if he has someone else to watch on the cameras and to dote on and to rape, maybe he'll be distracted enough to open up a window of opportunity. So I stopped making him happy. I allowed myself to show my age, started messing up his meals, began picking fights. All in the hopes that my suggestion that we get someone else to live with us here might have lodged in his head enough. That he would predictably start looking for someone else who's younger and prettier than me to fulfil his perfect wife fantasy, just like he did with Gemma.

That letter she wrote to me is still tucked away inside the first page of my notebook, hidden under the mattress. I pull it out, allow my eyes to flick over her words for the hundredth time, the words that changed everything for me.

To the next woman,
When I first started writing these letters they were for
myself. They were a way to try to keep who I really am
alive. A way to record any memories I could gather so that
the real me doesn't get lost forever. But now I sense that my

time in this cabin is coming to an end. Cal is getting bored of me. I'm getting old. Older than he'd like, anyway. And I'm pretty sure there's someone being kept in the barn. He keeps disappearing out there, more than he ever used to, and food is going missing. I hope to God I'm wrong, that I'm writing this letter to a woman that doesn't exist, that there's not going to be a repeat of what I went through. But my gut tells me Cal is preparing someone to take my place. If that's true, it's my duty to try to help you.

To the person reading this: don't give up. I've tried to escape three times. The first time he came home much earlier than I'd anticipated and I just barely got back in time to avoid him finding out. The second time I walked for two hours but ended up going in circles. This area of the Highlands is near impossible to navigate. My advice? Go at night and use the stars to guide you. Follow the North Star. As long as it's in front of you, you'll get out eventually.

That's what I did the third time. That time I thought I'd get away. I got further than I'd ever managed to. But he caught up with me and brought me back. I tried to pass it off as if I'd just gone for a walk and got lost, but he didn't believe me. He broke both my legs that night so that I wouldn't be able to attempt to leave again. That was the beginning of the end for me. I can barely walk, so I'm no longer the perfect wife he wants.

I'm going to attempt to escape one last time. It will end in one of two ways. Either I'll get away or he'll catch me and kill me. Either way, this will be the last letter I'll ever hide in this cabin.

If I ever do get out of here I promise I'll send someone to help you. Just please, please don't give up hope. Stay on his good side, pretend to do as he says, and get out at the first opportunity you see.

Good luck.

From Gemma (he calls me Mary)

From the moment I read that letter I knew this plan would work, that all I had to do was exactly what Gemma did. Stop being the perfect wife that he wants so that he would go out and find someone else. I hate Cal with every fibre in my body but I know him very well. I knew it would work.

And it has worked. There's another woman in the barn. Eventually she'll graduate to the cabin just like I did, and she'll be presented with her new wardrobe and her new name and her new life, just like I was, and then all I need to do is wait until a time when the blood has drained from his brain to his penis and he's too busy grunting and groaning to notice me slipping away.

I try to tell myself it's not as bad as it seems. It's survival. And as soon as I'm away from here I'll make sure to tell the police that there's another woman being held here. They'll come and rescue her and everything will be OK.

But then I look at the barn and I know everything isn't OK. No matter what, if she gets free in a few weeks, a few months, a few years, this will have happened to her and she'll never be the same again. I'll have done that to her.

I don't want to go to the barn.

So instead I continue to pace, I pick up a cloth and start absent-mindedly wiping down the dresser, I fold a load of laundry, even though the room is still barely illuminated by the moon because I daren't light the lanterns and alert him to me being awake. For all I know my cleaning and tidying is just making things messier. Anything to pass the time. He'll have to come out of that barn eventually.

He does. It's starting to get light by the time there's more movement outside, and I nearly miss it because my eyes are drooping so badly. When I see him though, I'm wide awake again. Adrenaline powering me. The woman isn't with him. Either she's still in the barn or she left without my noticing. I know which of those two options is the most likely.

I jump back into bed so quickly my foot catches on the side and I have to stifle a yelp. My eyes squeeze shut as I hear him coming back into the cabin. I purposefully breathe deeply, hoping it resembles sleep. Footsteps sound around the bed and I'm sure he'll notice my heart hammering.

He pauses, stood next to the bed. Why isn't he getting in?

'Mary?'

My name is not Mary.

My eyes twitch.

'Mary, I can tell you're awake.'

Oh no.

I roll over onto my back and peer up at him. He's silhouetted. No distinguishable features. Just a big, looming presence.

'What were you doing?' I mumble, my voice so small I can barely hear it myself. 'In the barn?'

'How much did you see?'

I hesitate, confused by his question. How much was there to see?

'I saw you going in there. And I saw the woman.'

The mattress depresses as he sits on the edge, back to me, and lets out a long, slow breath.

'She's a friend. Someone who needed my help.'

I shuffle up so that I'm leaning on my elbows.

'What kind of help?'

'She employed me to prune a tree in her front garden. Her husband...'

My heart skitters. She's married. That's a good sign. Maybe her husband will come looking for her.

'... He knocked her around. A lot. I wanted to check on her, make sure she was OK, and there she was. Bloodied up something good.'

A shudder works its way up my spine as I picture the scene. What this poor woman has already been through. Regret churns in my stomach.

'Anyway, she didnae want to go to the police. She was scared to run in case he found her. So I told her she could hide out in the barn until she had a proper plan.'

'I'll make extra breakfast,' I say, reaching for my dressing gown. It's too early for breakfast really but I'm overcome with the desire to make sure this woman is OK. 'Do you know if she likes anything in particular? She must be freezing in there. And with all those dead animals. Why don't you invite her to stay in the cabin? I can make her up a bed in front of the fire.'

I'm rambling. Cal won't like that, but I can't help it. I'm already gathering up blankets and cushions and brainstorming different baked goods I can offer her when Cal rests a hand on my arm.

'She's gon te stay in the barn, Mary.'

I drop the blankets back into their basket. Chills slink through me.

'Cal,' I whisper. 'She doesn't have to be in there. I said, didn't I? I said about having someone here to help out. I'm sure she'll be happy to.'

'She's going to stay in the barn. For now.' Cal gives my arm a squeeze. 'You're so kind-hearted to think of that though.'

I swallow. I'm not kind-hearted. I'm horrendously selfish. I think I might be one of the worst people I've ever known. No. I'm not kind-hearted at all.

I'm wracking my brains, trying to think of something I can say or do to undo this mess I've allowed to happen, to relieve myself of some of the guilt that's coursing through me, but Cal's mind is elsewhere. He sits on the edge of the bed and peers out of the window.

'The Bible says, "Wives, submit to your own husbands as to the Lord",' he says quietly. I'm not even sure he's talking to me. He seems to have gone off into his own little world. I respond anyway, knowing how much he hates it when I ignore him.

'Ephesians, chapter five, verse twenty-two.'

'Tha's what me mam always taught me. To run a good, Christ-loving, honourable home.'

I think back to the photo I found and curiosity consumes me. 'Why do you not like talking about your dad?'

He tenses but doesn't push me aside like he did last time. 'Why do you keep asking when you know I dinnae like talking about him?'

'We're going to have a baby in seven months,' I say, swivelling in the bed so that I'm facing him. 'I know nothing about this baby's paternal grandparents. I just . . . want to know.'

For a long time, Cal says nothing. The muscle in his temple pulses and I can see him turning things over in his mind. I hold my breath and wait.

Eventually, he swallows. 'He left early. To be honest, I dinnae really remember him. It were just me and me mam for as long as I knew.

That's probably why she raised me the way she did. Good Christian woman, she was. Always wanted a God-fearing family, a husband to serve. Always wanted to be a proper Proverbs 31 woman. She didnae get that chance. He took it away from her. So she brought me up good and proper so's I'd have the family she never had.'

His eyes seem to glaze over as he's talking, like he's not really in the room with me anymore, like he's disappearing into the past. I peer down at the duvet cover, uncomfortable. At least that explains his ideology, why he's so intent on living life like we've stepped back in time. But I've read the Bible. I've had to. Every night we do our devotions and study it together. I don't think this is what an all-loving God had in mind.

But then what do I know? I think, as I lie back against my pillow and try not to glance out of the window at the barn.

My plan worked. I'm definitely going to hell.

Chapter Nineteen

It's been fourteen weeks since I found out I was pregnant. That means it's been ten weeks since the woman first entered the barn. That also means I'm almost halfway through my pregnancy, and I still don't know what to do.

Life is so different now. I flinch when I hear Cal come home, which hasn't happened for years. I never know whether he's going to be in a good mood or a foul one. When he's in a good mood, it's like he can't do enough for me, like I'm all he needs in life to be happy. When he's in a bad mood, it's like it was when I first came here.

I'm still getting frequent headaches, and they seem to be getting worse. The heavy medical book suggests this is relatively common and might be due to many factors: dehydration, lack of proper sleep, stress. There is a big red box at the bottom of the page, however, that mentions something called pre-eclampsia, which severe headaches can be a symptom of. Apparently pre-eclampsia can lead to serious complications if it's not monitored and treated. I mentioned this to Cal last week and he didn't talk to me for three whole days.

So, I'm having to do my own monitoring. I've memorised the other symptoms of pre-eclampsia to look out for. Once Cal goes to work I head into the bathroom and strip down to my underwear, staring at my reflection in the mirror. I'm starting to show. Where my stomach was once toned and flat from years of hard labour, it's now distinctly round. Carefully, I work my way across my body with my fingers just as I do every day, pressing and feeling for any unusual swelling that might indicate these headaches are something to be concerned about. There's nothing as far as I can tell, and I lean on the edge of the sink as I breathe a sigh of relief.

'*Another day*,' I silently say to you inside me. '*We've made it another day.*'

I bend down to pick up my clothes and start dressing myself, but as I'm pulling my trousers up I move too quickly and a wave of dizziness hits me. My vision flashes and I grip onto the sink. Pain shoots from one side of my head to the other and back again like a ping-pong ball. Squeezing my eyes tight shut, I jab my fingers into my temple in a desperate attempt to stop the throbbing.

I peer feebly up at the pill box on top of the medicine cabinet. It's always been too high for me to reach, but now it looks even higher. Stumbling slightly, I grab the chair from the bedroom and shove it up against the sink. Even standing on the chair, though, the sudden weakness in my body means it's a struggle to lift my arms enough to reach the pill box. When I do manage to pull it down it's like a ten-ton weight in my arms. I have to balance it on the sink for fear of dropping it.

I take a moment to steady myself, the aches in my muscles worsening and my vision growing blurry as the headache continues to rip through my skull. My fingers tremble as I fumble with the opening.

It's locked.

A moan escapes my lips. I can't wait until he gets home, I just can't. It feels as though my head is going to explode. He keeps the key in his pocket, but maybe there's another one somewhere.

I stumble into the bedroom and make a beeline for the bedside table, though I'm certain there were no keys in there when I looked last time. He'll probably see that I've been rummaging in here again but at this point I'm beyond caring. All I care about is getting into that box, getting to those headache tablets. There's nothing in his drawer so I scan every other inch of the room.

Nothing.

The living area, then. Swaying slightly, I search once more through the coats – still nothing – so I move on to the kitchen drawers. It's ludicrous because I'm in those drawers far more than he is and I'd have noticed if there was a key being kept in them, but I hunt nonetheless. By the time I've been through every drawer, every cupboard, lifted every sofa cushion, even checked under the doormat, I'm dizzy with frustration.

And then my eyes land on it. An old toolbox sitting on top of one of the high kitchen cabinets. It's been there for as long as I can remember. We never use it, not since Cal brought home a nice new set of tools a good five years ago now. It's just sat there collecting dust.

I wonder.

The dining chair screeches against the floorboards as I drag it over to the kitchen counter, and its legs creak as I haul myself up onto it. Even standing on the chair my fingers just barely graze the toolbox, so I take another step up, this time onto the counter surface itself. It occurs to me too late that if I were to fall I could lose the baby, but I'm up here now and my headache is interfering with my common sense. I grab the toolbox, pulling it free from the cobwebs that have encased it over the years. A spider scuttles across my hand and I shudder. I lower myself gingerly down so that I'm sitting on the countertop.

For one horrid moment I wonder if this box will be locked too, but it isn't. The clasps pop open, a little cloud of dust puffing up into the air as they do. The lid is stiff but it opens. I peer inside. The tools in there look almost the same as the last time I saw them, despite their age. At first I can't see anything else apart from screwdrivers and measuring tables, but as I lift the centre compartment my breath hitches. There's a small collection of keys on a metal ring.

I hurry back to the bathroom, the sense of being within grasping distance of a painkiller overwhelming me. Prayers zip through my thoughts as I try one key, find it doesn't work, then try another. I go through four keys before one finally slots into the medicine box. When I twist the key a small click sounds and the lid lifts a couple of millimetres.

Yes.

I make a desperate grab at the box labelled 'paracetamol'. It says on the instructions it's safe for pregnancy and that I can take two, so I pop a couple of the tablets out into my sweaty palm and gulp them back hungrily. My eyes drift closed and I smile to myself, waiting for the sweet relief of the pills kicking in.

After a minute or so I feel better already, even though I know it's a placebo effect. If I'm honest with myself, it's partly just smugness at managing to get into the pill box. I open my eyes and look down at it as if it's a trophy I've won.

Something catches my attention and I frown. My vitamins are there too in their yellow box, though I've never seen it this close. Usually I see a flash of it in Cal's hand. He always gives me the vitamins themselves, not the box. I'm not sure what it is exactly, but something about the name on the side is jarring with me. I've read it somewhere before.

And then it hits me.

I hurry back to the living room and, with trembling fingers, pull the medical book from its shelf. There is the sound of a page ripping as I flip through too fast but I don't stop. My eyes dart wildly across the tiny text as I search.

There it is.

Yasmin is a type of birth control pill that may be offered to a new mother shortly after birth.

My mouth grows dry as I stare at the book flopping open in my limp hands, the truth finally sinking in. It's obvious now, plain as day. I can't believe I didn't see it before. It's why he reacted so badly when we found out I was pregnant. He wasn't giving me a vitamin each day to keep me healthy. He was giving me birth control pills. He doesn't want this baby. He never intended to get me pregnant. This was a mistake. A tiny, one in a hundred chance that a fertilised egg would sneak through despite his best efforts. And if he was purposefully trying to avoid getting me pregnant, what the hell is he going to do to you when you're born?

I feel as though I've been punched right in the stomach. My knees buckle and I have to steady myself on the sink. My hand catches on the medicine box and it clatters to the bathroom floor, the noise earth-shattering. As I crouch down to pick up the various pill packets I find my fingers don't work. My body has shut down. Even my brain isn't working anymore. I move from a crouch to a slump and I cry. I cry because I know I'll never forgive myself for not leaving sooner. If he had killed me it would have been better than having you born here.

I don't know how long it takes for me to move from that spot on the floor. For seemingly hours my mind is locked in a tornado of bitter memories and self-loathing. Eventually I manage to at least get all the pills picked up and back in the box. I've tried to place them back in the order they were in when I first opened it, but I can't be sure. I lock it up again, place it back in its high-up home and return the key to its hiding place. Then I stand in the middle of the kitchen unsure what to do with myself. For the last decade, my life has been centred around him. My purpose has been to be a good wife. I stopped that in order to get the new woman here, but now what?

I find myself drifting out into the garden, not bothering to slip my shoes on. Tiny sticks and stones embed themselves into my bare feet as I wander, dreamlike, past the vegetable patch.

If I kept going I could make my way to the loch.

I could fill my pockets with stones and throw myself in.

The realisation of what I'm thinking, what I'm doing, hits me like a truck and I stumble backwards. No! I deserve to be here. I have a life. Cal may control most things but he doesn't allow me to breathe, doesn't permit my heart to beat. And what's more, you're inside me. You can live without him too. But you can't live without me. You need me to be strong. You're relying on me to get us through this.

I storm back to the cabin and dust my feet off. As I do, water splashes down on my forearm and I think it's the roof leaking again, then I realise I'm crying. I swipe angrily at my face and move to the kitchen cupboards, pulling out pots and pans while biting hard down on my lip, forcing myself to get a grip. I focus on the dinner preparations, on the rhythmic, monotonous task of slicing and dicing, and by the time Cal returns it's nearly ready. Just as he likes it, only this time I haven't done it for him. I've done it for me and you. We need nourishment. We need to be strong.

When he walks through the front door he doesn't mention how good it smells, which already tells me what kind of mood he's in. I really should turn to face him, give him a welcoming smile and say how glad I am that he's home, but I can't bring myself to do it. I focus on the food instead.

His boots thud on the floorboards as he rids himself of his outerwear.

'How long till dinner?'

'It's ready now. I just need to dish up.'

Still I don't look at him. I feel him closing in on me, can sense him behind me. His breath touches my cheek as he peers over my shoulder and I resist the urge to pull away from him. He pulls a loose strand of hair behind my ear.

'You look like shit,' he says, taking my shoulder and manoeuvring me so that I have no choice but to face him.

'Do I?'

'Your face is all swollen. You been crying?'

'I just had a funny five minutes. Hormones.'

The words are thick in my throat and I'm struggling to get them out. Still, even facing him, I cannot meet his eye.

He grunts. The stale sweat from his day of work lingers in the air between us and I hold my breath, willing him to move away and let me get on with finishing up the dinner.

'I picked a name for little'un.'

The breath I'd been holding sputters out of me in a half-cough. 'What?'

'Mmm.' He nods, looking pleased with himself. 'I reckon James. Good strong biblical name.'

I swallow, the taste of bile collecting at the back of my throat.

'What if it's a girl?'

'Nah.' His hands creep up below the hem of my shirt and touch my belly. They're cold and all the hairs on my arms shoot up. 'I've got a sixth sense about stuff like this. That's a wee lad in there, mark my . . .'

His words trail off and his forehead creases. A jolt of panic shoots through me. He lifts my shirt higher and peers at my stomach, at the sides where my abdomen is clearly protruding. One finger slides down my right side.

'What the fuck is this?'

'What's what?'

I rack my brain for what he could be talking about, almost too scared to look for myself, but I have no idea. My eyes drop and I follow his gaze to where his finger is. It's pressed into my skin so that the area is turning white. I can see what he means now. There's a small, slightly purple stretch mark snaking its way towards my hip.

Before I can say anything he gives me a shove so that I stumble backwards and my spine collides with the kitchen counter.

'Why haven't you been using that cream I got you, eh?'

His face is twisted, a disgusted grimace distorting his mouth. My heart batters in my ribcage and the usual apologies play on my tongue but I force them back. I will not say sorry. I will not.

'It's disgusting!' he continues, too caught up in his rage to notice my lack of remorse. 'Pregnancy is not a fucking excuse to let yourself go!'

His hand reaches out and impacts with the nearest object – the utensil holder – and it goes flying across the room. Spatulas and ladles empty onto the floor.

'Clean up that mess and get out of my sight,' he spits.

I obey, picking up the utensils, giving them a wash, depositing them back into their holder and placing it back in its home on the counter. I glance at dinner which is starting to burn around the edges and my stomach grumbles, but I know better than to go against his wishes right now.

With a lump in my throat, I try to walk to the bedroom at a steady pace. As soon as my feet cross the threshold I shut the door behind me and hurl myself onto the bed, blinking back the tears as I lie hugging my knees. They press gently against my stomach. I press my face into the pillow so that I can cry into it without being heard and like this I stay, curled up just like the little person inside me, loneliness and sadness eating away at me.

I gasp as something flutters in my stomach. It's unlike anything I've ever felt. Like a bubble of gas popping but a little bigger, more definite. My hand shoots to where the popping was and I freeze, concentrating hard. The seconds tick by and I'm sure I must have imagined it, but then no, there it is again. A tiny, almost imperceptible movement. The movement of you stirring inside of me. Not his baby. Not ours. Mine.

It's like you're trying to tell me that you're here with me, a minuscule yet monumental reminder that I'm not alone.

My fingers tap back against my skin.

'I hear you,' I whisper, the tears now no longer able to be suppressed. 'I'm here. And I'm going to get you out.'

Chapter Twenty

Cal's getting worse.

He never came to get me after sending me away last night, so I went without the dinner I'd cooked. I could have waited until he fell asleep, presumably in the chair again, and snuck through to the kitchen, but I couldn't face another confrontation. So instead I stayed curled up on the bed and growing angrier and more bitter the longer I thought about him. Now I'm praying he'll get up and go to work soon so that I can finally have some breakfast.

This is like déjà vu for me. Feeling angry at Cal. For years my hatred for him was visceral, churning inside me every second of every day. But eventually I got used to being here. I got used to him. I never started to feel any kind of affection towards him. I've heard of some women being held captive who have fallen in love with their captor. That's not me. But it was exhausting being full of anger and hatred all the time, so I just sort of . . . stopped.

My eyes squeeze shut as I try to think back over the most recent years we've spent together. There were a few times he got unreasonably furious about the tiniest thing. I distinctly remember him ranting and raving one evening when I tripped with a pot of steaming stew in my hands and it went everywhere. It sprayed all up my legs and burned my skin but that wasn't his concern at the time. He was angry because it meant there'd be no dinner that night, not until I'd managed to cobble together something else at least.

There were other times like that too, but generally I chose to ignore them, chose to just survive in this nightmare.

But now I'm waking up again.

It's hours before there's movement outside the bedroom door, and the hunger is starting to make me nauseous. As the handle twists I remain in my foetal position, eyes tight shut in the hope that he'll think I'm asleep. I wonder if he can hear my heart pounding as he enters the room and stares down at me. It feels like knives jabbing me all over while I try to lie still.

Eventually he lets out a heavy breath and moves to the bathroom, and I can hear him brushing his teeth. I risk one eye open.

Based on how high the sun is in the sky outside our window, it's later than usual for him to be getting ready for work. Part of me wonders if he's done that on purpose, so that I'm without food for even longer. You flutter inside me and I place a reassuring hand on my stomach, as if I'm sending a silent message that it won't be much longer. He'll finish brushing his teeth, then he'll splash his face with water as he always does and then he'll be off.

Except he doesn't immediately head for the door once he's done in the bathroom. Instead, he lingers in the bedroom, and I have to snap my eye shut again and hope that he didn't spot me peeking.

'Mary.' His gruff voice cuts through the silence after a few seconds.

I do not move.

'Mary.'

There's a hand on my shoulder. He jiggles me so that I have no choice but to open my eyes. I peer up at him, trying to feign tiredness, as if I'm only just waking. We watch each other for a moment, and I wonder if he's going to apologise for last night.

'What time is it?' I say, when I realise he's not going to.

'Eleven.'

My eyebrows flick up involuntarily. No wonder I'm so hungry. I hadn't realised it was quite so late.

'Aren't you going to be late for work?'

'I decided I'm not goin' today.'

My stomach constricts. I've been waiting for him to leave all morning, not just so that I can eat but so that I can have a bit of space to breathe, to think. I don't want him here.

'How come?'

He inhales deeply through his nostrils. 'After last night, I felt I needed to be here. Clearly we need to work on our marriage.'

I say nothing. Just wait.

He cocks his head to one side, surveying me.

'You dinnae agree?'

Truthfully, I'm wondering what the latest is with wife number two in the barn. Surely at some point he's going to bring her out so that he can have double the doting on him, double the cleaning and cooking, double the sex. Why bother working on our 'marriage' when there's a fresh new one waiting just a few metres away. Maybe she's putting up more of a fight than I did. Maybe she's stronger than I was.

Of course, I can't say any of this to him. The last thing I want is for him to get angry again. So instead, I nod.

'I do. I do agree.'

His Adam's apple bobs up and down and he leans forward, elbows pressed against his knees.

'All right then. I think you need reminding what a good wife does. What's expected of you.'

He looks back at me, but not at my face this time. His gaze travels lower.

'When will you be ready for sex again?'

Ice travels down my spine. He hasn't raped me since I found out I was pregnant. I had assumed, since things have been so different, that it wasn't something he wanted to do.

'What?' is all I can manage.

'A good wife satisfies her husband, aye?'

Goosebumps are forming all along my arms and legs. I don't want him touching me. I think it might make me sick.

'I . . . I don't want to hurt the baby.'

It isn't entirely an excuse. The pregnancy books I've been reading all say that sex while pregnant is fine, that baby is well protected in the uterus and that they won't have the faintest clue what's going on. But the books also say that that's the case with a normal, healthy pregnancy. I have no idea if my pregnancy is normal or healthy because he hasn't allowed me to see a doctor to confirm or deny as much.

'Little'un will be fine. We're still husband and wife. That doesnae stop just because kiddies come along.'

I don't know what to say. I desperately want him to stay away from me. I've never felt more repulsed by him, and the realisation of that hits me like a ton of bricks.

His hand moves to rest on my thigh and I try hard not to recoil.

'Please,' I whisper, though it's so quiet I'm not even sure if I've actually spoken.

As he lifts my dress, my skin prickles with the cold. Even his hands are cold.

'I love you, Mary.' His lips are on my neck now, his breath tickling the underside of my chin, and my eyes prickle with tears.

But I can't say anything. My throat is locked as he leans towards me, the bed sinking as his weight presses on the mattress.

I close my eyes, and I force myself to think about anything else.

'Stop.'

He doesn't hear me at first. He's too wrapped up in his own pleasure. The bed continues to shake. His grunts continue to echo around the room.

'Cal, stop!'

I'm more forceful this time. I push my palms against his sweaty chest and heave him away from me. He gapes at me in shock, or is that anger on his face? I think he was nearly finished.

'What?'

'Something hurts.'

I ignore the look of indignation on his face and feel around my abdomen. There's a pulling sensation on either side that I've never felt before. My stomach churns and my heart rate quickens.

'Something's wrong,' I say, my voice wobbling.

There's clearly some kind of mental war happening in his head. Should he get angry or should he be concerned? I've never seen him so unsure of himself. His lack of response, though, only frustrates me more.

'Cal! There's something wrong with the baby!' My words come out a harsh snap, and they seem to jolt him back to life.

'Calm down. We dinnae know that for sure. Could be completely normal, what you're feeling.'

There's no holding them back this time. The tears roll freely down my cheeks. Why can't he understand? Why does he care so little? Surely he can't be so evil as to be willing to risk the life of his unborn child.

No. Not his child. Mine.

He watches me cry for a few seconds, his forehead creased.

'All right, all right. Stop that cryin'. Stop it.'

He places a hand on my thigh and I suck in a shaky breath, wiping my nose with my arm. I don't want him to comfort me.

'Perhaps . . .' He turns his head and peers out of the window, to the Highlands that stretch on and on. 'Perhaps we can get a doctor to come here and check you out. Make sure all's well with little'un.'

My eyes widen, but I daren't say anything in case I do something to make him change his mind.

He returns his gaze to me. 'That's if you promise to behave, aye?'

I press my lips tight together and nod.

Yes. I'll behave. If it means keeping you safe, I'll do whatever he wants.

Chapter Twenty-One

It's been two weeks since Cal said he'd get a doctor here, and I still haven't seen a soul. When I asked him a few days ago if he knew when they'd be coming, he just muttered something about them all being very busy and not considering my situation an emergency.

'They'll come when they come,' he had said with a tone that signalled he was quite done with the conversation.

The blessing, if you want to look at it that way, is that the pulling sensation stopped almost as quickly as it had started, and I haven't felt it again since. Cal was probably right. It was likely just a normal sensation that comes with pregnancy. According to the books, sharp pains and the kind of pulling I felt that night are merely a symptom of the uterus growing. But whether it was usual or not, I still want to see a medical professional. Also, though I've been careful not to mention anything of the sort to Cal, the more symptoms I experience the more I wish I had a mother to chat things over with.

'I hope you have a good day.' I smile as I help Cal into his work jacket. I've been especially nice to him, taking on my good wife act again in the hopes that it might be seen as 'behaving' in his eyes.

'Aye. What's for dinner?'

'I thought I'd do a shepherd's pie with that mince you brought in yesterday.'

He nods approvingly. Shepherd's pie is one of his favourites. He spent ages in the skinning barn last night preparing the mince. I try not to think about what else he might have done while he was down there.

He bends down to give me a kiss, and I try to make my kiss back feel as genuine as I can. Even though I've been back to waiting on him hand and foot recently, things still aren't the way they were. There's still something there, some layer of distrust from him lingering beneath every conversation, every kiss, every cuddle. It's like he's trying to figure out what I'm up to. I'm not acting well enough.

As he drives off, I watch him from the doorway, watch the dust flying up into the air and the rustle of the trees as he disappears into their thicket. Maybe, just maybe, today will be the day when he'll return with someone who can help us.

Clinging on to that hope, I make my way into the kitchen to get a start on preparing the vegetables for tonight's dinner. I prefer to slow cook mince throughout the day. It always tastes so much better. There's a slight whiff of off food as I open the cupboard and I make a mental note to check and rotate our supplies.

I pause, my hand lingering in mid-air in front of the shelves.

Potatoes.

Where are the potatoes?

I lift myself up onto tiptoes and scan the very back of the cupboard, moving various tins and jars aside to see if they've rolled behind something. Nothing. I chew on my lip as I pull back from the cupboard. How am I supposed to make a shepherd's pie without potatoes? I'm almost certain I had some left over.

Frustration eating at me, I haul on my coat and head out into the vegetable garden. My robin friend is there waiting for me on the fence, and I nod to him. I don't think there will be any potatoes ready for pulling, but I might as well check. If not, he'll have to make do with dumplings.

The thought stirs as I'm on my knees by the root vegetable patch. It's a crazy thought. Absurd. But it's there and it niggles at my brain making it impossible to ignore.

There were carrots missing too a few weeks back. He mentioned the lack of them in the stew I had cooked. It hadn't occurred to me as odd then, but I don't understand how I could have mistaken our food levels twice in such a short space of time. I have a fairly stringent stock rotation system. It's a necessary part of being a self-sufficient household. We need to know what we have and nothing can go to waste.

My eyes drift across to the skinning barn. Of course. There's food going missing because he's feeding it to her. What was it he used to give me? Steamed vegetables. Just enough to sustain me, to keep me alive, but lacking in nutrients enough to make me weak.

I fall back to rest on my heels, wishing I could take something more substantial to her. There was a padlock on the door last time I checked. But if I had a key, I could get to the cage.

The day crawls by at a snail's pace. The closer it gets to nightfall, the less confident I am in my plan, and the more my nerves start to get the better of me. Cal isn't best pleased at the lack of shepherd's pie when he gets home, but when I explain we've run out of potatoes he seems to drop it, which only confirms my suspicions. Dinner is more fraught than usual, I think. Perhaps he can see it in me. The disobedience. The insolence of what I'm planning to do. If he can, he does not say anything.

On and on the hours drag until finally we're clambering into bed, but still the seconds tick by at an agonisingly slow rate. I have to lie here, staring at the ceiling, not letting myself fall asleep while I wait for him to, though truthfully I have no chance of drifting off. I'm wired. Hyped up on adrenaline. I know now that I'm going through with it, despite any reservations I've had since I first made this plan. I can't not. The least I owe to this woman is a decent meal.

When he finally descends into a deep, rhythmic breathing and his usual snore starts to rattle through the room, the dread of what I'm about to do unfurls in my gut. I wait a while longer, maybe half an hour, maybe more, until I'm absolutely certain he won't wake. Then, so slowly and so carefully I'm barely moving, I slide out of bed.

His jacket is hanging up as usual. I creep over to it, being careful of where I'm placing my feet, avoiding the floorboards that creak. My fingers slide into his pocket and brush against his set of keys. When I withdraw them, I take a moment to study them. There's the little square one for the medicine box, the one I found the spare of above the kitchen cabinet. Next to it are two slightly larger keys with round tops. I assume one of these is the barn key. Next to those is the key to his truck. My thumb strokes it.

I could drive away.

But I've never even sat behind a wheel.

It can't be that difficult.

I need to wait until he's distracted. That's the plan.

To hell with the plan.

Where would I go?

I don't know.

I shake my head, forcing the argument to the back of my mind. Now is not the time. I need to focus on what I've been waiting all day and all evening to do.

Removing one of the round-topped keys from the keyring and gripping it knife-like between my fingers, I grab some of the leftover stew, slip on my boots and trudge outside. It's not like the last time I approached the barn. Last time I was wracked with nerves, terrified of what I might find. Though the fear still lingers, this time it's overtaken by a steely determination. I have to help her.

The moon is shining down on me, its light like a comforting hand on my back, encouraging me forward. The cameras that raise the alarm on Cal's phone are further out than this, near the 'no trespassing' sign, so he shouldn't be alerted to what I'm doing. I raise the key and will my hand to stay steady enough to slot it into the padlock.

The barn is larger inside than I remember. I had expected it to be cramped, packed tightly so that you could barely move. Instead it's spacious. A dark void. I blink a few times to help my eyes adjust now that I no longer have the moonlight to guide me, and a few details start to appear. Over to the left are the carcasses hanging up from Cal's most recent hunting session. I'm quick to avert my gaze. That's one of the reasons I've never returned to this barn since he let me out, because I can't stand to look at them. In the centre of the space, directly opposite me, are the larger power tools he uses and his tractor. To the right, shelves, though I can't quite see what they hold.

A shaky breath escapes my lips. Maybe she's not in here after all. Maybe he's got rid of the cage. I've convinced myself that my plan worked but perhaps that's just my guilty conscience talking.

My heart finally beginning to slow, I turn to leave. I'll lock it up again, slip the keys back into his jacket, slide into bed and he'll never know. But as I'm about to step back outside, something catches the corner of my eye. I retreat back into the belly of the barn and narrow my eyes. There's a boxy shape in between the shelves, pushed right up against the wall. It's large, large enough for a cow or some sheep. Or a human. The sight of it has unlocked something inside of me. A cold, creeping dread.

I take a few tentative steps towards it. Then a few more. As I get closer I can see details more clearly. Rows and rows of metal bars, locked shut with yet another padlock.

The air seems to close in around me.

It's the cage. It's still here. And there is a woman inside of it.

Chapter Twenty-Two

The breath has been punched from me. The air feels too thick to inhale, each gulp a laborious effort that doesn't seem to fill my lungs, as I stare down at the cage. My heart pounds against my ribcage, a frantic drum telling me to get as far away from this thing as possible. I told myself, swore to myself, that I would never lay eyes on it again. The desire to be outside of this barn, away from this horrific sight, is almost too intense to bear. The room spins as panic claws its way up my throat, a silent scream that can't find its way out. But this woman is in there because of me. If I don't try to help her I'm as bad as him.

'Hello,' I say.

She flinches. Undoubtedly she'd been expecting Cal. That's why she didn't react when I first came in. She's resigned to the routine he'll have forced onto her by now. Her head lifts slowly, her straggly hair parting awkwardly and sticking to her face. Her eyes meet mine.

A strangled cry escapes her that catches in her throat and causes her to descend into a coughing fit. Tears collect in my eyes as I remember it all too vividly.

'Help . . . me . . .' she wheezes through the coughs.

I want desperately to back away from the cage, to get as far away as possible, but I clench my fists and step closer. The smell hits me as I do and my eyes water.

'Please let me out.'

'I'm sorry, I don't have a key.'

The woman drops her head again and her shoulders begin to shake. The sound of her sobs cracks my heart in two. I can't watch her cry anymore, the guilt is too much, so I move to kneel by the cage and place the stew on the floor.

'I brought you some food.'

She glimpses it through the strands of her hair and shuffles forward. Weak, slow movements. The gaps in the bars aren't big enough to fit the bowl through so I dip the spoon into the stew, making sure to collect a large chunk of meat, and lift it up to her level. Drops of gravy splash onto the floor and I'm quick to wipe them up. There can't be a shred of evidence that I've been here.

Once she's finished she wipes her mouth with the back of her hand. 'Thank you,' she whispers. 'Is there any more?'

I shake my head. 'I'll try and bring a bigger portion next time.'

'When will that be? When will you be back?'

I swallow hard, wishing I hadn't said anything. I should have just placed the food on the ground for her and left. Talking to this woman is not only dangerous – all she has to do is mention me to Cal and I'll be joining her – but it's making me second-guess my plan entirely. Seeing her here, a picture of me ten years ago, is sowing seeds of doubt into my mind about whether I can actually go through with this, and they're growing like weeds. Can I really stand by and let this happen? Because it's not just the cage, is it? Even after she's free she faces being dehumanised at the cabin, turned into his puppet, raped without the ability to say no, and hurt and punished should she ever try to leave. If I could find the key to the cage I could let her out, give her a chance at escaping.

But I can't. Aside from the fact the cameras and his sodding alarm system would mean we wouldn't stand a chance at getting further than the 'no trespassing' sign, her keeping Cal busy is the whole reason she's here. If she gets out now then all of this will have been for nothing. She's the only way I'll ever get away from here. If there was another way, I wouldn't do it. If there was just me to think about, I wouldn't do it. I'd stay here and take it as I have done for all these years. But it's not just me and no matter how evil this makes me, no matter how much I know I'll never be able to forgive myself, I will do anything to protect you and get you away from this place. Even at the cost of another.

I back away from the cage.

Her eyes widen. 'Wait, please . . .'

'I have to go. I'm sorry.'

I turn, flee, tripping and stumbling as I go. My mind is a void. All I know is I need to get as far away from that cage and that woman as

I possibly can. As I burst from the barn, I clutch the edge of the door for support, the wood solid and real under my fingertips, a stark contrast to the surreal horror unravelling around me. My breathing is erratic, losing track of itself, ragged gasps that feel like they're stripping the world of oxygen. My body shakes uncontrollably. I squeeze my eyes shut and attempt to count backwards, anything to stop the panic. I curl in on myself, grip my hair in big, painful clumps and moan as the agony of everything I've lost and everything I still stand to lose sinks in.

The cabin stares at me, taunting. I don't want to go back there. He's there. Sleeping in my bed. But I have nowhere else to go. My gaze pans the surroundings. Trees. Hills. Beyond that the loch. Beyond that . . . more of the same. He chose our residence well, always said living out here meant he could make certain I was safe.

Not safe. Unable to get away. If ever you were going to keep someone against their will, this is the place to do it.

The trek back to the cabin is laborious, each step difficult, as if the cabin is pushing me away, warning me not to come back. As my fingers brush against the door handle I pause, a jolt of worry shooting through me. What if he's not asleep? What if he's sitting in his chair waiting for me? How will I explain where I've been at this time of night? How will I explain my tear-streaked face?

I pull back and move away from the front door, instead deciding to edge around the side of the cabin. My movements are so slow, so imperceptible, as I peer around the side of our bedroom window it takes me an age before I can actually see anything. He's still there. Seems to be asleep.

At the sight of him the panic returns. I lean my back to the wall and slide down it, curling up in a ball at the foot of the window and gripping my knees to my chest, trying to control my breathing. I need to get a grip. That woman in there needs me. She needs food. But the physical reaction I had upon seeing her, talking to her, was too much. If I'm going to take her anything else I need to be strategic. Food that's small enough to just pass through the bars without saying a word, but nothing that will leave behind packaging or anything that might hint at my having been there.

The Woman in the Cabin

It's an effort to drag myself up and into the cabin. Every limb aches. I feel like I've been hit by a truck. Every ounce of me is repulsed at the thought of getting into bed with him, so instead I collapse onto our threadbare sofa. If he wakes up I'll need to say I couldn't sleep or something.

And this is how I stay for hours. Staring at nothing in particular but thinking about everything.

Chapter Twenty-Three

At some point I fell asleep on the sofa. I know I did because when I open my eyes Cal has already gone to work. I wonder what he thought when he saw me out here. Why didn't he wake me up? In one way I'm glad he didn't, but part of me is terrified about what that means. Am I going to pay for sleeping out here when he gets back?

I close my eyes, trying to will away the images that flood my mind. The same question gnaws at my brain as the one I asked when he first locked me in that cage.

Why?

Why would he do this? He says his spiel about marriage and how wives and husbands are supposed to be, but surely he can't think I love him. Surely he can't believe in this lie he's built up. Marriage is supposed to be when two people meet, fall in love and decide to spend the rest of their lives together. They. Collectively. Together. It's not supposed to be one person deciding and the other being forced to go along with it and hurt and tortured into submission.

The answer, of course, is plain as day. He wanted someone to control. He wanted me cut off from my life, from the world, hidden away in this isolated cabin in the middle of nowhere, so that I was totally reliant upon him. If I had chosen to marry him there was always the chance I could change my mind. This way, I have no choice.

He's coming home. That's his truck's engine outside, in the distance. My heart thuds. On autopilot I jump to my feet and rush to the sink, where I start to busy myself with doing the washing up. Not that there's much to wash up. I haven't eaten or drunk anything, am too racked with guilt, so it's just his coffee mug and breakfast plate. I scrub them anyway as I watch the truck approach the cabin. My eyes flick over to the kitchen knives next to the sink and my fingers twitch. I could attack him as he comes through the door. Grab the keys from his bloodied body and jump into the truck, hurtle down the dirt path and find civilisation, someone to help me.

Cal gets out of the truck and I return my focus to the plate I'm cleaning. It's not worth it. I tried that once before and it ended up so, so much worse.

'You're up, I see.' His voice cuts through me as he comes in the front door.

'Sorry I wasn't awake to make you breakfast. You're home early though. In time for lunch.'

'Aye, only the one garden today. Work's drying up.'

I swallow. That means he's going to be home more often. He takes his boots off and starts hanging up his jacket as I finish off the plate. I wish there was more to do to keep my hands busy.

'How come you slept out here then?'

I bite my lip. There's an uncontrollable urge working its way through me to scream at him, pummel him with my fists, but it would be stupid. Who knows what he'd do to me. I need to stick to my plan. Until then, I need to act like nothing has changed.

'I couldn't sleep. I was tossing and turning and didn't want to wake you so thought it would be better to sleep on the sofa.'

I turn away from him, hoping that he can't see my ears reddening from the lie, and dry my hands with the cloth. His footsteps close in behind me on the floorboards. I can sense him right behind me, hovering. My grip tightens on the towel.

'Somethin' keeping you awake?'

Hands touch my shoulders and it takes everything in me not to flinch. He turns me to face him, gently but forcefully. I force a smile onto my face.

'Just the baby. You know how I worry.'

He watches me for a moment as if trying to decide if I'm telling the truth or not. His eyes, eyes that I found so sexy and alluring that night we met in the pub, burn into me like acid.

'Mmm,' he grunts, finally releasing me from his stare as he turns to his armchair. 'I told you, you shouldnae be worried. Lack of sleep is going to do far worse to you and little'un than anything else.'

'Did you manage to get a doctor's appointment yet?'

He slumps into the chair and rests his ankles on the footstool. 'There is no appointment. I spoke to a lad in town, local doctor. He reckons baby's absolutely fine. Nothing to worry about.'

I swallow again and take a deep breath. Mustn't lose my composure. 'How could he possibly know that without examining me?'

'How am I s'posed to know? Doctors, they're smart laddies, ain't they?'

'But you . . .' I pause, realising how high my voice is. Clearing my throat, I concentrate on keeping it steady and calm. 'You said you'd get him to come here.'

'I said I'd consider it.' There's a tone in his voice that I recognise, one of finality. It tells me that this conversation is done, that he's had the last say and that I better not push it. My eyes prick with tears but I force them back. Just in time, too, because he leans his head back and looks over at me.

'He also said it's fine to have sex while you're pregnant.'

My throat constricts. Before I can even begin to attempt to get any words out he stretches his arms above his head, then pulls himself to his feet.

'I'm going to go freshen up. Got a couple of deer to sort for this week's dinner and then we'll spend some proper husband and wife time together, aye?' He moves to me and slides his hands around my hips. 'I've missed you.'

It's all I can do to force a smile onto my lips. He kisses them, and I just know he can tell I'm not kissing him back properly, but my brain just won't let me do it. A small shudder works its way up my spine as I watch him disappear into the bathroom to clean himself up before heading to the barn. That godforsaken barn.

I wonder if that's what he used to do. Get home from work, take a few minutes to collect himself, stretch, wash his face, then head down to my prison to give me food and drink and ask me who I am. Just a normal day like any other.

A realisation occurs to me with a jolt. He's going to the barn. I still have the key. If he goes to open the lock and realises it's gone he's going to know I've been in there. I whip around and search frantically around the room. Where did I put it? When I got back from the barn

I was in such a mess. Panic ripping through me, I attempt to retrace my footsteps, acutely aware that he's left the bathroom door open. I can see the edge of his shoulder from here. All it would take is for him to poke his head out and he'd see me searching.

Think. Think, Mary. Think.

No. Not Mary. That's not my name.

I shake my head, forcing the thought from my mind. Now is not the time.

Think. I came in and collapsed onto the sofa and fell asleep. Trembling, I move as discreetly as possible over to the sofa and start rummaging around, digging my fingers down the edge of the cushions. They brush against a few crumbs and a hair tie, but no key. My face is flushed now, the blood rushing around my head and making me dizzy. Where could it be?

Wait, I didn't just come in and collapse on the sofa. I went up to the bedroom window first so that I could check he was still asleep.

I take another quick glance at the bathroom. He's getting changed out of his work clothes now. The last step in his routine. He won't be long.

I scurry over to the front door, flinching as it squeaks open, then practically fall over myself as I make my way back to the bedroom window. Something metal glints in the sun and my heart leaps. I have to be careful. If he comes out of the bathroom he might see me through the window. Taking a measured breath, I peek around the corner through the glass. The coast is clear. I snatch the key up and run back to the front door. There are mere seconds between me slipping the key back onto the keyring and into his pocket and him appearing in the doorway.

'You OK?' His brow furrows as he takes in my flustered appearance.

'Thought I saw a rat.'

I hold my breath, convinced he's going to tell me he saw what I was doing.

'Better make sure you're keeping on top of the housework. Cannae be having no rats chewing things up.'

I nod quickly, relief flooding through me at his response. 'I will, don't worry.' He grunts in acknowledgement before swinging his jacket onto his shoulders, key safely in his pocket, and heading out to the barn.

I am alone in the cabin once again.

With trembling hands, I sink down onto the sofa, my heart still racing from the close call. I'm too far gone with my plan now. That woman is here. I'm going to have to find a way out. If I don't then she's going through all this for nothing. But now that the clock is ticking and it suddenly seems so real, just the thought of trying to leave makes my blood run cold. The iron-shaped scar prickles.

What's worse? The fear of staying locked in this lie of a life, or the fear of what he might do to me if I try to leave?

I lick my lips, picturing it. His face if he were to catch me making a run for it again. I think back to the man who knocked at the door and asked for directions. I should have asked him for help. I could have begged him to take me with him, to help protect me against Cal. But I was so scared that Cal would kill him, and now he's long gone. The first person to knock at our door in all the years I've lived here. Who knows when we might get another visitor, if ever.

The sound of his heavy footsteps returning from the barn snaps me out of my thoughts. I shudder and brace myself, steeling my nerves as he walks back into the house. His expression is unreadable as he enters the room, his eyes flickering over me. The silence between us is thick with tension, each moment ticking by like an eternity as I struggle to maintain my composure.

He walks over to me, his gaze piercing through my facade of calmness. 'You've been acting strange lately,' he mutters, his voice low and dangerous.

I swallow hard, attempting to keep my face neutral. 'I'm just tired.'

He studies me for a long moment, as if weighing my words against some invisible scale. Finally, he holds out a hand to me. I have no choice but to take it, standing and hoping that my knees won't buckle.

'Let's go to bed then, aye?'

My blood runs cold at his words, the truth of what he's asking of me unmistakable. I can't live like this anymore. Not now you're relying on me to give you a better life. I need to get out of here. But now is not the time. I need to tread carefully. Follow the plan. Until then, I have to play the role of the obedient wife to perfection.

With a trembling hand, I reach out to touch his arm, mustering up all the false affection I can manage.

'You always know what's best for me,' I say, forcing a lightness into my voice that makes my skin crawl.

His face breaks into a smile at my words, but there's a glint in his eyes that sends a shiver down my spine. He leans in closer until I can feel his hot breath tickling my ear.

'That's right. I always know what's best for you.'

Chapter Twenty-Four

There's a phrase I think someone must have said to me at some point. Perhaps a friend from university.

Lie back and think of England.

It must have been something someone from before said to me, because there's no way it would have been in any of the books Cal has let me read over the years. It refers to, if I remember correctly, the societal expectation that women should endure or submit to sexual activity with their husbands, even if they are not particularly enthusiastic about it.

Yesterday I didn't lie back and think of England. I thought of the road sign. The image in my head that I had to paint, had to get out of my system.

Of all the emotions I've felt since I broke into the barn – the fear, the anxiety, the guilt, the dread – there's one that seems to trump everything else. The frustration. The life I had before Cal took me doesn't feel real anymore. It was all so long ago it's like it's another world, hazy like a dream. The time I wish I could forget, my imprisonment, is clear as day. But before that everything's a little bit smoky. I can picture my parents but not properly. I remember the way they used to hug me but can't conjure up the feeling of their embrace. I know what their voices sounded like but I can't hear it in my mind anymore.

I wonder what's happened to them since I was taken. Did they go on the news and do an appeal to find me? Was the strain of it all too much, leading to a messy, public divorce? Maybe they're not even alive anymore. I wouldn't know. The only technology in this cabin is what Cal has. His phone, which never leaves his side, and the cameras. No computers. No TV. All of it, products of the devil himself, according to Cal.

After I've handled my morning chores and fixed Cal his breakfast and waited for him to head out in his truck, I try to paint. It's the first time I've picked up a brush since my painting session with Cal. As I dip my brush into the paint, I can feel the familiar comfort of creating washing over me. It's a small rebellion, a secret act that Cal doesn't need to know about. The canvas becomes my sanctuary, each stroke a silent protest. This is better than simply writing it all down. Riskier, for sure. But better. With paint I can capture my parents' faces, the road I grew up on, the life that I was snatched from.

But even painting doesn't seem to bring me that same sense of remembrance that it used to. I stare at my work once it's finished, watching it dry in patches. The frustration boils within me. I need to remember. I crave it.

I nibble on my nail, realise what I'm doing, stop. Cal hates it when I have jagged, bitten nails. Instead, I pace the room, annoyance licking through me like flames as I look again and again at my painting, willing the sound of my mum's laughter or my dad's cheesy jokes to flood my ears. How can something so vital, so intrinsic to who I am, be kept from me? It's as if the universe itself is playing a cruel joke on me, dangling morsels of memory just out of reach.

In a sudden burst of fury, I snatch up the canvas and fling it across the room. The colours blur together in a kaleidoscope. It hits the edge of the table, tears, a jagged slice through the painted sky. The sound of it splitting is like a gunshot in the silence of the cabin. I freeze, my breath caught in my throat, as if waiting for Cal to burst through the door any second. But the only sound that follows is the ringing echo in my ears. I step closer to the ruined painting, scattered with broken wood and splattered paint like drops of blood on snow. With a heavy heart, I sink down and trace the tear with trembling fingers. Tears prick at the corners of my eyes. I need this to end. For ten years I have endured this existence. I need to either get out or give up and die.

You'd never know I'd even got the paints out by the time I settle myself at the kitchen table with a cup of tea. I make sure to get rid of any evidence of my attempt to remember, getting rid of the stray paint splatters with white spirit and burning the canvas in the wood burner. Once the easel and supplies were all packed away, I swept through the cabin doing my chores as fast as I possibly could so that Cal wouldn't turn on me, but not wanting to delay getting started on the next phase of my plan any longer. Then, I sat at the table, purposefully angling myself so that I could see any sign of Cal's return through the window, and started to strategise. I've retrieved the old notebook from under the bed. It's nothing special, but in these last five minutes of scribbling it's become my most treasured possession.

This notebook has allowed me to get it all out of my head and onto paper. The ideas that have been formulating. The how and what of any potential escape plan. And the why. I've used these blank sheets to remind me why I'm doing this. Why I have to leave. It's a collection of plans and ideas, yes, but more than that, it's a place to address any doubts, any fears about what might happen if I do manage to escape, and what might happen if I don't.

Chewing on the end of my pen, I flick to the next page and start to list out supplies I'm going to need if I'm to make this journey. I wish I knew where he kept his hunting rifles. I assume in the barn, but undoubtedly they'll be under tight lock and key. He wouldn't risk having me be able to get hold of them. Instead of a gun, I'll have to make do with listing out the necessities I'll need for survival. This cabin was built where it is for a reason. If you're going to imprison an abducted woman or two you're going to want to be as far away from civilisation as you can possibly get. How much of a trek I'm facing before I find any sign of life is anyone's guess. But it must be doable. That hiker walked here. That means there's hope. As long as I keep the dirt track that Cal travels down to get to work in my sights and don't veer off into the wilderness, I'll find a main road eventually. But I need to make sure I don't die of thirst or hunger before then.

This feels good. Sensible. The times I tried to escape when I first came here, there was no forethought. I just saw an opportunity and took it, planning be damned. This time, escape feels somewhat achievable.

He's coming home. I don't even have to see or hear the truck to know. There's a disturbance in the trees, the birds fluttering up into the sky, that signals something moving through the thicket. I close my notebook, the feel of its cover reassuring under my palm, and slot the book back into its hiding place. Once the notebook is safely stashed I make my way out into the garden and divert my attention to one of the raised beds, where I pick a few strawberries.

'Good harvest?' Cal says as he rounds the side of the cabin and comes to watch me.

'Welcome home.' I paste my best smile onto my face and offer him one of the strawberries. He plucks it from my fingers and pops it into his mouth.

'Now that's a good strawberry. What's for tea?'

'Pork chops and mash.'

He nods approvingly. 'Stick a few of them strawberries into a bag for me, will you? I want to snack on 'em while I skin them deer.'

I grimace and do as instructed, fetching a cloth bag from inside and dropping a few of the ripest strawberries into it. As I watch him head down to the barn my skin crawls and I try my best not to think about the cage.

But I can't not think about it. I can't not think about that woman.

My stomach turns as the thought of her settles, burrows itself into my brain. I retch, clasp my hand over my mouth and stumble over to the sink. I make it just in time.

Cal returns to the cabin half an hour later. Nothing about his demeanour suggests that he's holding an abducted woman in a cage, but then, I know that he's a master of lies and manipulation. My eyes flick to the barn and I consider trying to steal the key tonight to attempt taking her some food again, but I know I won't be able to. I can't even think about that woman without feeling another panic attack coming on, let alone go back down there.

No. I know what I need to do. I need to get away from here and then once I've found someone who can help, the police will be able to rescue her. Then I'll spend the rest of my miserable life trying to make it up to her.

'What you thinking?'

His words snap my eyes back to him.

'What?'

'You look right deep in thought there.'

My cheeks burn and though I know it's going to make me look guilty, I can't maintain eye contact with him. 'Oh. Just about the baby.'

My hand rests on my stomach, now substantially rounder, and the familiar flutter from you tells me I'm not alone, no matter how I might feel.

'Well, I've got good news on that front.'

He moves to his rucksack and starts rummaging about inside it. Curiosity overtakes me and I watch him, wondering what good news he could possibly bring me. He retrieves plastic bags labelled 'Waterproof Bed Sheets', a bottle of isopropyl alcohol and a box of latex gloves.

'Got these. That doctor friend of mine gave 'em me. Says it's the best things to use for the birth.'

My shoulders droop. Disappointment curdled with fear flushes through me. The thought of labouring and giving birth here, alone, with just Cal to help me, is too much to bear, and seeing these supplies is just making it seem all the more real.

'And,' Cal continues, placing the items on the table, 'we've agreed he'll come and supervise the birth.'

For a moment I think I haven't heard correctly.

'You . . . you mean it?'

'Aye. He's a good mate. Knows how to be discreet.'

Tears collect and splash down onto my cheeks as relief washes over me. A doctor! A real-life doctor. If I'm still here by the time you come I'm going to have someone who knows what they're doing to help, to offer his expert opinion if complications arise.

'Thank you.' The words are barely audible but my throat won't let me say anything else.

Cal must have heard me because he nods and heads to the bathroom to freshen up. I'm grinning so hard my cheeks hurt. Finally, finally something has happened in our favour. Someone is going to help us both survive this awful situation.

A glimmer of hope flickers inside me as I try to picture this doctor. I envision him as a kind-faced man, with a calming voice and gentle hands. There's a small niggle in the back of my mind telling me that if he's friends with Cal there's a chance he'll be as psychotic as him, but I push it aside. Doctors are good, kind people. Their job is to help people. Maybe, if I can somehow get him on his own without Cal around, I can tell him I'm being held captive here. Maybe, as well as helping with the birth, he could help us escape too.

'Somethin' on your mind, lass?'

I blink as his words snap me back to the present.

'Hmm?'

'You're starin' out the windeh.' He tilts his head towards the window, following my gaze. 'At the barn.'

I could kick myself. I hadn't even realised I was staring at the barn but he's right. Or rather, it's staring at me.

'Oh, I . . .' The words lodge in my throat. I had intended to act nonchalant, like I was just zoning out on account of my tiredness, but he can tell something's up. I'm sure of it. His eyes roam my face, searching for the lie, searching for what I'm trying to keep to myself. It will look even worse if I don't make eye contact, so I focus my gaze on the centre of his nose and pray that that's close enough.

He inhales, slowly, purposefully, as if he's sucking the very life out of the room. His fingers dance along the medical items on the table.

'You're proper pleased about the doctor, aye?'

I nod. I daren't try to talk.

He nods too, but still he's surveying me, scrutinising me.

'You'll carry on getting treats like that only if you're good, aye?'

All I can do is nod again.

137

Chapter Twenty-Five

'Mary?'

Cal's voice cuts through me. I wring out the cloth I've been using to scrub the bathroom floor and rest on my heels, groaning as my back clicks and pops. The housework has become tougher now that I'm further along.

'Mary, where are you?'

'I'm here, darling,' I call, ignoring the nauseous feeling that I get every time I call him that.

Just think about the doctor, is the mantra I repeat to myself.

It takes a good ten seconds for me to haul myself up from my spot on the floor. Aching and sore, I make my way out to the living space to find Cal standing in the hallway, his arms crossed over his chest. His eyes narrow as he takes in my dishevelled appearance.

'What were ye doin'?'

'Cleaning the bathroom.'

He nods approvingly. 'Come on,' he says, extending a hand towards me. 'Take a load off.'

He settles onto the couch and beckons me. I perch beside him and try to make myself comfortable, but comfort isn't really a thing anymore. I never expected pregnancy to ache so much. Cal notices my discomfort and grabs a cushion from behind him. He lifts my legs up onto the coffee table and places the cushion under my feet.

'Better?' he asks with a small smile.

I nod. For a moment, I allow myself to forget about our situation and just enjoy the feeling of being off my feet.

'So,' Cal begins, breaking the silence. 'I called the doctor this mornin'. Told him when you're due. We've just got te call him when you start havin' them contractions and he'll drive down. That sound okay?'

My heart rate quickens.

'Thank you,' I say cautiously. 'I think it will be good to have professional help.'

Cal nods in agreement. 'Aye, it will be good for you and our child.' His hand rests on my belly and I fight back tears. 'You know I'll make sure this wee bairn has everything they could ever need, aye?'

'Of course.'

What a load of crap. Everything Cal thinks is appropriate, more like. But not friends. Or school. Or proper healthcare. Or anything remotely resembling a normal life.

'Everythin' will all be good. Long as we understand each other, understand our roles in this family, long as you carry on bein' a good wife and doin' as you're told, we can be happy, aye?'

'Yes, Cal.'

'Good!' He jumps up from the sofa so quickly I flinch. 'Now we've got that clear, I've got a surprise for you.'

My face contorts into a grimace. A surprise is either going to be something he's brought back from work – a necklace or some new paints or something along those lines – or it's going to be something awful. I don't know whether to be scared or not.

I start to stand up and follow him but he waves me back down. 'You stay there. Relax for a bit. Won't be a moment.'

And then he's gone, out the front door. I stare forward, watching the flames in the fireplace dancing and jumping as if trying to show off for me. I could burn this whole place to the ground. That's an idea that hasn't occurred to me before. I'd like to see his cameras work after that. But then if, when, I got caught he'd probably make me build the whole cabin again from scratch. Even if I was on the verge of giving birth.

The image is torn from my mind by the sound of him coming back through the front door. I turn to see what this surprise is.

My mouth drops open.

She's here. The woman. He's brought her out of the barn. Out of the cage. I nearly collapse at the sight of her. Her skin is pale and waxy, and her eyes are sunken and hollow. She looks emaciated, weakened from the time locked away. Cal has her by the arm. He grips her tightly as he leads her into the living room. She shuffles along, head down, no fight left in her.

'Thought it was time you two properly met,' Cal says with a grin. The woman doesn't lift her head. Cal guides her to the couch and helps her sit. She winces in pain, eyes unfocused. 'I brought her in to warm up a bit.' He's saying it so casually, as if this is a normal everyday occurrence.

My heart pounds. I want to run to her, wrap my arms around her, apologise, tell her it's all going to be OK. But I stay frozen in place, uncertain what to do or say.

Cal goes to the kitchen and returns with a bowl of the soup I've had simmering on the stove. 'Here, drink this. It'll help.'

The woman accepts it with quivering hands. She takes small sips, spilling some down her chin.

I find my voice. 'Is she . . . is she going to be OK?'

'Oh aye. Once she warms up and gets some food in her, she should recover all right.' He pats her shoulder. 'This is my new bride, Mary. You'll be seeing a lot more of each other from now on. We're going to be a proper little family, the three of us.'

Chapter Twenty-Six

I feel sick. Cal claps his hands together, making both me and the woman flinch. 'Right! I'll leave you two to get acquainted while I finish up in the barn.' He heads outside and I'm alone with her. A knot of dread tightens in my stomach. The guilt I felt when she was just an idea, an abstract thought in my head, is nothing compared to this. Seeing her now in this state and knowing that I wanted this, that I planned for this, is making the gravity of my actions hit me like a ten-ton truck. I know all too well the horrors she has endured in that barn. Though her body may recover with warmth and food, the damage to her spirit will be beyond repair.

As she eats, I search her face for any sign of the person she once was. But her eyes remain downcast, dull and lifeless. She moves as if she's sleepwalking, detached from herself.

I hesitate, then slowly approach the couch.

'Can I sit with you?'

The woman doesn't acknowledge me. I'm not even sure she's heard me. I ease down beside her, every muscle tense. We sit in silence for several minutes. Finally, I clear my throat.

'I'm so sorry.'

The woman remains mute. She doesn't know what I did. If she did, if she knew that I had manipulated events to bring someone else to this hellhole in a desperate attempt at self-preservation, she'd probably turn and kill me on the spot. I would if I were her.

'Can you tell me your name?'

Her lips part, move, but no sound comes out.

'Pardon?'

I move my ear closer to her mouth, and this time a hoarse murmur escapes.

'Mary.'

A shiver criss-crosses along my shoulder blades.

141

'We'll get out of this,' I say, with a certainty I don't feel. 'Somehow, someday, we'll be free. But until that day you have to do as he says, OK? Don't try to run. Don't try to get away. If you try to leave, bad things will happen.'

Still the woman doesn't speak, so I do the only thing I can think of. I reach out for her hand. I expect her to flinch at the touch but she doesn't. Her eyes move towards me for the first time, but they don't look directly at me. They're looking at my stomach. My bump. A flicker of something crosses her face. Realisation, perhaps? Understanding of what lies ahead of her.

The approaching sound of boots breaks the moment. I release her hand as Cal enters, wiping his hands on a rag.

'There now, you lasses are getting on well, I hope?'

I lower my gaze. 'Yes, we're fine.'

'Good, good. And a lovely pair you make, too.' He grips her chin, tilting her head side to side as if inspecting livestock. She doesn't resist. Merely blinks slowly. 'Still a bit worse for wear, it seems. No matter. She'll bounce back soon enough with some rest. Now . . .' He disappears briefly into the bedroom. There's the sound of rummaging and hangers scraping against the rail in the wardrobe. When Cal returns he's holding a collection of my dresses.

'These ones will work for now. They're Mary One's, but as you can see she cannae fit in 'em right now.' He chuckles and I force myself not to roll my eyes. Mary One?

'Once you're feelin' up to it you can pick one to change into. You don't mind, do you, love? It'll help her feel more at home if she's in nice clean clothes.'

I shake my head, my throat tight. 'No, of course not.'

An ordinary man would expect his wife to go crazy if he brought another woman into the house proclaiming her to be his second wife, but not Cal. Cal's no ordinary man. Cal knows that only someone who wants their fingers broken would dare to question his choices.

'Come on then, Mary.' It takes me a second to realise he's not talking to me. His gaze is fixed on her. 'Mary, come and get changed, please.'

She doesn't move. I press my lips together, silently begging her to obey. He moves to stand directly in front of her and leans forward, face nearly pressed against hers. 'You've been through a lot and I know it will take some time before you properly accept that this is where you belong, so I'm gon' give you some leeway. But when I ask ye to do somethin', I'm gon' need you to do as you're told. Right, Mary?'

This time he is talking to me. I nod. 'Right.'

After a couple of excruciating minutes, she slowly stands up, her body looking like a puff of wind would knock her flying. She shuffles over to where Cal has laid the dresses on the coffee table. Her fingers brush over the soft fabrics, but her face remains blank. She picks up the top one. Blue floral. Smug, Cal leads her towards the bathroom and I sit and wait, unsure what else I can do. When they return, Cal stands back to look at her and she stands before us vacantly. The dress hangs off her thin frame.

'Oh yes. That's much better, aye?' He's directing the question to me. I nod, unable to speak.

He claps his hands together again and once more we both jump. 'Right, Mary Two, let's get you to bed I think. Mary One, burn those old clothes, will you? She won't be needin' them no more.'

Chapter Twenty-Seven

One hand rests on my stomach as I work my way through my list, placing food and water bottles and bandages into a neat pile on the table, forcing myself to ignore what's going on in the other room. I slept out here on the sofa last night. Cal wanted her in the bed for her first night in the cabin. I've been pushed out. Not that I mind, of course. It's what I'd planned for.

What I hadn't planned for, however, was the regret. Hearing the headboard slamming against the wall was bad enough last night, but I've woken up to it too. I'm doing this for you. I have to remember that. Any time a seed of doubt creeps into my mind I have to focus on what's important. Enough is enough. I will not let you be born in this place.

Mouth dry, I grab the final item on my list – water purifying tablets – and drop them on top of the pile. It stares back at me and I'm convinced I've forgotten something obvious. Something that I'll undoubtedly remember after I've been walking for a few hours and it will be too late to turn back.

My stomach clenches. I've tried not to think too hard about what will happen once I've actually escaped the cabin. I know in my gut that all those horror stories Cal told me about the dangers of the outside world were part of his manipulation, just another tool to keep me here like a good little wife. But it wasn't all lies. There are terrible people out there. I should know – I'm living with one. What if I end up facing worse dangers out there than I'm facing in here?

I peer out of the window and strain to see through the thicket of trees. It's useless. I've looked so many times at this point I've started seeing things that aren't really there. The other day I was convinced I saw a maniac with a bow and arrow charging towards the cabin. It was just a deer but it took a good half an hour for my heart rate to settle. This time, as I stare out of the window, there's no movement

144

at all, not even a rustle of leaves. It's a perfectly still day. No sign of bad weather, which is something at least.

I freeze.

The noises in the bedroom have changed. He's moving. Walking. *Damn it. I wasn't quick enough.*

I scoop my pile into the rucksack I've chosen for the journey. Heart skittering, I bound towards the back door and deposit my rucksack into the waterproof gardening trunk, along with my notebook. I can't keep it under the bed anymore, not now that another woman is going to be sharing our room. I'm never going to be in there alone. The gardening trunk is safe, for now. She's not doing any of the hard labour yet and Cal considers gardening a woman's job, so would never think to look in there. It's my little stash of secrets. I slam the lid down as quickly as I can and turn to head back to the cabin.

Cal is standing at the door. He's shirtless, hair still in disarray. His eyes are wild. Alert. Darting around as if he's trying to sniff out defiance. I try to tell myself that it's all in my head, but the more I look at him the less I'm able to convince myself of that.

'What're ye doing?'

Getting as far away from you as I possibly can, psycho.

I take a breath, hoping it will be enough to keep my voice steady. 'I thought I'd get out and do a spot of early morning gardening. The weather has brightened up so much recently.'

He squints at the sun, just beginning to peep over the tops of the trees.

'Hmph,' he grunts. He takes a step out into the garden. Blades of grass stick up between his toes. He walks all the way up to me, turns and sits on the trunk. I hold my breath.

The silence lingers on and it's unbearable. I feel like I should say something but I don't know what. I don't want to accidentally incriminate myself. So instead I stand and watch him, waiting for him to speak.

His fingers intertwine and he cracks his knuckles.

'What were you really doin', Mary?'

My name is not Mary.

'I . . .' My brain is suddenly racing at a million miles per hour, searching for something clever to say. I chew on the inside of my cheek. 'I realised I forgot to sort your lunch last night. I was going to grab some fruit and cucumbers and was hoping I'd be able to put it together before you woke up. I'm sorry.'

That was a smart answer. An admission of guilt to explain away my shifty behaviour, but not something that will land me in hot water. As long as he's not in a particularly bad mood, of course.

Cal regards me silently for a few moments, his expression unreadable. I try not to fidget under his intense gaze. Finally, he stands up from the trunk and stretches his arms over his head.

'You're right,' he says mildly. 'It's a right lovely mornin'. I think a walk is called for, what say you? How 'bout to the loch and back?'

'Are you not going to work today?'

'No work about. I told ye. It's drying up somethin' rotten.'

My heart sinks but I force a smile and nod. 'A walk would be lovely. Let me just get dressed.'

'Aye, I'm gonnae take a shower.'

Cal emerges fifteen minutes later dressed in jeans and a flannel shirt.

'What about Mary?' I ask, hating the way I have to call her that too and wishing I knew what her real name was.

'She's tired. She's gon' have a sleep. Just us two for today.'

He gestures for me to lead the way. I cross the threshold of our cabin slowly, delaying our departure. Something feels off, more so than usual, but I'm not sure what. I trudge forward in silence, hyper-aware of Cal's presence just over my shoulder. The morning sun filters through the canopy of leaves above us, dappling the ground with patches of light. It's quiet and peaceful. I wish I could enjoy the walk under different circumstances.

As we go deeper into the woods, Cal chatters animatedly about the plants and wildlife. He points out various species of birds and identifies edible berries. It's like nothing has changed. I suppose for him it hasn't. He doesn't know what I'm planning, that after all this time I'm going to attempt to make a run for it again. At least, I don't think he knows.

When we reach the shore of the loch, with its still surface reflecting the forest around it like a mirror, a desire stirs. The desire to shove him into the water. He'll be caught off guard, flailing in the cold depths. He can swim so it wouldn't kill him, but it would give me a chance to escape. It's risky, but it could work.

I flex my fingers, ready to push.

'Beautiful, in't it?'

I falter. My hands drop back to my sides.

'Yes, beautiful,' I murmur. It would never work. It was less of an idea and more a suicide attempt. He'd catch me easily once he managed to get out of the water, and my bag is back at the cabin. No. I need to be sensible here. I need to wait until he's distracted with Mary Two again. No altering the plan.

We sit together on a fallen log at the water's edge, sunlight dancing off the ripples. Trees stand tall around the perimeter like guards keeping watch. It doesn't escape me that it's stunning here. I don't often notice the beauty in things anymore. Cal drapes an arm around my shoulders and pulls me close. I stiffen but don't move away.

'I love it here, don't you? Just us and nature.' His words are a gentle caress on my ear, sending chills down my spine. 'No one to interfere in our wee world.'

I nod as if I hadn't pondered shoving him face first into the loch a moment ago. I take comfort in knowing that soon enough, I'll be free of him once and for all. As soon as the opportunity arises, I'll make my escape and never look back. The thought of freedom is like a warm embrace around my cold heart.

'Mary?'

'Yes, Cal?'

His grip on my shoulders tightens. Not enough to hurt, but it's uncomfortable.

'You're never gon' to try to leave me, are ye?'

I freeze under his hand, suddenly hot and claustrophobic.

He knows. Lord, help me. He knows.

Wait. Calm down. Maybe it's just a coincidence.

'Of course not.' I force a weak smile, attempting to feign amusement at such a ridiculous suggestion. 'Why would you even say that?'

He inhales, long and slow, taking just enough time that I fear my heart might actually rip its way through my chest, it's battering my ribcage with such ferocity.

'Tha's good. I know you wouldnae.' He carries on looking out over the surface of the water. His grip on my shoulders doesn't loosen. His other hand snakes over my hip and comes to rest on my stomach and it's all I can do not to squirm away. 'Jus' know if yous ever did try to leave me I'd take that there baby and drown 'em in that there loch.'

I blink. I'm not sure if I've heard him correctly. He can't be that bad. He can't be that crazy, surely.

'D'ya understand?'

I nod, tears brimming in my eyes.

Chapter Twenty-Eight

I don't realise she's joined me at first. The bacon in the pan sizzles loudly. I watch as it spits, little droplets of fat landing on the counters and the backsplash. I should turn it down really. There's going to be more to clean up. But it's hypnotic. So hypnotic, in fact, that when she coughs behind me I jump wildly.

I whirl around. She's directly behind me, wearing my dressing gown, peering over my shoulder at the bacon. She's been gradually looking better since he let her out of the barn. Her skin isn't quite so pale and drawn anymore. But there are still dark circles under her eyes.

'Sorry, I didn't mean to startle you.'

I force a smile. 'No bother. I was lost in my own world there.'

We watch each other awkwardly, waiting for the other to speak. This is the first time I've been alone with her since she was let out. After Cal took me to the loch I had expected to see her for dinner, but instead he took a tray into the bedroom for her. By the time night rolled around she was already fast asleep. I had thought Cal would ask me to sleep on the sofa again, but instead he positioned himself in the centre of the bed so that he had her on one side and me on the other. I'm not sure if that's a permanent situation or not. Later today I'm going to suggest we take it in turns, so that he has one night sharing the bed with her and one night with me. That will help – having a set schedule so that I know when he's going to be with her. That way I can prepare myself for my opportunity to leave.

She's still looking at me and I have to drop my gaze to the floor. It's almost like she can tell what I'm thinking, can see the betrayal as a physical life force between us. My hand rests on my stomach again and I focus on you, attempting to justify it to myself. You are my priority. Not her. It has to be that way.

'Is Cal still asleep?' I say when I can't bear the silence any longer. I turn back to the bacon and flip the strips over one by one, watching the undersides turn from pale pink to crispy brown.

'No.'

It's just the one word, but it makes me start, nonetheless. I hadn't expected her to reply at all. She's been so quiet this whole time.

'Oh, is he coming out for his breakfast, then?'

'He told me to come help.'

I nod. Of course he did. One day to acclimatise. A lifetime of service.

'Oh, well, great,' I say, forcing cheer into my voice. 'Can you grab some plates out of that cupboard there? Toast is on the grill. The bacon will be done in just a minute.'

She nods and moves slowly to the cupboard, taking down three plates. They rattle as she lowers them to the counter. Her hands are shaking. The silence hangs heavy between us. I want to ask how she's doing, if she's feeling any better, if she needs anything, but the words stick in my throat. Instead, she's the first to speak.

'How did you end up here?'

I pause, spatula hovering over the frying pan. 'I imagine in the same way as you.'

'How long have you been here?'

My lips press together as I hand her the block of butter and a knife to start spreading the toast. I know what she wants to hear. That I've only been here for a few weeks, like her. That we were both kidnapped at the same time and that this baby isn't Cal's and that the only reason I haven't escaped yet is because I haven't had the chance. She doesn't want to hear how long I've really been here. If she hears that, it opens up the possibility that the same might become true for her. But what am I supposed to do? Lie?

'A while,' I say eventually, hoping she doesn't push the matter.

'And you've never tried to leave?'

I don't say anything to that. I'm not stupid. If Cal sent her in here to help with breakfast he's probably listening on the other side of the door. Telling this woman about my various escape attempts will make him angry, and I'm not in the mood to deal with that. Not when I'm so close to my plan working.

'You said . . .' She steps closer to me and lowers her voice. 'You said yesterday that if I try to leave bad things will happen. What bad things?'

She needs to stop talking. Right now. It's coming across as disobedient. She's figuring out what her next play should be, how to increase her chances of getting away. She's going to end up getting both of us locked in that cage.

'Why would you want to leave?' I force out a laugh. 'This is your home now.'

Her mouth drops and at that moment the bedroom door opens. I turn, pluck the butter knife from her hand and start sorting out the toast.

'Well, isnae this a nice sight. The two o' you cookin' together.'

I place his plate on the table first, with the largest portion, then give the second largest to her and put the smallest in front of myself. As I sit down I avoid looking at either of them.

'So, how're my two favourite lasses this mornin', eh?' Cal says through a mouthful of food.

I stare down at my plate, pushing a piece of crust around with my fork. Across from me, she does the same, silent. Cal looks between us expectantly before clearing his throat.

'Well? Someone say somethin'.'

'We're fine,' I reply quickly. 'Just tired.'

He nods, shovelling more food into his mouth. The clinking of forks on plates fills the silence until he speaks again.

'I was thinkin' we could go on a little trip today. Jus' the three o' us. Maybe a picnic by the loch, get some fresh air. What do you reckon?'

I glance up to see him looking at her, gauging her reaction. She tenses, fingers tightening around her fork.

'That sounds lovely,' I say, before she can respond. 'Doesn't it, Mary?'

I will my eyes to meet hers, hoping she understands my warning.

She glares at me. 'Yes, a picnic sounds nice.'

'Excellent!' Cal beams, pleased with her response. 'Mary One will get some sandwiches sorted and we can head out in a couple of hours.' He shovels the last of his food into his mouth and sits back in his chair, clutching his stomach. 'Tha' was a good feed. Great team effort. Make me another drink, will ye, love.' He scoops his empty glass up and hands it to the woman. I hold my breath, watching her as she surveys the glass.

Don't do anything stupid.

She hesitates for a moment. Glancing at me as she takes the glass from Cal's outstretched hand. I try to communicate with my eyes – *just do as he says.* With a small nod, she turns away and crosses to the fridge to refill his drink and I let out a slow breath, returning to my food.

The noise shatters the quiet. I don't even realise what's happened at first. One minute she's pouring orange juice, the next she's snatched up a knife from the block beside the sink and has plunged it into Cal's chest. Cal lets out an anguished roar. His chair crashes to the floor as he lurches to his feet, face contorted in rage and pain. Blood blossoms across his shirt as he staggers towards her. It's not his chest. It's his shoulder. If she meant to kill him, she's missed.

'You crazy bitch!'

She backs away, bloody knife clenched in her fist. My heart hammers against my ribs. What has she done? She's just ensured her own death and likely mine as well. Maybe he'll even have me kill her as the ultimate punishment.

She tries to dart out of his way but he's too fast. He grabs her wrist and twists. She screams, her hand releasing the knife. It clatters to the floor and she hunches over, cradling her hand. It's bent at the wrong angle.

Cal grabs her by the shoulders and bashes her against the kitchen counter. His face is wild as he presses it right up against hers.

'Mary!'

It takes me a second to realise he means me.

'Tell Mary Two why she must never try anything like this again.'

My mouth opens and closes like a fish. He turns his enraged eyes on me.

'I said . . . tell her why.'

'Mary, you must never try to hurt Cal again,' I finally say, the spiel I remember him making me repeat when I attempted something like this all those years ago sticking in my throat. 'He only wants what's best for us, even if we don't understand it yet. We're lucky he's so patient and forgiving.'

'And what will happen if she does try anything like this again, eh?'

The words taste like bile in my mouth but I force them out. 'He'll break your other hand.'

'And?'

'And even if you kill him it won't do any good. You don't know how to get out. It's too far. You'll just die out here with him.'

Disbelief is smeared across her face. Cal's grip on her shoulders loosens slightly as he nods his approval.

'Tha's right. You're a good wife, you are. Shame Mary Two here isnae as good as you. I think another spell in the cage is wha's needed.'

Her eyes widen and she struggles against him, panic rising. 'No! I won't do it again! I'm sorry!'

'Cal, wait!' The words escape me before my brain even comprehends what I'm doing. 'You don't have to do that. She made a mistake. It's her second day here. I'll teach her.'

Cal pauses, his hand on the doorknob. 'Clear this mess up,' he says.

I wince, unable to watch as Cal drags her out, her feet scrambling for purchase on the worn floorboards, her nails clawing at the wood.

'Please!' she shrieks, twisting in his grip. 'I'll be good. I promise!'

Her pleading eyes find mine, wordlessly begging me to intervene. *Help me*, she mouths.

Silence falls over the cabin as the heavy door is slammed shut.

Chapter Twenty-Nine

One month later

It's the dead of night. Cal's snoring is echoing around the cabin, almost loud enough to make the walls rattle. I can't sleep. I'm propped up in bed, laser focused on my stomach. I'd already been struggling to get to sleep when I felt it. The twinge. The pulling sensation. Since that first one I've felt similar twinges three times. I'm currently trying to figure out just how long I've been awake waiting for the feeling to come again, and just how many times I need to feel it before I should wake Cal up.

Now that we're closer to the birth, I've allowed myself to think more about what happens afterwards. About being a mum. Here. It's something I've always wanted, to have kids of my own, but now when I think about it I'm faced with a tremendous sense of loss. I'm grieving for the life we should have.

I've not gone anywhere near the garden trunk. It's risky. The rucksack and notebook are still there, have been for weeks, and if I'm not going to use them I really should put everything back and burn the book just in case he were ever to go snooping. Cal's warning from the day at the loch has made me realise what I'm up against, how foolish I was to think I could just run away. Not only that, but my plan has gone to shit. The whole point of having another woman here was to distract him, to keep his focus off me so that I'd have more of an opportunity to get away, but she's been back in the barn for weeks again after her 'episode', as Cal likes to put it. Who knows how long she'll be in there. Even so, putting everything back and getting rid of the notebook would be officially giving up and I can't bring myself to do it. I refuse to let the last of my hope flicker away. There's still the doctor. He's still going to come to the birth and if he does decide to help me at least the rucksack will be there, ready.

I tense as another twinge pulls through my belly. This one is stronger, lasting longer. I slide my legs over the edge of the bed and stand slowly, one hand on my swollen middle. My body feels foreign to me these days, cumbersome and awkward.

I tiptoe across the creaky floorboards, wincing as they groan under my steps. Every step I take sounds thunderous to me. The nerves beneath my skin spasm and shiver. Cal's snores hitch but don't falter. I pause in the doorway, listening. When his snores resume their steady rhythm, I slip out into the night.

The cool air raises goosebumps on my skin as I walk to the garden, each step cautious in the dark. I find the trunk by touch and memory, heart thudding. My fingers tremble as I work the clasp and lift the lid. The rucksack sits there patiently, a promise waiting to be fulfilled.

I sink down beside the trunk, one hand still cradling my belly.

'I haven't given up,' I whisper. 'I will find a way. I promise.'

I sit here for a long while, stroking my stretched skin. The twinges have subsided. Lucky Cal gets to sleep for another couple of hours. Even you have gone still, as if my whispered promises and caresses have lulled you to sleep too.

And then a noise breaks the night. A faint wailing.

I freeze, straining to hear through the stillness. For a long while nothing happens and I think it must have been the wind, but after a few minutes the noise comes again and my stomach lurches. It sounds like an animal. A lamb bleating for its mother, or a vixen calling for her cubs. But it's not an animal at all. It's human. Mournful and pleading. Her.

The cry comes again, more insistent now. This time it's an unmistakably human voice, rising and falling in anguish. I stand, peering into the darkness. The moon casts the farm buildings in silver and shadow.

I don't know what to do. The sensible voice in my head is telling me to go back inside, pretend I heard nothing. But the woman cries out once more, her voice raw with despair, and I think back to how I did the same. All those months screaming out in the hopes that somebody, anybody, might hear me and help me. Before I can think better of it, I'm following the sound. Past the garden, into the field, to the barn.

Closer now, it's clearer. A primal, tortured wail that chills my blood. At the barn door I pause, heart hammering. The sound is definitely coming from inside.

'Hello?' My voice shakes.

There's a brief moment of silence, then the wailing resumes, louder now, more desperate.

With shaking hands, I reach for the latch, then curse myself. I don't have the key. Didn't even think about it as I made my way over here.

The woman's cries intensify and I look back towards the cabin, biting my lip. All this noise is going to wake him, I just know it, and then he'll see me here next to the barn and God knows what he'll do to me, to both of us.

I shimmy around to the wall I know the cage is pushed up against.

'Shh, please.' I knock gently on the wood, hoping she'll hear me but praying Cal won't. 'You need to be quiet. He won't like it. Please.'

But she doesn't stop. On and on it goes, piercing through the night. I chew down on my lip so hard I taste blood, expecting to see Cal's silhouette in the cabin doorway any second.

'Listen, I'm going to help you. I'm not going to leave you in there. But you need to stop screaming, please. I have to go. I'm sorry. I'll be back.'

I scurry back to the cabin, the woman's wails filtering out the further away I get. Or perhaps she is actually quietening down. Did she hear me? Did she hear my promise? I have no way of knowing.

Cal was still fast asleep when I returned. I lay awake for most of the night, listening intently for any more of the woman's cries, but there was nothing. Even after eventually falling asleep and having a few troubled hours of rest, I still thought of her as soon as my eyes flicked open, and I haven't stopped since.

I've promised her I'm going to help her. I've given her a glimmer of hope. That means I can't go through with my plan even if he does let her out again.

I think back to seeing her for the first time, that day that Cal led her to the barn under the pretence of it being a safe haven from her abusive husband. The irony. She had no idea what was coming.

I've committed myself now. I promised that woman that I would help her. I can't break that promise. But I have to think of you too. Really, I should have left that evening after we went to the loch, but Cal's warning scared me into buckling. Now, I fear I'm too far along to attempt an escape. I'm large now, unsteady on my feet, and I get out of breath quickly. I'm not sure I'd be able to get as far as the loch without descending into a wheezy mess, let alone much further. Will it be even harder once you're born, though? The idea of carrying someone so small and young and vulnerable as I try to get away from here is unthinkable.

The lack of sleep is getting to me. My eyes are sore and my head is scrambled. I get up and make myself a cup of coffee. For a long time I avoided it, but the pregnancy books says that one cup a day is safe, and I need something to get me through, to help me function. I sip it mindlessly, eyeing the gardening trunk through the window. Today, once Cal has gone to work, I need to retrieve the notebook and go over my plan again, then alter it. I'll need two scenarios: one for trying to escape while pregnant with just the woman by my side, and one for escaping with you in my arms, too. The more I think about it the less doable it seems and I curse myself for hesitating for so long. If I had left when I planned I might be home right now, with my parents, receiving ultrasound scans and buying furniture for the nursery.

My hand flies to my stomach as another twinge twists its way through me, this time more severe than the sensations that woke me in the night. I wince. The coffee churns uneasily in my stomach. It's not painful, exactly, but it's there. A niggle that I've never felt before. Surely this isn't the start of labour. It's too soon. I've got three months left.

Trying to control my breathing, more to stop myself from going into a panic than to relieve any discomfort, I pull down the pregnancy book and start flicking through the pages. The book is separated into forty chapters – forty weeks – with each chapter detailing what you could expect and what might go wrong at this stage. I find my week and follow my finger down the tiny text until I come across something called Braxton Hicks contractions. My brow furrows as I concentrate. It certainly sounds like what I'm experiencing, and according to this book it's nothing to worry about. It's just a sign that my body is readying itself for labour.

Appeased only slightly, I attempt to distract myself by tidying the cabin, but the sensations continue and before long sweat is breaking out on my forehead. It's when I go to the toilet I see it. Three tiny red spots in my underwear. Small enough that I would probably have missed them had I not been specifically looking for signs that something might be amiss. I pause, heart hammering in my chest as I stare at the spots of blood in my underwear. This can't be good. The pregnancy book didn't say anything about bleeding when it spoke about Braxton Hicks.

I consider my options. I could wait and see if the bleeding gets worse. But what if something is really wrong with you? No, I need to tell Cal. If something is wrong I'll need help.

Waking Cal up is not something I've ever attempted, nor ever wanted, to do. He's sprawled out on the bed, mouth hanging open. I stand over him for a moment, watching him rise and fall, thinking how easy it would be to plunge a knife into his chest right here, right now, if only I had the nerve.

'Cal,' I say softly. No response. I reach out a tentative hand and shake his shoulder. 'Cal, wake up.'

He stirs, blinking his eyes open. When he sees me standing over him, his face twists.

'What the bloody hell are ye doin'?'

He sits up abruptly and I take a step back. 'I'm sorry. But something's wrong.'

'What're ye talkin' about?'

'I'm bleeding. And I've been having these pains all morning. I think something might be wrong with the baby.'

Cal scrubs a hand over his face. 'It's probably nothin'. You're overreactin'.'

'But what if it's not? What if something is really wrong?' My voice rises in panic.

He glares at me. 'An' what exactly do yous expect me to do about it, eh?'

I stare at him helplessly.

'You need to get the doctor here. We can't wait until the birth. We need him here now.'

Cal's eyebrows flick up. The muscle in his temple pulses, as if there's a living creature in there trying to break free.

'Oh, I do, do I?'

I chew down on the inside of my cheek, forcing myself to stay quiet. There's a fine balancing act to be done. I can't be too forceful.

When he's satisfied that I'm not going to attempt to retort, he swings his legs out of bed and makes a meal out of stretching, groaning as he reaches up above his head and circles his wrists and ankles.

I wonder what you'd be like if you'd been stuck in a cage for months, I think, but of course I don't say it. I remain quite still and silent while he clicks and cracks each joint. He's taking his time on purpose. Making me wait.

Finally, he stands and edges past me, which is quite a feat now that my belly is ballooning across the width of the space at the end of our bed, and goes out to the kitchen where he pours himself a cup of coffee. I follow, fists clenched, heat prickling beneath my skin.

'Cal,' I venture, hovering in the doorway.

'Aye?'

'Please.'

His coffee is slammed down with such ferocity it sloshes over the edges of the cup. 'For God's sake, woman! I've only just woken up. I've got te be at work in an hour. Can you at least let me drink my coffee without naggin' at me?'

'I'm sorry,' I whisper. The words taste sour on my tongue.

He rolls his eyes, as if my very presence is annoying him. 'Clean that up,' he says, jabbing a finger at the drips of coffee working their way down the cupboard door. Hatred and annoyance bite, but I do as he says and grab a cloth to wipe up the spillage. He disappears back into the bedroom with his cup and slams the door behind him. Once he's gone I place a hand on my stomach and pray that you can feel me, can sense my reassurance. 'Just hold on, little one,' I whisper. 'Stay strong for me.'

After a moment, once it seems as if Cal is going to be locked in the bedroom for some time, I consider stepping out into the garden to start coming up with a Plan B. But just as I make a move to do so he calls through the closed door.

'Mary. Come 'ere.'

I sigh and walk into the bedroom. He's shirtless, and my eye flicks to the scar on his shoulder where Mary Two stabbed him. He never got it looked at properly. I did my best dousing it in alcohol, sewing it back up, but the scar is thick and raised. He doesn't look at me as I enter.

'So happens that first garden I'm working on today isnae far from the doctor. If you're good I'll ask him to come back with me once I'm finished. I want this place spick and span when I get home, you hear. Not a single grain of dust or I'll be sendin' him home. And for Christ's sake, make yourself look presentable. You're s'posed to be a wife, not a maid.'

'Of course.'

His eyes glint and he waves his hand at me. 'Off with you then. Let me get ready.'

Cal goes to work without even so much as a goodbye and I immediately get to work on my chores. The twinges have stopped, and I'm not sure if that's because they really are just Braxton Hicks contractions or if it's because I'm distracted, but I want the doctor here nonetheless. There was still the blood.

I grab a duster and polish the living room furniture, working my way clockwise around the room. As I'm doing the fireplace my eye drifts, as it always does these days, to the barn. I should go down there today while he's gone. Try to talk through the wall to her again. Just the thought that someone is on her side could be enough to keep her going.

As I'm polishing, the big problem with my escape plan glares at me. The cameras mean I'm really only going to be able to try to leave while he's at work. He'll know I've left but it will take him however long it takes to drive back before he can catch up to me. But if I'm to get that woman out I'll need the keys, both to the barn and to the cage, but the keys are only ever here when Cal is, which means I'll only be able to escape with her if he's home. There's also the issue of not knowing what kind of state the woman is going to be in by the time I can get to her. If she's dehydrated, starved, weak, is she going to be able to run?

One problem at a time. I need to figure out the key situation first. Perhaps there's a spare set somewhere, a set that I can use even if he's got the originals at work.

And just like that, I have my plan for the day. I need to search this place from top to bottom.

Chapter Thirty

I wear my yellow long-sleeved dress with the white cuffs, the one he always says he loves on me. It's a little bit tight around the top of my stomach but flows nicely at the bottom. I tie my hair back and pop on a light layer of makeup. It seems ridiculous, faffing with these things when I only have a finite amount of time to search for another key, but the last thing I want is for him to arrive home with the doctor and for me not to be ready.

I study my reflection in the mirror once I'm done, looking myself up and down. This is a dress for him. It's not one I'd choose. In fact, none of the dresses I own are ones I'd choose. I squeeze my eyes shut and try desperately to remember the sort of clothes I wore before I came here. I had a fabulous black sleeveless dress that just barely covered my bum. It was always my pick when I went out for an evening with my friends. It made me feel confident and sexy. Cal would say disgusting and whoreish.

Now that I'm ready for his return, whenever that might be, it's time to force myself to focus on the matter at hand. I need to see if there's another set of keys hidden around anywhere.

I start my search in the living room and kitchen. I rifle through the drawers, even though I've been through them a million times and know I would have seen a set of keys if they had been there. One potential hiding spot down, Lord knows how many to go. I bite my lip as I search, checking over my shoulder every few seconds, certain Cal will rush in and catch me in the act. I sift through the depths of the cupboards, then do the same for the bookshelves, carefully removing each book and checking it thoroughly, even flicking through every page, before sliding it back into place. Nothing. I run my hands along the underside and back of each drawer, feeling for any secret compartments. Still nothing.

Frustrated, I move on to the bedroom, though my hope is dwindling fast. I already searched the cabin thoroughly the first time I went looking for a key. I can't imagine anything's changed since then.

I go through his bedside table, his wardrobe, the dresser. I even check inside his shoes. No spare keys.

Dejected, I sit on the bed and pull out Gemma's letter, the one I saved, rereading it. I've read it so many times I don't even have to have the physical letter in my hands anymore. I know what it says word for word. But I like having it, even though it's risky. Feeling it under my fingertips is like a security blanket.

Go at night and use the stars to guide you.

Gemma's advice lingers in my mind as Cal's truck pulls up in front of the cabin and I tuck the letter away once more. At least if I go at night I won't need to worry about finding another key to the barn. But it's risky. So, so risky to attempt to leave while he's here. I picture Gemma begging for forgiveness as he broke her legs. A horrid tingling sensation works its way up my shins and my thighs and I have to shake them. What happened to Gemma? She said she'd come back for me and she never did. Does that mean he caught her? Is she lying in a shallow grave beyond those trees somewhere?

And once again, as they always do when I look out of the window these days, my eyes flick to the barn.

My actions have meant I'm no longer his perfect wife. I thought I was being clever, suggesting he bring someone else here. I thought it would take some of the heat off me and make it easier to escape. But when he brought me to the barn, his next 'Mary', Gemma knew her time was up.

Does that mean mine is up too?

Cal steps out of the truck and slams the door shut behind him. The doctor isn't with him. My heart sinks. Cal strides towards the cabin door, and I scramble to sit at the table before he enters. When he does, his eyes immediately find me.

'Where's the doctor?' I ask, my voice wavering only slightly.

'Nice to see you too.' He shakes off his coat. My eye flicks to the pocket in which I know he keeps the barn key. When Cal turns back to me his lip curls. 'There was a time I'd come home to a nice home-cooked meal on the table.'

'It's only three.'

'A cup o' tea then. Anything?'

Forcing my lips together to stop me saying something I shouldn't, I head to the kettle. Once it's boiling I take a chance again.

'So, the doctor, he . . . he wasn't there, or?'

'He's a busy man, Mary. Says ye dinnae have anythin' to worry about. A bit o' bleedin' is normal.'

I clench my jaw and grip the edge of the counter to steady myself as I pour the water into two cups. Normal. How could he possibly know what's normal? Cal didn't even see the blood. Didn't even ask how much there was or what it was like. I know with absolute certainty that he didn't even speak to a doctor. Why would he? That would mean revealing I'm here. I doubt there's a single person in the world other than him who knows that.

'Well, that's . . . that's good to hear.'

Cal is at the table now, boots up, waiting expectantly.

I bring him the tea and he takes it without looking at me. I sit across from him and wrap my hands around my own mug, seeking its warmth.

'I was thinking,' Cal says, leaning back in his chair. 'It's been a while since we had a nice dinner together. Why don't you make us something special tonight?'

Something special. I know exactly what that means. The thought makes my skin crawl.

'Of course. What would you like?'

He grins. 'Surprise me. Impress me.'

I take a sip of my tea so that he won't see the look of disgust on my face. It burns my lips and my tongue.

'I'll make one of your favourites,' I say once I've managed to swallow the scalding liquid.

He beams, satisfied. 'That's my good wife.'

'Drink your tea and then why don't you go and get cleaned up? I'll start the prep.'

One more evening. That's all I need to get through. I just need to keep him happy until he falls asleep.

'Oh, I almost forgot.' Cal jumps to his feet and rummages about in his coat pocket. He pulls out something circular and silver. My mouth drops open.

'Is that a . . .'

'CD player. Aye. Old one. They don't really make 'em like this anymore. But figured some music might help to cheer the place up a bit. Think it's needed lately, aye?'

He places the CD player on the table and presses one of the buttons. The room erupts into music. Violins and cellos swell together, dancing around each other, weaving a tapestry of sound that I swear I can see in the air between us. It's been so long since I've heard music that my eyes sting with tears. The last time must have been before . . .

Cal grins at my reaction, mistaking my tears for something else entirely. 'Thought you'd like it.'

'Thank you,' I stutter, my voice shaking.

'No problem, hen.' He leans over and kisses me on the cheek before downing the last of his tea. I watch him leave the kitchen, his heavy footsteps retreating into the bedroom. Then I do something I haven't done in a long time. I let out a deep breath and allow myself to weep silently into my hands.

I only cry for a few minutes, long enough to get it out of my system so that I can focus on what actually needs doing. Then I get to work on making the heartiest, most filling pie I can muster. I want him full. I want him drunk on the whisky I'll serve him with dinner. I want him dozing off by the fireplace this evening, barely able to keep his eyes open. I want him to sleep deeply.

Cal inhales deeply as he comes back out to the kitchen, drinking in the aroma of simmering broth. I have to admit, I've outdone myself this time. The very smell of it is making me so hungry I can almost forget about everything. Almost. The planning, the scheming, is still there. It's always there these days, churning over in the back of my mind. I need to make sure I eat enough tonight that I'm satisfied for a good leg of the journey, but not so much that I'm sluggish and slow. I also need to make sure I'm leaving enough leftovers to put into a Thermos to take with us. That poor woman in the barn is probably starving.

'Smells great,' Cal says, patting me on the back. He leans over me and plucks the spoon from my hand, ladling up some of the sauce and tasting it. His mouth makes a horrible slurping noise as he does it. 'Could do wi' a touch o' parsley, me thinks.'

He disappears out to the garden and I grab the spoon just in time before it sploshes back into the pan. I'll wash it up, get the pastry prepped and then I'll start him on the whisky. That gives him a good couple of hours to get sufficiently inebriated.

'Mary?' Cal's voice calls from outside just as I've started rolling out the pastry.

'Yes?'

'Come 'ere a moment, will yous?'

Annoyed at the interruption, I wash my hands of flour and wipe them on my apron before heading to the garden.

The sight that awaits me makes me want to throw up. Cal is sat next to the open trunk, my stash of supplies and my notebook on the floor by his feet. I freeze in the doorway as if I've walked face first into a brick wall. Cal's expression is unreadable as he looks up at me.

'What's all this then?'

His voice is a scalpel, precise and cutting. My mind races, trying to think of some plausible explanation, but nothing comes. He's caught me red-handed.

I take a breath. 'I . . . I can explain.'

'Can ye now?'

He stands slowly. I've always known he's a big man, tall and broad, but right now he seems to fill the space in front of me, blocking out the sun. He stares at me directly in the eyes, waiting for this explanation that I apparently have.

I take a step back instinctively. 'It's not . . . I didn't . . .'

'Not what? Didnae what?' he spits. 'G'on. Explain.'

My mouth opens but no words come out. I'm trembling now. My brain has melted into a useless muddle. I can't string a thought together, let alone a sentence.

He picks up my notebook, flips through the pages. Potential routes, supply lists, scribbled notes. Evidence of my planned escape.

'One. When Cal gets home, get him drunk,' he reads, beginning to pace in front of me. 'Two. Tire him out. Sex? Is there anything I can slip him? Three. Wait at least two hours to be sure he's in a deep sleep. Four. Smash his phone so that the alarm doesn't go off when we leave.'

I shake my head, willing him to stop.

'Cal, please . . .'

'I knew ye were up to something,' he says, head snapping towards me. I'm astonished to see his eyes are shining. 'Sneaking around, hiding things from me. After everything we've been through. Ten years of marriage and this is what I get, eh? Leaving me in the middle of the fucking night!'

His eyes flash with anger. Or madness.

For a split second I'm overcome with the urge to scream at him that what we have isn't marriage, that he's crazier than I thought if he really believes this to be a real marriage, but the look on his face makes my words die on my tongue.

'Did you really think it would be that easy to leave me, eh?' he snarls.

Without another word his face twists. He throws my notebook to the ground and lunges towards me. Before I can react, he grabs my arm in a vice-like grip, dragging me away from the cabin. I cry out in pain and shock, stumbling to keep up with his long, determined strides.

'Cal, stop! You're hurting me!'

My cries fall on deaf ears. His fingernails dig sharply into my skin as he wrenches my arm, propelling me forward.

We're a good halfway across our land before I realise where he's taking me.

'No. No, please. Stop.'

I try to twist away from him but he's too strong. The barn looms in front of us, almost as menacing as him. As we reach it, he fumbles in his pocket, pulls out the key that I was planning on stealing in just a few short hours' time, and rips open the padlock.

As he shoves me roughly through the open door I lose my balance and fall hard onto the dirt floor. Pain explodes in my kneecaps and I shriek. Hay flies up around me in a dusty cloud as I scramble to

167

my feet. Cal slams the barn door shut behind us with a resounding thud. I try to search around me for somewhere to go but there isn't another entrance. No way out except through the door he's blocking.

He grabs me by the arms, spinning me around forcefully and seizing the back of my neck. Every cell in my body recoils and he pushes me closer and closer towards the cage. Digging his fingers into my neck, he yanks my head forward so that my nose is nearly touching the bars. Mary Two stares back at me, eyes wide, face gaunt, a mirror of what awaits me.

'You're showin' signs of it,' he growls.

I blink back tears. 'Of what? Cal, please . . .'

'Signs o' the devil.'

He forces me closer still to the cage. My face presses against the cold metal and my heart stops.

'Maybe you need to go in here for a spell, aye?'

'No.'

Suddenly, I'm right back where I was when I woke up inside that thing. The terror, the hopelessness that I felt back then comes rushing back in a sickening swell. I scream. He just lets me, holding my head down, pressing my cheek into the cold metal. I squeeze my eyes shut, try to block it out, pretend it's not really happening, but my world is twisting and distorting. I'm having a panic attack again, just like when I broke into the barn. I gasp for air like a drowning woman. My chest feels as though it's going to explode from the sheer effort of breathing.

Finally he spins me around and slams my back against the cage. The hard edge juts into my spine, causing me to howl. A small smile creeps onto his lips.

'If ye dare disobey me again I'll do it. Dinnae think I won't. An' this time I'll leave ye in there until that baby comes out'a ye or dies. Whichever comes first.'

Chapter Thirty-One

I have been the perfect wife for five weeks now. Five long weeks. I've done everything right. The meals he likes have been on the table waiting for him at the exact right times. The cabin has remained spotless. I've worn his favourite dresses, altering them where possible to allow for my bump, applied enough concealer to hide the dark circles under my eyes from all the sleepless nights, and brushed my hair in the right way to disguise the fact I've been losing it in patches. Stress, I have to assume. Or maybe it's pregnancy related. Regardless, he's unaware. He just knows I've been the perfect wife. He's even stopped asking if he can trust me to be alone before he goes to work. My counterfeit vulnerability is working.

It hasn't escaped me. How easy it's been these past few weeks. Now that he thinks he's back in control. He's been kind, gentle, attentive. In many ways it would be so much easier, so much safer, so much better to just stick with this life. I did it for years. I could just . . . carry on. But then a sharp jab to my ribs is all it takes to shake the notion of staying. No matter how easy it might seem to do nothing, I can't do it to you. I can't condemn you to a life of being raised by a madman. A chilling detail of Cal's threat five weeks ago in the barn lingers in my mind.

His face had been filled with joy. He had enjoyed every second of my terror.

The items I've been stashing have been chosen with care and precision. I mustn't make the same mistake of trying to take everything I could possibly need in a big rucksack. I need to think smaller. Smarter. Less obvious. So it's been a discreet process: a biscuit wrapped in cling film instead of being dunked in my tea one week; a singular bottle of water the next; a tin from the very back of the cupboard on week three. Each item chosen with deliberate care. A small collection he won't notice or miss, hidden under the floorboard along with Gemma's one remaining letter. The space down there is tight. Despite only adding one small thing every now and again, it's already nearly so full I soon won't be able to lower the floorboard flush. That means it's time.

Evening isn't far off. One last stint of normality to get through. And I do. I play the part with precision, do everything he expects of me. After dinner Cal sits in his armchair by the fire, pipe in hand, already half asleep after his dinner. I pause in the doorway, watching him. This man who has become my captor. I sit next to him and read, and I force myself to lean close to him, to rest my hand on his thigh and seemingly enjoy this time together. After an hour or so my eyes flick to the window. The sun is sinking below the horizon, casting long shadows across the valley. I rise slowly from my chair, wincing as my swollen ankles protest.

'Is it OK if I head to bed?' I ask softly. Cal nods, barely looking up.

I make sure to be well out of his line of sight before I release my sigh of relief. He doesn't want sex tonight. Thank God. I move into the bedroom and sit on the edge of the bed while I go over the plan in my head one last time. Then I slip under the duvet and wait. Now that I've gone to bed he shouldn't be far behind.

As if he can read my mind he stays up long after I came to bed. Typical. Any other night he'd join me within half an hour at the most, but the one night I need to stay awake he takes his sweet time. I lie still under the covers, trying to keep my breathing even and calm. The minutes drag on endlessly. I strain to hear any sounds from the other room over the pounding of blood in my ears.

Finally, there's the thud of his footsteps crossing the wooden floor. I listen to the familiar sounds of Cal preparing for bed in the bathroom. The splash of water, the creak of floorboards. Then silence. I squeeze my eyes shut and try to feign sleep as he climbs into bed beside me.

The mattress sinks under his weight. His breath is sour with whisky as he leans over to kiss my forehead. 'G'night, lass,' he mumbles. I don't respond, keeping my body limp and relaxed. And then I wait some more.

When his breathing becomes slow and heavy with sleep I still don't move, though I allow myself a tiny sigh of relief. Gingerly, I open my eyes and glance at the window. The moon is high, casting a pale light into the room. I lie completely still, listening to Cal's rhythmic breathing. After fifteen agonising minutes, I peel back the covers. The bed creaks slightly as I slide my legs off the side, every muscle tense. I stand up, moving at a glacial pace to avoid any sudden noises. As I move I remain hyper-aware of any hitches in Cal's breathing, and as I tiptoe over to the clothes I laid out to change into I periodically pause to check that he hasn't stirred, but he remains deeply asleep.

Once dressed, I move quickly but quietly to the loose floorboard and prise it up. My small stash of supplies is still there, undisturbed. A few scraps of food – just enough non-perishables to avoid starvation – the bottle which I'm planning on refilling with rainwater or water from the creeks, a torch, an extra pair of socks. I gather them up in my arms and scurry across the room, feeling my way along the familiar walls. At the bedroom door, I glance back once more at the lump under the duvet. My sleeping captor. A flood of emotions wells up inside me – fear, anger, sadness – but I force it down. Now is not the time. I slip out into the hall, my bare feet making no noise on the cold wood floor.

The final pieces needed for my escape are in the kitchen. His rucksack, currently filled with odds and ends from his work, sits by the front door. I gently tip them out and replace them with my own things. They look pitifully inadequate in the cavernous depths of the bag, but they'll have to do. I reach for my coat but pause, my hand hovering in mid-air. After dithering for a few moments, I take down Cal's hunting jacket from the hook beside the door. It's far too big for me but it's warmer than mine and waterproof. I slip it on and pull on my boots. I reach into my pocket, his pocket, and my fingers clasp around the key to the barn. Gripping it between my fingers, I take one last look around the kitchen that I've spent so many hours in. My eyes stray to the carving knife, its blade glinting dully. I pick it up and place it into the other pocket. Just in case. Then, still holding tightly onto the key, I make my way into the cold damp of the night.

A few steps away from the cabin I glance back, half expecting to see Cal lunge from the darkness, grabbing for me. But there's only stillness and silence. You shift inside me, as if sensing my adrenaline.

'It's OK,' I whisper. 'We're getting out of here.'

I walk steadily at first, then quicken my pace, my heart galloping with urgency. White clouds of breath billow out in front of me before dissipating into the darkness. My boots sink into the mud but I push forward. Freedom is close now. So close I can taste it.

As I reach the closest wall of the barn there's a sound interrupting the silence. I strain to listen. Someone is crying. More like a whimper, really. The woman. She's still alive. I know I'm wasting valuable time by trying to get her out, but if I don't, who knows what will happen to her once he figures out I'm gone. He'll want his new wife, ready and willing, and if she's not as obedient as me, as weak as me, he might hurt her more than he ever hurt me. It's my fault she's here. I'll never forgive myself if I don't try.

I press my face up against the freezing wood. 'I'm here. I'm going to get you out.'

The crying stops only for the briefest of moments, as if she's unsure whether she's hearing things or not. I feel my way along the wall to the door. My hands shake as I fumble to fit the key into the rusted padlock. The scraping of metal on metal echoes too loudly in the stillness.

'Come on.'

My heart sinks as the rusted key grinds uselessly in the padlock. Why isn't it working?

'D'ye really think I'm that stupid?' Cal's voice sends my blood running cold. I whip around. He's there. On the other side of the vegetable patch. It's too dark to see his face, but I can imagine what it probably looks like.

'I changed the lock after you broke in the last time. The one you're lookin' for is right here, lass.' He holds his hand up. A key dangles from his finger. 'Now, why don't you come back 'ere before you do somethin' you're gonnae regret.'

I glance helplessly at the barn door. The useless key still hangs from the padlock.

'Come on, Mary. Nothin' for you to do. Nowhere for you to go.' His words are like knives slicing into me, slicing into any hope I had of getting away from here. 'If ye come back now we'll pretend this never happened, aye?'

I stare at Cal, paralysed. He starts to walk slowly towards me, his boots crunching on the frosty ground. Now that he's closer I can make out his features, but I wish I couldn't. There's a vein pulsing in his neck like a snake ready to pounce. His eyes are dark. His fists clenched.

'It's over, Mary,' he says. 'You've got nowhere to go. That wee bairn in your belly needs its daddy.'

At the mention of you, something snaps inside me. A rush of primal, protective fury. Before I even realise what I'm doing, my fingers close around the knife in my coat pocket. I whip it out and point it at Cal with a trembling hand.

He stops short. Even in the darkness I can see his smug expression morph into surprise.

'Stay back,' I warn, my voice cracking. Cal's eyes flick down to the knife, then back to my face. After a moment, he lets out a hollow laugh.

'What exactly is your plan here, lass?' He spreads his arms wide. 'You gonnae stab me? Carve me up like a Sunday roast?' His voice drips with contempt.

My eyes flick from Cal to the knife and back again. He's right. I can't stab him. I don't have it in me. But I'm not as weak as he tried to make me.

I place one hand on the barn door.

'I'm sorry,' I whisper, even though I know she can't possibly hear me. Before Cal can take another step, I turn and sprint. My boots pound the sloppy earth as I run faster than I ever have in my life. The tote slaps against my side.

'Mary!' Cal's voice booms. It's not just a call; it's a hunter's cry.

I don't dare look back. I run, heavily pregnant though I am, and I run until I approach the edge of the trees, and then I'm in, weaving between the shadowy trunks of pines. The roar of blood in my ears and the crackle of underbrush beneath my feet fills my ears, and then something else.

His truck's engine.

I veer away from the dirt road, plunging myself deeper into

the undercover of trees where the truck can't follow. Why it didn't occur to me to steal his car key so he wouldn't be able to follow me, I do not know, but it's too late for regrets now. Beneath the cover of the trees, I falter to a hurried walk. Pain shoots across my stomach and jabs me in the sides. The frigid air burns my lungs. I knew running when this heavily pregnant would be hard but it's like my entire body is screaming at me. Behind me, there's a screech and a skid and I assume the truck has stopped, that he's going to follow me on foot. In my mind's eye I see him wielding his hunting rifle, aiming at my skull. I have no idea if he has one of his guns with him or not but I wouldn't put it past him. I pick up the pace again.

'Mary! Stop!'

I jump, head ducking instinctively, but on I run, ignoring my body's protests. Sharp branches whip against my arms and face, stinging my skin. I run as if the devil himself is on my heels.

The devil himself *is* on my heels. And I'm going to be free of him.

Chapter Thirty-Two

I'm further than I've ever been without Cal's company since I first came here. I know he's not managed to follow me this way in the truck. The way is narrow, cutting directly through the forest. Some firs arch so densely here they block the night sky. But I won't allow myself to relax. He can't follow me in the truck but he knows I've escaped and my refusal to look back means I have no idea when or if I lost him. He's not going to stop trying to catch me. He's out there, tracking me like an animal. All those years I spent watching him go off to hunt and now I'm the prey. But the cabin itself is no longer visible beyond the trees and that itself gives me comfort.

I'm walking quickly now instead of running, but even so it doesn't take long before my muscles start to ache and perspiration wets my forehead even in the cold of the night. There's a stitch in my side too. I try not to panic that it could be radiating from my womb and press on. The pain blots everything from my mind. Keeps me focused on the task at hand. I need to head north, which makes it easy to follow the stars, and I've drawn out a rough route as best I can on the back of Gemma's letter. It's one of the items tucked into my rucksack. Directly opposite the loch Cal took me to those few times there is a marked hiking trail and that's where I am heading. It's a good mile trek to the loch, and I've no idea what awaits me beyond that point, but a marked trail means civilisation at some point, eventually. I glance up at the sky, at the stars. It will start getting light around eight o'clock, so I guess in around five hours' time. I need to get a move on if I'm to continue to be able to use the stars to guide me and have the cover of darkness on my side.

As I travel deeper into the woods, the light from the moon is lessened, shielded by the canopy above me. I rummage about in my rucksack for the torch. It flickers a few times as I turn it on. I worry briefly that the light might act like a signal to anyone looking. But it's too dark for me to care. I need some kind of visual or I'll end up breaking my leg on one of the many protruding branches. The trees seem to be leaning in, their branches reaching down, their leafless winter twigs acting as fingers trying to grab me, to pull me back.

Suddenly my quick walk diminishes to a silent tiptoe. My eyes dart around. I think someone is watching me. It's a sense in the air, a disturbance in the bushes. I freeze like a deer with a gun aimed at it. My ears strain to catch any hint of movement. Nothing unusual. I spin on my heel and scan the forest behind me, but all I can see is a tangle of trees like shadowed arms intertwining, reaching for me. It would be so easy for someone to spy on me from the depths. I try not to think about the stories Cal told me, about the dangerous people I could meet if I were ever to venture away from the safety of the cabin. I know he said it to keep me compliant, but his words and warnings ring in my ears nonetheless. I have to remind myself that no matter who or what I might possibly run into out here, it would be hard-pressed to be any worse than what awaits me back home.

Not home. The cabin is not my home.

Heart racing furiously, I wait for a few moments longer, but I know I can't let paranoia stop me from pushing on. Keeping my attention trained on my surroundings, I hurry north, checking my position by the stars. I should be fairly close now. But before I can go too far the toe of my boot catches on something. I stumble, barely catching myself before I hit the ground. I think of you the second I go down, how much you're relying on me.

I press a hand to my belly as I push myself back up, whispering reassurances. *We're going to make it. It's going to be OK.* I shine my light to see what tripped me. A boot . . . connected to a jean-clad leg. I stifle a scream as the torch illuminates a body sprawled on the forest floor. The face is unrecognisable. Decomposed and half-eaten. But I recognise the shirt, stained with dark blood. It's the hiker. Cal said he'd driven him to the main road. Shown him how to get out of the remote Highlands.

A sob erupts from my throat. This is all my fault. This man is dead because he saw me. Because he knew I existed. Cal couldn't risk letting him go, couldn't take the chance that he'd recognised me from the newspapers, alert someone to my being held captive. If I hadn't let him in, Cal would never have known about him. If I'd sent him away the second I saw him he'd still be alive right now.

No. This is not my fault. It's Cal's. He's a monster.

With a renewed sense of hatred I scramble up and continue to run. I don't stop even as my lungs burn and my legs feel like they might give out. The image of the dead hiker is seared into my mind but I use it as fuel, forcing me forward. I have to keep going, have to get free of this nightmare.

The stitch in my side has spread, gripping my abdomen like a vice, pulsing. We're so close. Just a little further. The terrain grows steeper, my boots slipping on loose rocks and gnarled roots. I use the slender trunks of young birches to pull myself up the incline, their papery bark peeling beneath my grasp.

At last, I crest the ridge. The land slopes downwards again and loose earth moves under my feet as I slip and slide. Ahead I can make out a faint glow – the moonlight reflecting off the loch's surface. I'm close. Breaking through a final line of trees, I stumble onto the shoreline. The wide expanse of water stretches out before me like liquid silver, dark and calm. Somewhere on the other side is the marked trail, my route to freedom.

I peer down at the lakeshore and run my fingers along the surface. The water is thick, syrupy. I shudder at the thought of falling in. That would as good as seal my fate. If Cal doesn't get me the hypothermia will.

My eye travels along the edge of the loch, searching for the hiking trail. I try shining my torch but the beam isn't strong enough. It doesn't travel far. I squint, trying to remember where I'd seen it the last time. I think it was over to the left somewhere.

There!

It's there, the sign, a slight darkening in the otherwise undisturbed landscape. Between me and it, a sheer cliff face. I'm on the wrong side. When I came here before we followed the dirt path. We approached the loch at the top of the hill, close to the trail. This time I'm at the bottom. My heart sinks. The cliff towers above me, an impenetrable wall of rock. There's no way I can climb it, not in my condition. I could go back into the woods and circle to the other side, but doing so means risking running into Cal.

I glance back over my shoulder nervously, peering into the dark forest. It's silent and still, no sign of pursuit yet. But I know it's only a matter of time before he thinks to search the loch. My other option stares at me, daring me.

Taking a deep breath, I start making my way along the rocky shoreline, moving as quickly as I can manage. The footing is precarious, loose stones shifting under my boots. I have to watch each step to avoid twisting an ankle or worse. Weariness drags at my limbs as I navigate the terrain. I don't know how much further I can push myself. The stitch in my side has become a throbbing ache, building in waves. I press a hand to my belly, praying you're all right. We have to keep going. There's no other choice.

I force my legs to move, one step after the other. My eyes periodically shift to the cliff face looming above me as I clamber. I'm watching for any break, any place where the steep slope levels out enough to attempt climbing up. But so far the rock wall is sheer, with no handholds in sight.

Before I'm even halfway to the trail my foot drops, missing one of the stones and plunging in the frigid water. The cold seeps through my boots. It's paralysing. I bite down a scream and press myself against the rock wall, wishing I could go back and change my mind, venture back into the woods and take the long way around, but I've come so far there's no point. I have as far to travel back as I do lying ahead of me.

I force myself to keep moving, shivering as the freezing water sloshes in my boot. My teeth chatter violently. I clench my jaw and wrap my arms around myself in a futile effort to retain some warmth. The cold is penetrating, numbing my foot and sending spikes of pain up my leg with each step.

Up ahead, the cliff face seems to taper slightly before rising sharply again. It's not much of a slope, barely angled, but it may just be enough. Gripping the icy rock with numb fingers, I hoist myself up, scrabbling for any grip I can find. My boots slip dangerously on the inclined surface as I claw my way higher. Loose pebbles cascade down behind me, plinking into the dark loch below. Slowly, painfully slowly, I hoist myself up and finally emerge onto the verge, metres from the hiking trail. My movements are laboured, my mind dazed with tiredness. I roll onto the grass, blades stiff with frost, and lie on my back, chest heaving. Each breath burns my lungs. The stitch in my side feels like a fiery poker skewering my abdomen. I know I need to keep moving but my body is screaming for rest.

Just a few minutes, I tell myself. I'll close my eyes only for a moment before carrying on. Exhaustion is overtaking the cold and the fear. But almost as soon as my eyes close, pain radiates through my body. Something is wrong – terribly wrong. This is more than just exhaustion or the strain of the climb. This pain is deeper, visceral. I try to slow my breathing, to calm myself enough to assess what's happening.

That's when I feel it – the first hard clench across my belly. A strangled cry escapes my throat as the force of it steals my breath. I curl inward, knees drawing up instinctively. My fingers dig into the frozen earth beneath me. Fear like I've never known lances through me. Out here, alone in the remote wilderness, I know neither of us may survive this.

Please, not now, I beg. I don't know who I'm begging. You. My body. God. Gritting my teeth against the pain, I force myself to stand on shaking legs. I can't rest here. It's too open. Too easy for Cal to spot me from a distance. I need to find some kind of shelter, to take a few minutes to sit and ease my body, to eat and drink. I realise too that I'm desperate for the toilet. Dizziness washes over me as I stagger forward, my boots tripping from grass to path as I meet the trail, and I follow it.

On and on it seems to go, winding this way and that. There, not far away, is a stand of pine trees, their branches still green in the winter air. It's as good a place as any. I stumble towards them, each step a battle against the growing agony. At last, I reach the shelter of the trees and collapse behind a fallen trunk, out of sight from the trail. You kick feebly, as if sensing my panic.

'Shh,' I soothe, as much for my own benefit as yours. I'm not sure what to do first. Sleep, eat, drink or pee. I choose the latter, balancing the torch on a flat rock, lowering my trousers and squatting, the cold air wrapping around me.

I see the blood moments before I feel it. The release. The gush of liquid.

My waters have broken.

Chapter Thirty-Three

It's too soon. Much too soon. I'm not ready. We're not ready.

Another pain, a contraction, as I now know, wrings my abdomen ruthlessly. I should have brought the pregnancy book. It's so heavy and I didn't think I'd need it, but at least I could have looked at what to do. I squeeze my eyes shut and try to remember what it said, how long I might have now that it's started, but my mind is frazzled. My head is awash with thick fog. The contractions are coming fast now since my waters broke, each one harder than the last. There will be no stopping this. You are coming. Demanding to be born.

I should have stayed. The frozen ground beneath me offers no comfort, only bitter cold that seeps through my clothes. I crave the shelter of walls and a fire's warmth, not the whispering pines surrounding me. I have nothing. No pain relief. Not even a warm bath to lie in. And what of you? What happens when you come? What if there's something wrong? Before I was terrified of doing this without a doctor present but at least Cal would have been there to help. He could have gone and got someone if things took a turn for the worse.

The screech of tyres on gravel makes my heart stop. I freeze, listening hard over the frantic pounding in my ears. It can't be. The slam of a truck door shatters the silence.

He's here.

Contraction after contraction racks my body as I remain motionless behind the fallen tree trunk. As the next contraction comes I bite down on my lip and it's only when the wave is over that I realise I've bitten right through it, blood pooling in my mouth.

The crunch of boots on frosty undergrowth grows louder. He's searching. Hunting. My lungs burn for air but I don't dare breathe. Silent tears stream down my cheeks. I squeeze my eyes shut and beg for this to be a nightmare I'll soon wake from.

But the snapping of branches and rustling of bracken tells me this is all too real. He's close now. So close I imagine I can hear his steady inhale and exhale mingling with the winter wind. I clench every muscle, willing my body to be silent and still. The pain is excruciating but I throw one hand over my mouth and squeeze, stifling the screams I'm desperate to release. I fixate on an ant crawling over a pine cone in front of me.

The footsteps draw nearer. Crackling twigs under heavy boots. My fingers dig into the earth, grounding me. I count slowly, timing the waves of pain. Breathe. Focus. The footsteps stop somewhere to my left. I can feel him standing there. Hovering. I imagine him with his head tilted, listening for me, scouring the loch for any sign of movement. My heart hammers against my ribs. I'm certain he can hear it.

Then the footsteps start up again, moving away. I stay frozen in place as the engine rumbles back to life, the truck reversing and turning. Only when the sound has faded completely do I finally release the wail of pain I've been sucking in.

Safe, for now.

But of course, I'm not really. It's not safe to give birth outdoors, especially not in winter. Nothing about this is safe.

The hours drag by and still the baby isn't born. I move from lying on my back to lying on my side to rocking on all fours. Leaves mixed with dried blood stick to my palms. I can't focus. All I can do is groan. Throw my head back and sob. I'm weak and I'm getting weaker by the second. My hands scrabble in the rucksack and find one of the energy bars. I feel so sick I can barely face the thought of eating but if I don't I know I'll pass out. I rip the packet open with my teeth, pause as another contraction rips through me, bursting me apart, then take a bite in the lull. I immediately throw it back up.

Squatting is better. It eases the pain but increases the pressure. I feel around to see if I can touch your head, but there's nothing there. I let out a frustrated howl, no longer attempting to stay quiet. I don't want you to come but I don't know how much longer I can go on. I feel so light-headed I have to grip onto the fallen trunk beside me to steady myself. I snatch the bottle of water up and glug it greedily.

The liquid mixes with the blood from my chewed-up lip, metallic to swallow. Sweat drips from my head.

The pressure intensifies and suddenly I'm pushing. It's not a conscious thing. I don't choose to push. It just happens, my body taking over. It's unlike anything I've ever felt, like all of my insides are trying to force their way out of my body. My legs shake, quaking with fatigue. The world blurs before my eyes. My screams sound far away, separate from me. I grit my teeth and cry and push and wail and shake my head and scream and push. There's a tearing sensation and the pressure eases a little before returning with a vengeance. This will be it. I'm sure of it this time. I strip myself bare from the waist down and lean my head against the tree trunk. My fingers find the top of your head and it's a perfect head, the tiniest whisper of hair. I break into a smile despite the pain and bear down. A surer nudge, a slick against my thighs, and my heart rate skyrockets. The urge to get you out of me is so strong I couldn't resist even if I wanted to. I take everything I have left, every ounce of energy, every semblance of sanity, and focus it into these last few pushes.

And then I look down and there you are, lying on the floor, doll-like. Still.

It takes just half a second for the instinct to kick in. I scramble, scoop you up in my arms, leaves and blood and mud and bodily fluids congealing between my fingers. There's no crying. Babies should cry. That's what they do when they're born. I lay your tiny body face down across my arm. I'm not sure how I know what to do. I don't question it. I rub and pat your back, whispering prayers into your perfect ear, willing you to respond.

It feels like an age. Far too long. But it does come. The most incredible sound I've ever heard in my life. You scream, as if suddenly realising you're no longer in the comfort and warmth of my womb, and curl your tiny fists and bring your knees up to your chest. I flip you over, pull you into me, wrapping my coat, his coat, around you.

I lean my head back and close my eyes. We've survived. For now. Who knows what's going to happen next. But we've survived.

Chapter Thirty-Four

You're a girl. I haven't chosen a name for you yet. Back at the cabin I had pored over potential baby names, lining up favourites for both a boy and a girl, but none of them fit. You've fed from me. It's bizarre. I've never breastfed in my life and yet it feels like I always have. Now you're asleep, for the first time ever, and you're warm, nestled against my bare chest, absorbing my heat. I'm starting to get cold but I don't care. You can have it all. Every last bit of warmth I have.

I've spent the last hour, maybe more, I can't be sure, taking in every last detail. The shape of your lips, your eyes, your nose. All me. None of him. I know I need to move but not yet. Right now, Cal isn't out there searching for me. Right now, there's no danger lurking outside this shelter of trees. Right now, it's just us.

I shift in my position and feel the umbilical cord brush against my thigh. The placenta hasn't expelled itself yet. I'll wait for that and then I'll use the knife, the one I took for protection, the one I had no idea just how much I'd need to cut the cord. For now, we're connected. I trace my finger over the perfect curve of your cheek. Your skin is still blotchy and smeared with blood and vernix, but to me you are the most beautiful thing I've ever seen. Your rosebud lips work silently in your sleep. What dreams stir behind those paper-thin eyelids? Nightmares? Do you already sense the precarious nature of your existence? That your first breaths were drawn in a remote forest instead of a warm bed?

When the afterbirth slips free about ten minutes later I'm overwhelmed with a sense of loss. I begrudgingly reach for the knife. It's a sturdy blade. Cal used to use it for gutting fish. The handle is smoothed from use. I position the knife close to your belly and cut through the gristly cord. You stir but don't wake.

I know I can't stay here forever. As much as I want to remain in this little bubble, just me and you, I know the longer we stay here the more I'm putting you at risk. The batteries on my torch are running low, too. I'm not usually one to be scared of the dark but out here I feel so much more vulnerable, and all it takes is a cloud cover shrouding the moon and we'll be plunged into a whole other kind of darkness. I take a few more minutes to drink and eat, taking small nibbles this time for fear of being sick again. Once the energy bar is gone I adjust, trying to find the best position for us both to make this unthinkable journey. I manage to tie my top in a way that you're supported, kind of like a sling, though my arm still grips you tightly from below so that I can be sure you won't fall. Then I splash water from my bottle onto my legs, attempting to wash away some of the blood and mess that stains my skin. I pull my trousers on, not bothering with underwear, and drape my coat over my shoulders.

It's when I go to slip my feet into my boots that I realise it. My toes, the ones that dunked into the loch, don't look right. Frowning, I shine the torch at them. There's a slight bluish tint to the skin. I gingerly poke my big toe, expecting to feel searing pain, but instead I don't feel anything. They're completely numb.

I'm not sure what it means, clearly nothing good, but I can't focus on this right now. Gritting my teeth I find the spare pair of socks that I was sensible enough to pack and put them on, then the boots. My body screams in protest as I slowly get to my feet. Every muscle aches. There's an empty feeling in my womb now that you are out and I'm so, so sore between my legs. I can't decide what's worse: trying to walk so fast so soon after giving birth or trying to bear weight on my foot. The toes themselves are still numb but everything else, the sole, my ankle, my calf, tingle and sting with every step. Every couple of metres I have to stop, lean myself against a tree trunk and take the weight off that leg.

You're not making a noise. In one way I'm glad – a baby's cries would echo around the Highlands and draw him closer to us – but the other part of me is terrified something is wrong with you. I refuse to let my head go there. I just need to get to civilisation and they'll be able to help you. They'll be able to get you all the care you need. All the care I should have been able to provide as your mother.

I follow the hiking trail as it winds its way through the rugged landscape, my eyes scanning the horizon for any signs of life. I clutch you closer to me, trying to share what little warmth I can as the wind whips my hair wildly around us. You're a warm, soft weight against my chest. I glance down at you, brushing a gentle finger over the downy hair on your little head. You look so peaceful curled up in the makeshift sling.

I swallow the lump in my throat and blink away tears, fixing my eyes ahead. All I can see for miles is more of the remote Highlands – craggy hills and endless moors blanketed in heather. I've started hearing things, too. Not the sounds of the Highlands that I've been hearing since I left – the whispering of the trees and rushing of the wind – but voices. As if someone is whispering to me, trying to tell me something. Perhaps I'm going mad.

The trail seems endless, just leading me deeper into the remote Highlands with no town in sight. I want to scream out in frustration but swallow it down, knowing any noise could echo for miles in this emptiness. I've been walking for what feels like hours now but still there is nothing surrounding us. But I don't stop. I can't stop. I know that if I do I'll never start again.

The morning is drawing nearer now. In the distance, the rising sun is just beginning to peek over the mountains. It won't be long before we're completely exposed. Just as the thought crosses my mind, I hear it – something approaching. The rumbling of an engine. At first it's faint, almost indistinguishable from the wind. But it steadily grows louder, the unmistakable roar of a truck approaching.

His truck.

I whip my head around, wide-eyed, chest heaving, searching for somewhere to hide. But there's nothing. The forest is long behind me, back near the cabin. Here on this trail there's just open moorland all around. The road is still not in sight, but the truck sounds close now. I clutch my baby tighter to me and run, forcing myself to ignore the protests screaming from my leg.

The engine sounds thunderous now, echoing off the mountains. I listen intently. It's definitely a truck, not a car. I have to assume it's Cal. Who else would it be out here? As I run I suddenly become aware of a warmth spreading through me, sweeping across my chest and stomach. Wet warmth.

I look down. You shiver. You've peed all over me. I didn't even think about it. I've got nothing. No nappies. Nothing to mop you up or even change you into. Right now it's warm but it will quickly get cold. Almost as soon as I've realised what's happened you begin to cry and I cower, desperately trying to shush you, to rock you, to bounce you. Anything to stop you crying.

'Shhh, please,' I beg, 'he'll hear you.'

My pace quickens and the momentum seems to calm you a little. That or you've got no energy left to cry either.

Run. For God's sake, run. If you don't keep on running he'll catch you.

The words reverberate around my brain, forcing my legs to keep moving. My eyes water as the crotch of my trousers rubs against my wounds. Every part of me is on fire. Your little face presses against my chest, and for a moment I'm terrified that I'm smothering you. You're so still. I pull you back an inch, make sure your mouth and nose are free from fabric, and your nose twitches and I choke back the tears. Tears of relief. Tears of fear. Tears of pain. Tears that this is the entry to the world that I've given you, that the start of your life has been nothing but running for our lives.

Don't stop. Keep going.

The pain is so severe now that my vision is blurring. I blink, chew down on my tongue to distract myself, to give myself a different pain to focus on.

And then, is that . . . headlights?

I blink, trying to unsee it. But it's there. It's real. I slow my run to a walk, every fibre of my body on high alert. It's too dark. I can't tell if it's his truck or not. You make one of your little noises that I've heard for such a short amount of time but already know so well, and I kiss your forehead.

'Mummy will look after you,' I whisper against your skin.

The headlights grow closer, two blinding eyes.

It's not him.

Now the truck is closer there is enough morning light to see the white exterior. His is blue.

And now I'm weeping, not because of the pain, but from the sheer relief flooding my body. Someone is coming to help us. Finally.

I wave my free hand in the air.

'Please!' I scream. It echoes back to me and I'm momentarily petrified that the sound of it is enough for him to find me, but I don't need to worry anymore. He won't be able to catch me before this truck gets to me.

'Please, help!'

They're not going to stop, I think. They can't see me.

I'm about to place you on the edge of the road, bundled up in my coat so that I can throw myself in front of the car. Even if I die they'll have to stop and they'll see you and you'll be safe. But before I can do that there is a change in the sound of the approaching engine. They're slowing down.

'Help us!' I cry again, my arm waving even more frantically.

The car pulls over and the window rolls down. A woman with frizzy grey hair shooting off in all directions peers out, her wrinkled forehead creasing in concern. She has a kind face. A new face. Her eyes flick over my bloodied, mud-stained appearance, then from me to you.

'Lord above, are you OK?'

She clambers out of the car and I try to speak but no words come. Instead I stagger and fall forwards, into this total stranger's arms with you nestled between us, and I sob into her shoulder. We're going to be OK. We're going to be safe.

Chapter Thirty-Five

I wake with a start.

I'm back. In the cabin. With Cal.

But as my eyes search the room I realise that's not the case at all. I have no idea where I am. It's a room I've never seen before. It's very white. Very clean. There's an odd smell that I can't quite place. A deep ache sits in my body, making it so that I don't think I could even sit up from this bed if I wanted to. But then memories filter back to me, slotting together like the pieces of a puzzle, scratching at the surface of my brain. The cabin. Cal. Running through the trees. Falling into the loch.

I jerk bolt upright as one thought hits me harder than all others.

My baby. Where is my baby?

'It's OK. You're safe. You're in a hospital. Everythin' is gon' te be OK.'

The voice is like silk stroking my ears, despite the strong Scottish accent. I rub my throbbing head and peer round to my left, where the voice came from. The old lady stands in the doorway, tray in hand. She's smiling and I think it's the kindest thing I've seen in months. I can't quite believe I'm looking at another human being. The first new person since my replacement.

At the thought of the hiker my stomach turns and my head starts to throb. The old lady must see my discomfort because her face twists in concern and she steps towards me, placing the tray on the table next to me. It holds a glass of water, a glass of orange juice and two slices of buttered toast.

'Ye need te get your strength back,' she says, passing me the glass of water. I sip it gratefully. It slides down my dry throat and feels divine.

Her words finally register.

'Did you say I'm in a hospital?' My eyes dart around again. This doesn't look how I remember hospitals to be. It's cosier.

'Aye. Not one of the big city ones, mind. This is a small, specialist ward. But you've made excellent progress these past few weeks.'

'Few weeks?' The panic descends again. A few weeks without you. What's happened to you? How have you been fed? How could I have missed the first few weeks of your life? I hunch over, tears overtaking me. I know I need to stop, to calm myself down enough to talk to this woman properly and explain everything that's happened, but the sobs need to come out of me as sure as you did when it was time for you to be born.

Finally, I catch enough breath to get out a few words in between my blubbering. 'The baby. Is she . . . OK? Where . . . is she?'

I try to untangle myself from the bed sheets. I need to get out of this room. I need to get to you. To make sure you're all right.

The woman rests a hand on my arm. 'Mary, listen to me. Everythin' is gon' te be all right.'

'No, I . . . I need to see her.'

I can't breathe. If my heart doesn't calm itself I'm going to end up having a heart attack. Something stirs then, a moment of realisation. I stare at the woman, at her kind, kind face.

'I never told you my name.'

Her eyebrows flick up for the briefest of seconds. 'Your husband told us your name.'

Fear like I've never felt erupts inside of me. I've been lying here for two weeks. Unconscious. Vulnerable. And he's been here. He's been saying who knows what. Oh God. What if he's got to you?

'No, listen to me, you can't trust him. He's not my husband.'

'Aye, we're aware. Ye told us yesterday. And the day before tha'. And the day before tha.''

'What are you talking about?' The fear is being taken over by something else now. Annoyance. This woman, the angel I thought was my saviour, is talking absolute nonsense. I haven't spoken to her since she found me on the hiking trail. She must have me confused with another patient.

'I've never told you about him.'

Her lips fold in on themselves, making her look vaguely familiar but I'm certain I've never met her before. She leans over and pulls a clipboard out of the end of the bed, resting it on her lap.

'Your doctor says physically you're very well. You've recovered nicely from your ordeal near the loch. He was able to save your foot, though it will be sore and you need to keep it bandaged for a wee while. There doesnae seem to be anything physiologically wrong. No head injuries.'

I frown. 'You're not my doctor?'

'I'm a different kind o' doctor. A psychologist. My name is Dr Stewart.'

I stare at her blankly, confusion clouding my mind. A psychologist? What is going on here?

It's then that I see them. The restraints attached to the edges of the bed. One for each of my wrists. One for each of my ankles. A cacophony of alarm bells erupts in my head but I force myself to try to remain calm.

'I don't understand. You just said I'm fine. I need to see my baby.'

Dr Stewart regards me steadily, her eyes filled with sympathy. 'Mary, I know this is very confusing for ye.'

'My name's not Mary!' The words come out a strangled scream, my attempts at calm lost, but Dr Stewart is unfazed. She pauses, waits for me to finish, then resumes her sentence. 'But you've been through a significant trauma. It's normal in situations like this for the mind te need time to recover.'

I shake my head sharply, panic rising in my chest. 'No. Listen, I need to get out of here. I need to find my daughter before he does.'

Dr Stewart places a gentle hand on my arm. 'Mary, I want ye to take a deep breath with me.'

Against my better judgement, I follow her lead, inhaling and exhaling slowly.

'Good, just like that,' she encourages. 'Now, I want ye to really listen to me. There is no baby. You arrived here alone four weeks ago, exhausted and talkin' of a deranged man holding ye captive. But there was no sign of an infant with ye.'

I want to scream. Attack this woman. Curse at her. Make her see the truth.

'No! You have to believe me. I left him. I escaped.'

'I know you think ye did, but tha's where the line between reality and delusion starts to blur.' She pauses, her gaze never leaving mine. 'Mary, we've been over this. You've been having delusions. Your brain has conjured up this entire story. Paintin' your husband as a monster when in reality all he's been doing is tryin' te help you. The pregnancy. The baby. It's all part of a traumatic stress reaction to what really happened to ye. What your parents did to ye that made you leave and go off grid with your husband in the first place.'

'But . . . I . . .' I trail off. Images flash into my mind: your kicks, the hunger, the pain, the birth. But when I try to piece them all together they scatter like autumn leaves in the wind. Dr Stewart nods encouragingly as if she can read my mind.

'You're wrong,' I say. 'I gave birth to her, I saw her.'

Dr Stewart's expression softens. 'I know this is hard te hear, but we all have your best interests at heart. Your husband explained about your infertility. About how long you've both been tryin' for a baby. I believe you've been sufferin' from a delusional pregnancy. It's not uncommon in situations like yours, especially with the isolation and stress of livin' out in the middle of nowhere without having properly dealt with your issues.'

'That's not true!'

'This isnae the first time you've been with us, Mary. Your husband has been beside himself with worry. You've been actin' strangely for weeks, accusin' him of things that aren't true. He tried to help you, Mary.'

'My name isn't Mary!'

'Then what is your name?'

I open my mouth to respond but nothing comes. It's there, my real name, drifting in front of me, but I can't quite seem to reach out and snatch it back.

'He's manipulating you,' I whisper instead. 'Please don't believe anything he's telling you. I'm not crazy. I'm not.'

Loss blossoms inside me. I scream and thrash and soon there are hands gripping my arms firmly and a sharp scratch in my upper arm and the feeling of the restraints on my wrists and ankles and suddenly things are twisting, distorting, clouding.

Chapter Thirty-Six

The drugs are making me woozy. There's always a dull ache behind my eyes and a bitter, metallic taste in my mouth. The drugs. I've lost count of how many times they've sedated me. Each time I wake it gets harder and harder to cling to reality. To cling to you. I sleep a lot and when I wake I spend my days in a sort of haze. I can't get up and stretch my legs or get any fresh air because of the restraints. My mind feels sluggish, thoughts moving like molasses. I can barely think straight. I get told about a lot of things that have happened since I've been here. Conversations that I've had with my psychologist that I don't remember. I'm told Cal asks to visit often and I refuse to see him, yet I have no recollection. Nothing feels real anymore.

I try to focus on you. Try to picture your face, conjure the weight of you in my arms and the smell of your skin, but they keep popping pills into my mouth and injecting me with whatever it is that makes me fall asleep when I try to fight back, and each time the image of you becomes less and less clear. I'm questioning everything. My sanity. My memories. Even your existence.

I don't know how much time has passed. The days bleed into one another, a monotonous blur of medication and therapy sessions. Dr Stewart is understanding and empathetic when she talks to me and I have a vague sense in the back of my mind that I hate it when she talks to me like that, like she's pitying me, but I lack any real self-awareness. It's like I'm watching myself through a thick pane of glass. Everything is blurred and muffled.

The only time I'm not restrained is during our sessions. Dr Stewart says I'm making progress. She tells me of how I met Cal, how I instigated our whirlwind romance and insisted we get married and move as quickly and as far away as possible to get away from my parents. Apparently I told her all this the last time I was admitted a few years ago, when the delusions first started.

'You made progress then, too,' Dr Stewart says. 'You accepted reality and you went home. Unfortunately, it happened again.'

She goes on to explain how I burned all my discharge forms in a desperate attempt to pretend it had never happened, so that I wouldn't have anything reminding me of the truth, so that I could go back to my alternate reality that I'd fashioned for myself. The other woman in the cage doesn't exist. The woman who fled her abusive husband to come and live in the middle of the Scottish Highlands with Cal: she's me. I'm her. Except it wasn't a husband. It was abusive parents. And there was never a cage. No abduction. Cal and I were happy for a long time. I sit stock-still as I listen to Dr Stewart explaining everything that's wrong with my brain. Sometimes she asks me to confirm or deny facts and I do neither. I don't even know what the truth is so how could I possibly answer her?

'What about the letter from Gemma? It was in my rucksack. You should have it.'

'You wrote that letter. A handwritin' analyst has confirmed it. It must have been an attempt to prove the delusion to yourself. Same reason you came up with the idea of "Mary Two". If there was someone else it happened to then you couldnae possibly be makin' it up.'

The argument dies on my tongue. This is how it goes. Every time I think of something that might help to prove I'm not crazy, both to Dr Stewart and to myself, there's an explanation.

'Why would I want to create a reality where I'm being held captive? If I insisted on us getting married and moving away like you say, surely I should have been happy? I got what I wanted?'

Dr Stewart leans back in her chair. 'It's one of the great mysteries of the brain. My best guess is that your mind knew it still needed to process trauma, but since you wouldnae allow it to deal with your true issues it invented a new trauma to deal with.' She pauses to allow her words to sink in. 'Once you made Cal the enemy in your mind, you had someone to fight against without having to accept who and what you really need to fight against: what happened with your parents.'

'What did happen with my parents?'

'You tell me.' Dr Stewart taps her chart. Her old fingers look like knobbly tree branches. 'We've never been able to get you to tell us. I dinnae think you've ever allowed yourself to remember. Not since you've been under my care, anyway.'

I fall silent. Once more, like so many times before when I've painted that road sign and thought about the people who gave birth to me, I try to picture their faces. But it's still just smoke. Maybe the doctor is right. Maybe it's just too painful to think about them. My mind just won't let me do it.

'What's wrong with me?' I whisper. 'Why can't I tell the difference between what's real and what's not?'

After God knows how many of these sessions, I'm officially diagnosed.

'It's a severe form of post-traumatic stress disorder,' Dr Stewart says. 'You've created these memories because it's easier than facing what actually happened to ye.'

My brain is healthy in the traditional way. I wasn't in a car accident, I didn't crack my head open, I didn't fall. There's no actual damage to my brain at all. But it's not really healthy. It's confused and twisted. I wish I could take a saw to my skull and pull it out, inspect it and fiddle with it, make it work the way it's supposed to. Occasionally I actually consider doing it. The more time I spend with Dr Stewart the more I understand that I do have the capacity to get better. Like she said, I've done it before. But I'm terrified that it will happen again, another 'psychotic break', as she calls it. Sometimes I can't even remember what's wrong with me.

I'm staring out of the small window of my room when Dr Stewart knocks unexpectedly. I turn my head on the pillow to glance her way.

'We don't have another session, do we?'

'Not a usual session, no.' She moves into the room and undoes my ties. I sit up with a groan, place my feet on the floor and ground myself. It's always such a relief to stand and stretch. I move tentatively over to the window and resume staring out of it. Dr Stewart sits in her usual chair. After a moment she pats the bed to encourage me over. I stay where I am. I like it here, by the window. I feel less like a prisoner when the outside is just there, on the other side of the glass.

'It's time to start talkin' about your home plan.'

'My what?'

'We need to put a plan in place for gettin' you back home. With your husband.'

Home. The word pierces me. I want to go home so badly. I want to be better, to feel confident in my brain's ability to not splinter the second I'm back there, without Dr Stewart to ground me in reality. But I'm not sure I'm there yet. I don't feel ready.

Dr Stewart must see it in my face because she smiles with understanding. 'It won't be immediate, dinnae worry. But you are making progress. And we can start to implement the transition, gradually.'

I nod, though my neck is stiff. 'What do I need to do?'

'A good step would be to talk to your husband. We could schedule a visit at the end o' the week. Do you think you can talk to him this time for me?'

A shiver runs down my spine. I gulp down the lump in my throat and force another nod.

'Good, Mary. Good.' Dr Stewart beams her approval. 'You get some rest. I'll let him know te come.'

She stands and goes to leave the room.

'You're not going to do my restraints?'

She stops, glances back at me, smiles. 'I dinnae think there's any need, do you? You're getting better, Mary. You need to start believin' in yourself.'

And then she's gone and I'm alone with my thoughts again. I rub my wrists where the restraints should be and look back out the window, trying to focus on the calming effects of staring at nature. The dreary Scottish countryside stretches endlessly before me, the rolling hills and scattered trees a constant reminder that I've gone from one form of isolation to another. At least at the cabin I could garden. I could go out and feed the chickens and chat to my robin friend, though thinking about it now, that was probably just another sign of my insanity. I long to feel the wind on my face and the crunch of leaves beneath my feet.

I limp around the small confines of my room, being careful not to put any pressure on my bad foot, my mind swirling with apprehension. The thought of seeing Cal makes my stomach knot. I haven't spoken a word to my husband since the day I was committed here. The day my world fractured into a myriad of jagged pieces. I know I need to apologise to him. The fact he's stuck by me all this time while I've fallen from reality so far and accused him of such horrors is really quite remarkable. But something inside is stopping me.

As I try to rehearse the conversation in my head I get hot, sweat collecting under the collar of my nightgown, and it feels like it's strangling me. I rip the papery fabric off over my head and stand hunched over in my underwear, attempting to focus on inhaling and exhaling. Once my body has cooled a touch I stand back up and focus once again on the window. If I concentrate hard on counting the leaves of a nearby tree it seems to do the trick. I can stop myself from going into one of my panic attacks.

I count slowly.

One.

Two.

Three.

I place my hands on my hips, steadying myself.

Four.

Five.

Six.

Wait.

My fingers brush against something, catching on raised edges of skin, sending an icy chill down my spine. I peer down.

There, barely visible but shining ever so slightly purple in the light of the window, is a stretch mark.

Chapter Thirty-Seven

I have to get out of here. I need to get to you. The drug- and therapy-induced haze has finally lifted. I am awake.

When Dr Stewart came for my afternoon therapy session I realised her role in all of this. She's the one with all the power. She's the one who says whether I'm well or not. She's the one who gives me the drugs and comes at me with a syringe when I'm not behaving as I should. She's the one who can sign the papers to let me out of here. So now that I've convinced myself of my sanity I need to convince her. I know from all our sessions so far that trying to convince her of Cal's *insanity* is futile, that if I insist my original story of my escape from a madman is true I'll never see the outside of these four walls. So, instead, I need to make her believe I've seen the light. I have to tell her exactly what she wants to hear.

I've decided to call you Robin. It's stupid, I know, naming you after a bird, but to me, that robin represents freedom and hope and kindness. I wanted to name you because it solidifies you in my mind. It helps to make you real. You are real. You're not a nameless idea but an actual, living person. I will not allow them or Cal to make me doubt you ever again. I'm going to find you and we're going to get out of this hellhole together. You're all I can think about, though of course I mustn't let the good doctor know that. If anything happens to you, if he does anything to you, I'm responsible. I should have left earlier. I shouldn't have waited so long, shouldn't have timed my escape so close to my due date.

I don't take the pills Dr Stewart hands me on the daily. Instead I slip them under my tongue and wait for her to leave before spitting them into the toilet. The only trouble with that is I'm also no longer taking any painkillers, which means the pain in my foot has intensified. I don't care though. My head needs to be clear, and as the fog lifts the more I'm certain of the truth. I say the correct things during our therapy sessions, agree when I'm supposed to, cry in the correct places. It turns out it's easy to cry on demand. I just have to think about you and those weeks we've had stolen from us. Dr Stewart's guard is slipping, I can sense it. Maybe it's the way she no longer writes in her notepad as fervently, or how her questions seem to hold a note of complacency, as though she already knows my answers before I even give them. She's getting ready to send me home. All I need to do is talk to Cal like she wants. She'll send me back with him and then I can find you.

I close my eyes and think back to the last time I saw you, the last time I held you. Will you remember me? My voice? My smell? Will you have any comprehension that I'm your mother? I have to pray that you will. I wish I could go back to that last moment with you and press pause, make those few seconds last an eternity.

Something hits me then and I can't believe I didn't think about it before.

Dr Stewart was the one who rescued me that night. She was driving near the hiking trail when she found me delirious and bleeding.

When she found us.

A wave of nausea rolls through me as the realisation hits. Dr Stewart was there. She saw you. She knows you exist. I collapsed into her arms, sobbing as I clung to her, begging her to help you.

You are real and Dr Stewart knows it.

My mind races, piecing together the implications. Dr Stewart brought me here alone, without you. She claimed I was delusional, that there was no baby. But she was lying. She must be working with Cal. It's the only explanation that makes sense.

I think back to that night, replaying Dr Stewart's reaction. When she saw me on the trail, dishevelled and clutching my newborn, there was a flash of something in her eyes. Was it shock? Confusion? Or was it recognition, like she had been expecting to find me?

Rage wells up inside me, hot and visceral. That monstrous woman looked me in the eye day after day, coaxing me to doubt my own reality, all while knowing you were out there somewhere. I know now that I cannot wait until the end of the week in the hopes that she's going to decide I'm well enough – no, *compliant* enough – to leave. If she is working with Cal she's dangerous. Who knows what they've done with you or what they'll do if I don't find you soon. I have no idea how close I am to the cabin, how far she drove me to get here, but I'm going to have to try.

I approach the threshold of my room, beyond which I've not even attempted to venture. Saliva gathers in my mouth and I take a deep breath, forcing myself to remain calm. Panicking will only make things worse. I pause at the door, pressing my ear against it. Beyond it, everything is quiet. She's not returning to my room. Not yet.

Slowly, I turn the handle, wincing as it creaks. I peek out, expecting to see a long corridor with other rooms just like mine branching off of it, a receptionist's desk and waiting room perhaps. Instead I'm met with floral wallpaper and sofas and a coffee table and a fireplace. My time here rolls in my mind like a highlight reel. I've not seen a single doctor besides her. She said I'd been seen by someone else, someone who assessed my physical health, but that was while I was out cold. I have no way of knowing if there actually was such a person. Surely if this were a real hospital I should see other people? Nurses, attendants, cleaners? Surely the psychologist shouldn't be the one bringing me all my meals and checking I'm in bed when I'm supposed to be.

The truth is obvious now and I hate myself for not seeing it sooner. This is not a hospital. Dr Stewart is not who she says she is at all.

I slip out, my uneven steps silent on the plush carpet. There's no sign of her or anyone else. I know I'm not going to be able to make it to the cabin, however close or far it is, if I'm wearing nothing but a nightgown. I need to find a coat and shoes at the very least. I grimace at the thought of putting shoes on over my bandaged foot. I haven't had a chance to peek under the wrappings yet but I can tell the skin is covered in blisters just by attempting to walk on it.

As I move into the living room this whole situation seems even more bizarre. On first glance I'd say this was the home of a kind-hearted, innocent old lady. The stereotypical kind you read about in books. There's a basket of knitting yarn next to the armchair. A display of plates adorned with cat faces strung up on the wall. An array of family photos in antique frames next to a cup and saucer on the side table, still with the dregs of her last cup of tea sitting in the bottom.

It's quiet. Unnervingly so. I have no idea where she's gone or how long she's been away, I know I need to get a move on, but something catches my eye in one of the photos. I pick it up and inexplicably want to laugh.

Cal.

Little boy Cal.

That's where I recognised her from. When I didn't say what she wanted me to say, when she gave me that look of disappointment, I had a gut feeling that I'd seen her before. And I have. Though only in photo form. She was in the picture I slid out of Cal's wallet when I first went looking for the key.

Dr Stewart is Cal's mother.

A faint noise pulls my attention away from the picture and I cock my head, listening hard. At first I think it's a lamb bleating, but then I realise it's coming from inside the house. Upstairs, I think. I strain my ears and my feet move of their own accord, instinctively following the noise. I find the staircase and creep up, pausing on each step to check there's no sign of Cal's mother. It's as I near the top and I can hear it more clearly that I allow myself to believe the sound is indeed what I think it is.

My pace quickens, all thoughts of blisters on my foot erased from my mind, and my heart smashes against my ribcage as I frantically search for a way into the attic, scouring the ceiling looking for a hatch. The cries grow louder, more insistent. It's you, I know it is. You're here.

The sound of footsteps pounding up the stairs make me spin around just in time to see a syringe plunging towards my neck. I duck. My hand flies up and grabs onto Cal's mother's wrist. She's not as frail as she looks. Her eyes are wild as she tries to push against my grip, aiming the sharp point of the needle for my skin. It's the exact look that was on Cal's face when he trashed our room. The resemblance is uncanny now I can see it. Crazed.

I push hard against her arm and though she's stronger than she looks, I'm more so. The needle twists, points towards her. She gives an earth-shattering screech as it pierces her skin and burrows deep into the muscle above her collarbone. I stretch my thumb up and push the plunger down, depositing whatever drug she was planning on using on me into her bloodstream.

It doesn't take long for her to slacken under my grasp. Her eyes roll back in her head and I lower her down to the floor. She sits slumped against the wall, legs at an awkward angle, like a broken puppet. I don't bother trying to adjust her position. Leaving her where she is I begin throwing open random doors, searching, searching. When the third door opens your cry suddenly grows louder and I know I'm in the right place. I sweep my gaze over the bedroom. It's coming from the far corner. I rush over, tears of relief already streaming down my cheeks. But as I approach, my elation turns to horror.

It's not you.

It's just a screen, perched on the side table, showing the feed from one of Cal's cameras and crackling with the sound of your cries.

Chapter Thirty-Eight

You're not anywhere in the house. I've searched every inch, even the outbuilding in the garden. You're not here. After checking every room again one last time I make my way back to the master bedroom and curl up in the corner, cradling the screen, tears streaming. I couldn't see you on the video feed. He must have been holding you just out of its line of sight. We got so far away from that cabin and you've ended up right back there. I feel sick at the thought.

You've stopped crying so there's no sound coming from the speaker anymore, but I press it against my ear and rock, praying that I'll hear the tiniest little noise. Nothing. I peer at the screen again, squinting, scrutinising the familiar view of the area just outside the front door of the cabin. There's no hint of movement. He's not there anymore. You're not there anymore.

A shudder works its way down my spine as I watch the motionless screen. It wasn't just Cal watching me all that time, making sure I didn't attempt an escape. It was his mother, too. No wonder I never got away with it. No wonder Gemma got caught.

I know I haven't got that long until she'll start to come to and I know I need to be formulating some kind of plan, but I'm out of ideas and out of hope. I've never felt pain like this. I almost wish I'd overdosed on those blasted drugs they were feeding me if only to put me out of this misery. Almost. I'm no good to you dead.

A noise on the other end of the monitor startles me and I scramble to listen. It's hard to make out what it is. Rustling. Perhaps you moving around. Starting to wake up. And then, yes, your little voice, strong and clear as you cry and bellow.

'Shhhhh.'

My blood turns to ice.

'It's OK. Your da's here. There. Dinnae cry.'

I squeeze my hand over my mouth. My fingernails dig into my

203

cheeks. You're crying and instead of me being there to comfort you it's him. Anger curls up inside of me like a snake and I stand, launch the screen across the room. I stare out at the land surrounding the house, chest heaving, fists clenched. For my entire adult life I've only ever seen the Highlands from one view. Seeing it from a different angle is disorientating, but I think I recognise the largest mountain that stands near the loch. If I'm right, that means the cabin is in that direction. But it's far. So far. I attempt to wiggle my toes and fire shoots through my entire foot and ankle. There's just no way I'm going to be able to walk that kind of distance.

My gaze drops to the ground. Cal's mother's truck is parked up outside.

Unlike Cal, his mother keeps her keys easily accessible in a little dish near the front door. After getting changed into a top and pair of jeans, courtesy of Cal's mother's wardrobe, I pluck the keys from the dish and hurry out. Cal's mother's trainers are a tad too tight for me, but it was that or bare feet. When I get outside, I realise just how much of a charade I've fallen for. The house I've been kept in is the least hospital-like building imaginable. It's quaint and reminds me of descriptions of cottages in fairy tales. While the inside of the house was fairly tidy, the front is unkempt, long grass in desperate need of cutting and overgrown bushes providing privacy from the outside. Through the tangle of grass weaves a stepping-stone path, moss-covered and cracked. Beyond the path, the driveway and truck, and beyond the truck, looming trees. I look around as I make my way, trying to be sure of my position. I don't have the stars to guide me this time.

I open the driver's door and slide behind the wheel, my hands shaking. My body tenses as I slip the key into the ignition. When I first thought about attempting to use the truck to get back I didn't think I'd ever driven before, but sitting here behind the wheel sparks something. It feels familiar. Not a memory, as such, but a hint of recognition. Yes, I had a few lessons all those years ago, around my seventeenth birthday. Flexing my fingers, it's like my muscles know what to do. I turn the key. The engine rumbles to life, a dormant beast stirred from its slumber. My foot hovers over the pedals, hesitant at first, then presses down. The engine roars but the truck doesn't move. I look around desperately, sure that at any second Cal's mother or even Cal himself will throw open the door and drag me out. My eyes land on the stick in the centre console. *Yes, I've seen this before.* I don't allow myself to think too much, just allow my hand to do what it needs to do. I shift the stick down to the 'D' and try the pedal again. This time the truck lurches forward, and I grip the steering wheel so tight my knuckles whiten.

'Come on,' I mutter to myself, willing strength into my voice. The path back to the cabin is etched into my mind, a trail of breadcrumbs that now leads me back to hell. Or salvation. Once the road becomes too narrow for the truck I veer off, making sure I keep the hiking trail in my sights so I don't lose my way. Trees blur past as I force the vehicle along the track, jerking the wheel left and right to avoid the rocks and potholes that threaten to unseat me. The land becomes hillier and I feel an alertness come over me. I'm closer to the cabin now. Closer to danger.

My hands are slick with sweat on the steering wheel. As I approach a particularly sharp bend in the road, I ease off the accelerator too late and the truck bounces over a large rock, causing me to jolt forward in my seat. I grip the wheel tighter, preparing for impact. It doesn't come though. The truck steadies itself and I'm back on route.

Finally I see it. The cabin in all its run-down glory. I can't believe I'm back here. Voluntarily, at that. As I near the clearing, I kill the headlights and slow down. With a shuddering sigh, the truck nestles into the anonymity of the treeline, hidden beneath the dense canopy. I cut the engine and the world falls silent.

I don't have time to second-guess – I slip out of the truck and press myself against its cold metal, scanning the area. I hadn't really thought this far ahead. It's all very well getting back here, but I have no idea what my next move is. I wish my head wasn't so sluggish still.

Fortunately, a plan presents itself to me.

'Fuck!' Cal's voice is so loud and sudden as he bursts from the cabin a flock of birds take flight. I don't blame them. Even from my obscured position I can tell he's fuming. Perhaps his mother has got in touch, let him know that his poor, pathetic, weak captive bested her. He strides away from the cabin, urgency in his step, and throws himself into his own truck. He doesn't see me. He can't. I'm nothing but a shadow here, a ghost in his world.

The moment he disappears into the forest, I dart towards the cabin, my feet barely touching the ground, light and soundless. Weeds are growing through the gravel and a strange instinct comes over me to pluck them out. Cal won't like it if he gets home and sees weeds. I scold myself and carry on. Every cell in my body screams at me to run, to get far away from this place that reeks of dread, but I push forward. This is my one chance to slip inside unnoticed.

I hurry to the cabin as best I can, slowed by my foot. The bandages are damp and I'm pretty sure it's either bleeding or the blisters have burst, but I can't think about that right now. There's snow on the way. I can feel it in the air. If it snows I may as well give up trying to get away from here once I've found you. Time is of the essence.

I nudge the front door open and shoulder my way inside. It's colder in here than it is outside, if that's even possible. He's clearly not been keeping up with the things I used to do like prepping and stoking the fire. The wind whistles through the cracks in the walls and the ceilings and I hate him even more for not even making sure you're warm.

I search the cabin, though it takes much less time than searching Cal's mother's house. My breath quickens as I move from room to room, each inhalation sharp and ragged. My heart is a frantic drumbeat urging me on. Fingers trembling, I scan the bedroom, the room in which I had imagined you spending your nights by my side, back when I believed in my life. I squint in the dim light, desperate for any sign of you.

'Where are you?' The words are a whisper, a prayer floating through the stillness.

No coos or cries answer me; no soft gurgle to guide me to you. The cabin is empty, mocking me. Panic claws at my chest, but I shove it down, refusing to succumb to fear.

I move back into the kitchen and the rumbling of my stomach reminds me that I haven't eaten all day. I pull open the cooler and grab the first item of food I find. A container of soup. Prising the lid off, I sniff at its contents. It doesn't smell terrible. I grab a spoon and eat it cold. As I do so I catch sight of my reflection in the mirror above the mantel. I look nothing like my old self. Such a short period of time and the difference is unbelievable. I shudder and stare into my sunken, bloodshot eyes, ringed by deep dark circles. My cheeks are hollow, bones sticking out so that my entire face looks sharp and angular. My skin is dry and flaking, almost grey in the unlit room, as are my lips. I'm a shell of who I once was. I look almost dead.

Having forced down a few mouthfuls of the cold soup I press my fingers to my temple and try to think where he could possibly be keeping you. The obvious answer is staring right at me. I can feel it through the window. I don't believe he could be so cruel as to keep a newborn baby there. But of course, that's exactly where he'd keep you. Away from prying eyes. Away from me.

Cal's jacket hangs forgotten on its hook, a small victory for me. It's a new one. No doubt the one I took was too covered in afterbirth and blood for his liking. Its fabric is rough under my fingertips, reeking of woodsmoke and pine. *Pockets. Please let the right keys be here.* My hand closes around a cold metal ring, heavy with promise. I pull the keys out, confirming that they are indeed the set he dangled so smugly in front of me, and clutch them like a lifeline as I slip back out the door, every sense alert.

I make for the barn, a dark monolith against the afternoon sky. The key slips into the padlock easily, not like the old rusted one. I edge the door open, just enough to slip inside, the hinges protesting with a faint groan that sets my nerves on edge. Inside, darkness wraps around me, thick and oppressive. My eyes strain, adjusting to the lack of light, searching the shadows for a hint of movement, the soft texture of a blanket, anything.

There's nothing. No cot, no bassinet, no sign of life. Just the hulking shape of the cage. I swallow hard, the taste of fear metallic on my tongue.

I can't leave her. The other woman. I promised her I'd come back for her.

With reluctant steps, I approach the cage and my stomach twists as I realise she's lying on the floor. Not moving. I've left it too late.

Warning signals telling me to stay away emanate from it, seeping into my bones. I flick to another key on the ring and slot it into the lock, turning it with a click that sounds too loud in the silence. I brace myself, steeling my nerves for what I'm about to discover.

The door creaks open. I force myself to look. She stirs.

'Come on,' I urge, my voice barely above a whisper. 'We have to get out of here.'

I reach for her hand, cold but alive. Her eyes lock onto me, wide and glassy with confusion. I squeeze her fingers, trying to ground her back to reality. My eyes search her face for any hint of understanding, of recognition. I think something flickers in her gaze, a tiny ember of awareness that hadn't been there before, but it's gone before I can tell and she just blinks at me, the dim light of the barn casting shadows across her gaunt face.

My shoulders droop, but seeing her like this has only bolstered my resolve. I give her hand a gentle tug.

'We can't stay here. Can you move?'

I try to gesture at what I want her to do. After a few agonisingly long moments she seems to understand and pulls herself to standing. She groans and I know all too well that feeling. Aches in your bones like nothing you've ever felt before. I hold my arm out to her and support her as she steps out of the cage.

'Good. That's good. This way.'

The woman moves so slowly, barely a shuffle, that I'm second-guessing my decision to let her out. I should have found you first. This is taking too long.

'I don't suppose you've heard a baby cry . . .'

My words are cut short and my head flies up. An engine cuts through the stillness outside, shattering any illusion of safety I have.

Chapter Thirty-Nine

Cal

'Ma?' I'm not sure which emotion is stronger. The anger that the bitch has done what she's done, or the worry that Ma might be more hurt than she made out on the phone. I burst into the cottage. 'Ma? Where are ye?'

'Upstairs, lad.'

I storm up the stairs and find her crumpled on the hallway, slumped against the wall. Her head lolls forwards and though she's awake she's not fully with it. I crouch beside her.

'What did she do, Ma? Did she give you somethin'?'

Ma's lips move, sound escapes them, but I can't make out what she's saying. Moving my ear closer to her mouth, I strain to listen.

'What d'you say?'

She places a hand on my neck, pulls me even closer. Her grip tightens. Fingers digging into my muscle. Nails cutting into my skin.

'This is your fault. You're a disappointment.'

She pushes me back, releasing my neck, and I sit in the hallway beside her.

'Ma, I'm . . . I'm sorry.'

Her eyes roll back in her head. 'Didnae I tell you, Callum? Didnae I teach you properly so's this would never happen?'

'I tried.' She's the only one who can make me feel like this. Small. Like a scared wee lad again. Having her talk like this to me is taking me right back there, to the cupboard she'd lock me in every time I didnae do exactly as she said. I've been kinder to my wives than she was to me. Least I gave them food and drink. She'd let me sit

209

and rot in that cupboard, starving, gasping for water, until I'd properly learnt my lesson.

'I've never questioned your choices,' she says, snapping me back to the present. 'Not once did I raise my eyebrow when you brought those girls home. All I said was that I didnae want nothin' to do with it. That it was up to you to keep 'em under control.'

'Ma, I tried. I did exactly what you'd have done.'

'Clearly not! I've had to get involved, haven't I? "Ma, Ma, help me, she's escaped and I cannae find her." Draggin' me out, makin' me get in my truck at that hour o' the mornin' and go lookin' for her, askin' me to bring her back here and sort her out because you're not man enough to control her yourself.' She shakes her head, disgust seeping into her features. 'You're just like your pa. Spineless. I thought I raised you better.'

I stare at Ma, her harsh words cutting through me like knives. Even now, when she's hurt and drugged, she knows exactly what to say to break me. She's right, of course. All my bravado about being in control, about knowing best, it's all a sham. I'm a sham. Man of the household my arse. I get to my feet, steadying myself against the wall.

'Tell me how to fix this,' I say.

She scoffs. 'Ye need to drive me back to your place. That's where she'll have gone. She'll be lookin' for the baby.'

Chapter Forty

Mary

Instinctively, I halt, pulling her back with me into the shadowed recesses of the barn, as I listen to the approaching engine.

'Cal,' I mouth silently. He's returned. Our window for escape is rapidly closing. We stand together, our breathing shallow, as the rumble of his truck grows louder, closer. The sound drills into my skull.

I peek around the corner of the door. I can see the truck from this angle. My muscles coil, readying myself to sprint, with or without this woman, but before I can do anything the truck grumbles to a stop directly outside the barn. He must have noticed the door was open. I freeze at the sight of Cal's mother, slumped in the passenger seat. She's awake but her eyes are half closed, the effects of the drugs evidently still wearing off.

'Come on,' I hiss, urgency sharpening my voice to a razor's edge.

She flinches, eyes wide. I grab her arm, pulling her towards a stack of hay bales shadowed by the barn's eaves. 'In there. Quick.'

She stumbles into the hiding spot, her movements jerky. I press a finger to my lips, signalling silence.

'Stay.'

With no idea whether she understands me or not, I slip away from her. I find my own refuge in a pitch-dark alcove behind an old plough, draped in cobwebs and dust.

I squeeze into the narrow gap, very nearly standing on an old rake that's been left lying points-up on the floor. Sound becomes my only way of knowing what Cal is doing. The crunch of gravel underfoot outside. The distant rattle of his breath. Time stretches, thin and taut. The barn's timbers groan in the wind.

He's close now. He moves methodically, searching with a predator's patience. A match ignites and for a moment I think he's going to burn the barn down with us inside it, but he's using it to help him see. The walls are bathed in flickering light. Shadows dance across them as he moves.

A hay bale shifts, a rustle of straw, and I will the other woman to be silent. I crane my neck but I can't see her from my hiding spot, not without giving my own away. I can see Cal though. He's closing in on her. And he has one of his hunting rifles in his hand.

'I know you're here, Mary. I can hear ye.'

A drop of cold sweat trickles down the nape of my neck. He stops right in front of where she's hiding.

'Come out, come out, wherever you are,' he sings.

Fear laces my spine. The warning in his sugary tone is as clear as the loch. He moves again, angling himself more in my direction. I risk shifting to track him. His eyes are chips of flint, hard and merciless. I know that look. I've been on the receiving end of it too many times. He's strung tight as a cable about to snap. He's seconds from finding that woman and I don't even want to think about what he's going to do to her when he does. She's so weak and fragile from her time in the cage. She's not going to have a chance at fighting back.

I'm not even sure it's a conscious decision on my part. There's a moment of stark clarity, a realisation that I cannot – will not – allow him to find her. His footsteps carry him to a stop right next to her. I straighten in my hiding spot, drawing a deep breath. My fist closes around the rake handle.

As I emerge from my hiding spot a smile creeps onto Cal's lips, one that doesn't match the victorious look in his eyes.

'Oh my love,' he says. 'I've missed you.'

He takes a step towards me and I stagger back, pointing my feeble rake weapon towards him. His forehead crinkles and he places the gun down, leaning it against one of the hay bales. He raises his hands in mock surrender.

'You're nay still scared of me, are you, lass? Doc told me you was getting better.'

I shake my head in disbelief. He's not really going to try to keep this up, is he? 'I know the truth, Cal. I know she's your mother. I know you've got my baby.'

'Mary, you've been through a lot. Come home and we can talk about this properly.'

He holds out his hand to me but I hold the rake firm, making a jabbing motion towards him.

'No! I'm not coming anywhere with you. I know the truth!'

Cal lets out a sigh, drops his head. 'The truth is you're sick, Mary, love. Yes, OK? Dr Stewart is my ma. I asked her to help you because I trust her. Way more than any doctors out there.' He gestures behind him at the wilderness that nearly killed me. 'She were a psychologist for years before she retired to be a wife and mother. She knows what she's doing. You're in good hands with her.'

'Stop! I don't want to hear it!'

'You never want to hear it, Mary. That's the problem. Every time we try to tell you the truth this is what you do.'

'You stole my baby.' The words come out choked and tears splash down my cheeks, much to my annoyance. I don't want to show any weakness in front of him.

He folds his lips in on themselves, the cogs of his brain whirring as he tries to formulate another lie. The air between us crackles with tension, thick enough to choke on.

'We thought it would be for the best.'

I blink, taken aback.

'Just until you're better,' he continues.

'You . . . you admit she's real?'

'Ma didn't think you were in the right headspace to be raising the little'un and I agreed. But she's fine. She's healthy. She's waiting for you to get better so you can come home and we can be a family, just like we've always wanted. Please. I love you so much.'

The air seems to thicken around me. Doubt gnaws and nibbles at me. No. This is what he does. He makes me think I've lost my mind but it's all just control and lies.

'Where is she, Cal?'

He licks his lips, looking briefly at a loss for words. 'This isn't the

213

time or place. You need to come home with me, get some rest. Once you're feeling more your old self you can see her.'

'WHERE IS SHE?' I screech at him, strangulated and desperate.

Something flashes on Cal's face then. A new expression, one I've never seen before. Some kind of concoction of anger and realisation and understanding. Isn't that something? To live with someone for so many years and still have the capacity to see an expression for the first time.

He blows out the match and we're plunged back into darkness. He lunges for me, the space between us closing in an instant, pushing the rake out of his way. It's so old it snaps and splinters almost instantly. I drop it, stumble back, and turn to run. He's blocking the doorway but if I can lure him further into the barn somehow . . .

He's quicker than me, though. He grabs my shoulder and yanks me back. His arms snake over my front, wrapping around me, holding me tight to his chest.

'Stop fighting me, Mary.'

He pushes me forward and I realise what he's going to do.

'No, please, not in there. I can't.' The familiar panic works its way up inside me. I'd rather die than go back in there. I struggle against him but he continues to force me towards the cage. His chest pushes against my back and I'm face down on top of it, the edge pressing into my stomach. One of his hands moves to my head, entangling his fingers in my hair and he presses down, the cold bars digging into my cheeks.

It isn't until he's yanking my underwear down that I understand. He's leaning on top of me, crushing me, breath reeking and hot on my face. He kisses along my neck, three little pecks that make me want to throw up.

I open my mouth to scream but no sound comes out. My lungs are compressed. He's suffocating me as he bears his weight down on me. I writhe and buck as best I can but he just presses down harder and I think my ribs might crack under the pressure. There's the sound of his zip undoing.

'You're mine,' he says, so close to my ear I can feel his lips moving. Tears roll silently down the sides of my face. I can't do anything.

A sharp crack shatters the air, the noise alien and jarring. Cal's head snaps towards the sound. It's only a moment, a heartbeat, but in that fragment of time, his grip weakens. I suck in ragged breaths, the pressure on my lungs lessened. I twist and strain to see what it is that's distracted him. A figure emerges. The late afternoon sun glints off a metallic object in her hand.

The other woman. She's holding the hunting rifle.

Chapter Forty-One

The gun trembles in her hand as if it weighs more than the sum of its parts, more than metal and mechanism. My eyes flick between it, the woman and Cal. He seems to have momentarily forgotten I'm here, though I know if I move under his limp grasp he'll be quick to tighten it again.

Cal turns to face the woman, slowly raising his free hand in a gesture of surrender. His eyes lock onto the rifle barrel.

'Easy now,' he says, his voice low and steady. 'No need for that. Put the gun down before someone gets hurt.'

Her knuckles whiten as her grip tightens. Her piercing green eyes flash with defiance. She doesn't speak.

'Mary, what's gotten into you?'

It takes me a moment to register that he's not speaking to me but to her. 'Pointing a gun at your own husband? Think about what you're doing here.'

I try to twist away from him but he pushes me back down against the cage.

'Don't listen to him. Your name's not Mary. He's not your husband. He took you, just like he took me. You've got a life out there somewhere. A family.'

Cal's fingers dig into my neck like talons, a silent warning to stop talking. The woman tenses. Her brow furrows ever so slightly but her aim doesn't waver.

'This woman is confused, love. She's trying to hurt us. Please, put the gun down.'

Still she doesn't speak. Her eyes drift to mine and I pray to God that she can see the pleading in my eyes, can see that I'm to be believed and not him.

'Whatever she told you,' Cal continues, 'it's not true. I love you. You know I do. Put the gun down and we can go home.'

She blinks hard as if trying to clear her vision. Cal lowers his voice, dark, dangerous.

'Listen te me. If you help me deal with this psychotic woman I promise you you'll be safe. Nobody will ever hurt you ever again. You can have anything you want. I'll spend the rest of my days tryin' to make ye happy.'

His words are like a shock wave. Something clicks inside me and there's a bizarre moment where I want to apologise to him. I squeeze my eyes shut and shake my head. When I open my eyes I see it's had the same effect on the other woman, too. She cocks her head to one side, confusion etched across her features.

'You know it was her idea to bring you here,' Cal continues, and my throat constricts. 'She said to me 'bout getting someone else to come live with us. You're here because she made it so.'

Fear and shame curdle inside me. I can't even deny it, can't even tell her he's lying, because he's not. Slowly, surely, she moves the gun so that it's pointed at me.

This is it. I'm going to die. My plan, my actions, my selfishness. They're going to be my undoing.

No. Not before I've found you.

With all my strength, I wrench myself from his grasp and yank his arm so that my face is just covered by his shoulder, a sort of human shield. A deafening crack shatters the silence of the barn. Cal cries out, howling and grasping at his upper arm. I don't stick around to see what damage the bullet did. Probably quite a lot. I'm almost certain it was the same shoulder she stabbed him in. I sprint out of the barn, gunshot still ringing through my ears, head ducked low in case the woman tries to fire again. Cal's mother is no longer in his truck. I have no idea where she is, didn't see her get out, but I don't have time to worry about that right now. I make for her truck, still hidden amongst the trees, grass whipping around my legs, pain exploding in my foot with every step. The keys are dangling from the ignition where I left them. I wrench open the door, then freeze.

I can hear you crying.

My eyes scan my surroundings wildly. Where are you? I follow the sound of your cries. It's like a homing beacon, guiding my steps as I make my way around the side of the cabin. It's not like when I heard you on the baby monitor. This time I can feel your presence. It gets stronger as I get closer.

It's her. Cal's mother. She's standing in the garden, amongst the vegetable patches, chickens clucking at her feet, a pram next to her, and she's rocking you in her arms.

My heart leaps into my throat. The urge to rush forward and snatch you away is almost more than I can bear, but I daren't for fear of what she might do. The old woman seems lost in her own world, gently swaying and murmuring soft soothing sounds. As I approach, a twig snaps under my heel and her head snaps up.

'Please,' I whisper, my voice cracking. 'Please let me have my baby back.'

She smiles at me and it's the same smile Cal gave me. Knowing. In control.

'You've been such a bad wife,' she says. Her voice is ice and it sends a shiver skittering down my spine.

I shake my head. 'I'm not his wife.'

'This wee one says otherwise.' Her hand strokes the top of your head and my skin crawls.

'I don't understand,' I say. 'Why are you doing this? Why are you both doing this?'

She tilts her head towards you and stares, eyes intense and dark. 'When you're a mother you'll do anything for your child. Dinnae you know that yet? My son deserves a good wife. He deserves a better wife than you.'

I swallow. No wonder Cal is as crazy as he is. His mother is deranged. He never stood a chance. But I can't do anything all the time she's holding you like that.

'That's why the other woman is there, right? Because I wasn't good enough for him?'

She doesn't respond, just carries on stroking your head.

'And what about Gemma? Was she not good enough either?'

There's a flicker of confusion on her face at the name, then recognition. 'That bitch tried te leave him. I know what it's like te be abandoned by the person you love. I'll never let him be hurt like that. I had no choice but to kill her.'

A gasp escapes my mouth. My stomach constricts. *She* was the one who killed Gemma? Not Cal? A sickly feeling swirls in my stomach as I realise just how dangerous the person holding you is. I have to get you away from her.

I take a careful step forward, hands raised in surrender. 'I understand. You'd do anything for him. But I'm begging you, please. That's my child.'

'No. This is my grandchild.' Her arms tighten around you. 'My son's child. I wanted ye to be right for him. I told him. I said to him "Just give her one more chance. Just give her some time wi' me. I'll talk her round. I'll make her see sense." Why couldnae you have just been his wife?'

Tears build in my eyes. 'I know you want to protect your son,' I say gently. 'But this isn't the way. Keeping women here against their will. It's only going to end badly.'

'You dinnae know anything about bein' a mother. About the sacrifices it takes.' Her eyes flash and I stop in my tracks, not wanting to take another step towards her, not wanting to set her off. As I take in her expression I see that she too is on the verge of tears. 'I wanted a good life for him. So bad. I wanted him te have a better life than I did. One with a good wife who would care for him like I do.'

I don't say anything. I don't know what to say anymore.

'All I ever wanted was for him te be happy. He'd have made such a good daddy.' She's gone distant again, looking back down at you and swaying. Suddenly, as if a bomb has gone off inside her, she moves, jerking you wildly to the side.

'Please don't!' I scream. I lurch towards you, not knowing what she has planned but desperate to protect you from whatever it is. She flinches, glares at me, her gaze cutting right through me, and places you down in the pram.

Confused and terrified, I watch as she gives you a light kiss on your forehead. She doesn't say anything else. Just straightens herself up and drifts away, disappearing into the cabin.

I stand frozen for a moment, unable to process what just happened. My eyes stay fixed on you in the pram, watching the gentle rise and fall of your tiny chest. You seem unharmed, just drifting back to sleep after the sudden movement.

Slowly, I force my legs to carry me towards you on shaky steps, still hesitant that this may be some cruel trick. But she is gone. We are alone. I reach the pram and a sob escapes me as I gaze down at your perfect little face. My whole world. I stroke your cheek ever so gently, barely daring to breathe in case I wake you. Then the concept of waking you is suddenly not enough to stop me. In one swift motion I lift you into my arms, holding you close against my pounding heart. The familiar warmth and weight of you brings fresh tears spilling down my cheeks. I press kisses to your downy hair, breathing in that sweet baby scent I was so sure I would never experience again. You stir slightly, scrunching your nose, then nestle into me with a contented sigh.

'It's all right. I'm here,' I whisper through my tears. 'We're going home.'

Chapter Forty-Two

Amy

There's something Cal doesn't know about me.

I never told him. As far as he is concerned, I agreed to come with him to his cabin in the Highlands because I was scared Rich would find me. But that's not the case at all. I came with him because I needed somewhere to disappear to, where the police wouldn't find me.

Because they'll be looking for me. I'm not sure exactly how long it will have taken them to discover Rich's body, rotting in the kitchen. Leaving him wasn't enough. I needed to make sure he'd never follow me. I needed to make sure he'd never do the same thing to someone else. I needed to kill him.

I'll never forget it. How freeing it was bashing his skull in, bringing the cast iron skillet down on his head again and again and again until long after he went still. Every time I went for it I thought of all the women I'd be saving. And that's what I did to someone who beat me around when he'd had too much to drink. What Cal did was much worse. But he did it to the wrong person.

The man who has held all the power is pressed terrified against the wall. I'm holding his life hostage at the end of a gun. Me. The woman who he thought he could control. He clearly underestimated the might of a woman pushed to the brink.

I can almost taste the adrenaline that courses through me, a bitter tang on the tongue. The gun in my hand trembles as it points at the heart of our shared nightmare. My fingers twitch on the trigger.

'Amy, please . . .' Cal's voice fractures the charged silence, his plea scraping against my ears. He used my real name. His words are slick with desperation and I lap it up.

221

The gun feels cold and alien in my hands. I've never held one before but I love it. With every thud of my heart, I am reminded of everything he's done. I think about the cage. I think about the other woman he's had locked up here for God knows how long. I think about him breaking my hand. Cal's eyes widen with the realisation that his world is tilting on its axis. He can read my mind. Knows what I'm thinking. Knows what he's done.

'Amy, I love you,' he tries, the words hollow.

I peer down at the trigger beneath my fingertips. It would be so easy – just one squeeze, a burst of fire, and then silence. Justice served cold on the barn floor.

I stare him directly in the eyes.

'Get into the cage.' My voice doesn't quiver. It doesn't break.

Cal's face pales. His gaze darts to the cage, then to the door, frantic calculations etched in the furrows of his brow. The muscles in his jaw twitch. He's trying to think of a way out of this. But he's cornered, an animal in a trap he set himself. His eyes search mine, looking for a sign of weakness, a glimpse of the woman he once manipulated. But she's gone, replaced by someone stronger. He sees it. The steel in my glare that wasn't there before. The transformation from prey to predator.

'Please . . .' he starts again, but there's a finality in my stance that tells him all he needs to know.

The gun doesn't waver. Neither do I.

'I said . . . move.'

He glances at the cage, gaping open like a grave. With a ragged exhale, he stands, takes a step forward. Then another. Each movement is slow. Delaying. His feet drag across the dusty floor, the sound grating.

I watch him, unflinching, as he crosses the space between us. He now seems smaller somehow. His rugged features are twisted into a mask of resignation. His boot hovers over the threshold of the cage, and for a fraction of a second, he pauses – a final silent plea in his eyes. But there's no mercy left in me to give. With a nod that's more a shove, I urge him on.

And then he's stepping in, crossing into the box that will be his cell.

I stand sentinel, watching as he lowers himself down. This is justice. Not the kind found in courtrooms or in the pages of law books, but raw and primal. My hand hovers for a moment before I slam the cage door shut. A heavy metallic clank reverberates through the barn. The sound ricochets off the walls. I step back, my breath visible in the frigid room, a mist of triumph and exhaustion mingling before me. For just a heartbeat, as the lock clicks into place, everything stills. No pleas or threats, no wind howling its mournful tune outside. Just the quiet thud of my pulse.

Turning, I see her. The other woman, standing in the barn door with a pram secured in her hands. My unexpected ally. Our gazes lock. There's an unspoken conversation in that look, volumes of shared fear, anger and resolve passing between us without a single word. I step towards her, pulling her attention from the cage and the pathetic excuse for a man curled up inside it, and we pivot together, the door now just an exit, not a barrier. The pram wheels and our steps echo. Limping from our ailments but purposeful. We cross the threshold and share a glance, unspoken understanding knitting us together.

The silence fractures with a single, spoken word.

'Amy,' I say. 'My name is Amy.'

She repeats it, her face breaking out into a sad smile. 'Amy.'

'Who are you?'

She considers me for a moment, and then whispers, 'Lauren.' I can tell it's the first time she's said it out loud in all the time she's been here. Her real name. She looks down at the pram and her chest swells. 'And this is Robin.'

With nothing more than a nod, I start to walk again, granting her space to breathe. Our hands brush against each other, fleeting contact that grounds us in the here and now.

'Amy?' Lauren says.

'I know. Let's not look back.'

We're at the edge of the woods now. The cabin and the barn are well behind us. The ground beneath our feet crunches, a frozen carpet of pine needles and brittle leaves. The sky stretches endlessly above us. Evening is closing in. The truck sits waiting for us. We approach and Lauren glances at me.

'Can you hold her? There's no car seat.'

For a moment I'm petrified at the thought, but my face softens as I look down at the pram and nod. I make sure the blankets are still snugly wrapped and give Lauren a little squeeze on the arm to reassure her.

Lauren slides into the driver's seat and we climb in beside her. The engine's growl is like a final declaration of our departure. Once we're all buckled in Lauren manoeuvres the truck onto the narrow track. The tyres crunch over the gravel. Despite myself, I glance quickly into the wing mirror, and I watch the cabin and the barn disappear behind a line of trees.

Chapter Forty-Three

Lauren

The fluorescents above hum with a monotonous drone. My fingers trace the delicate knit of your baby blanket, the soft fibres a stark contrast to the hard plastic chair I'm sitting on. You're in the pram beside me, swaddled. A bundle of serene innocence. I lean closer, drinking in the peaceful rise and fall of your tiny chest. The faintest whiff of baby shampoo mingles with the musty air.

The world outside this police station is uncertain. But you – you are light.

I glance at the clock. Time stretches and compresses, each tick both fleeting and eternal. I find myself planning. A shop on the way back to our temporary accommodation, the one with the cheerful yellow sign. I'll stock up on baby-proofing gear: plug socket covers, cabinet locks, corner cushions. It's ridiculous. You're nowhere near rolling over, let alone getting around and hurting yourself, but I'm going to do it anyway. I'll ward off any and all danger. Always.

There's a vibration in my pocket and I pull out my phone. It's an old one. Second hand. They gave it to me along with various necessities I'd need to at least feel human. I'm not sure what the protocol is when two women turn up with a baby and nothing but the clothes on their backs, but there certainly seemed to be a plan in place when Amy and I first arrived in town. There was lots of talking. Lots of explaining. Lots of paperwork to fill out. They figured out who I was pretty quickly by scanning the missing persons database and asked if I wanted to be reunited with my parents. I told them I wasn't ready. From then everything happened pretty quickly and you and I were placed in a flat, nothing fancy, but a place to call our own even if it's just for now.

Cal's shadow looms in the recesses of my memory. At night, I wake screaming, the image of his features twisted into that all-too-familiar sneer imprinted in my mind. It's not just the memory of his touch that chills me. It's the icy tendrils of fear that still cling to my thoughts.

I'm told I need to go to therapy and I don't disagree. I need to sift through the wreckage he left behind. I need to dissect the lies until I can see the truth of who I am beneath them. The idea of unravelling the knots of our shared history is daunting, but necessary.

My thumb hovers over the screen of my phone. Amy's message glows underneath. She's been through it since we escaped, too. It turns out the reason she was hiding out with Cal in the first place was because she had killed her husband. This fact had surprised me when I found out, but didn't faze me. I can't judge her. Turned out, neither could the jury. She was found guilty of manslaughter, taking into account the severe and prolonged abuse she suffered at his hands, and was given a four-year suspended sentence. As long as she reports to her probation officer regularly, attends counselling, stays in the area and doesn't commit any further offences, she's free to live her life. I guess everyone thought the same: she's had more than enough punishment for her crime already.

Amy's text message is simple.

Have you done it yet?

I hesitate, my reply a confession of procrastination.
I type back:

Not yet.

She responds almost immediately.

Let me know when it's done. Coffee after?

I reply that yes, coffee would be great, and the screen dims. I tuck the phone away. Coffee with Amy. A step towards normality. Or at least the illusion of it.

Officer Barns' voice startles me from my reverie.

'It's time.' I know this police officer. I've seen him many times since my escape and he's disconcertingly kind. He's the one who told me that they'd found Cal in the cage, weak from blood loss, just about clinging on to life. He's the one who arrested him and kept me updated on every part of the trial, who told me I wasn't expected to be there or face him, that both Amy and I could give our testimony over a video call. He told me they'd found Gemma's remains, and that her family finally has the answers they so desperately craved for over a decade. And he told me what the sentence was. Cal will spend the rest of his life in prison with no chance of early release. From captor to captive. A fitting punishment, I think. He also told me what became of Cal's mother. After she disappeared into the cabin it seems she found the sharpest knife in my drawer and slit her wrists. A permanent escape from accountability.

Escape isn't an option for me. I thought getting away from Cal, from the cabin, would mean freedom. Turns out it doesn't. I'm still suffering, just in a different way. But I have to keep going. I must walk forward, navigate the debris, build something better from the ruins. If not for myself, for you. Your future stretches out untouched and full of possibility.

Officer Barns waits, his patience waning. I meet his eyes, glimpsing a flicker of understanding. I take a deep breath, steadying myself. Gripping onto the pram handles for support, we walk together into the next room.

I make out two familiar figures rising from plastic chairs along the wall. Mum and Dad. I freeze, overcome. They rush forward, enveloping me in their arms. I melt into their embrace, the solid warmth of their bodies, the familiar scent of home. I'm not sure why I put off seeing them again. Shame? Fear that I'd let them down, allowing myself to be hypnotised by Cal, to be abducted by him? I don't know. But for the first time in I don't know how long, I feel safe.

No words need be spoken in this moment. We cling together and sob. After a long while Dad pulls back, smiling through his tears. He squeezes my shoulder gently. Mum continues to hold me close, stroking my hair.

'My girl,' she murmurs. 'I knew you'd come back to us.'

My heart swells and I choke back a sob. After everything, they never gave up hope. Never stopped searching. I've seen the social media campaign they had going. #FindLauren. It went viral. There are YouTube videos by amateur detectives analysing my case that have millions of views. There were neighbourhood search parties and annual appeals. I've had to be shielded from a lot of it. Newspapers wanting to hear my story. Requests for interviews. Even an offer of a book deal. Apparently I don't even have to write it. I can just tell the ins and outs of what happened to someone and they'll turn it into something people want to read. I've turned down all such offers. I want to forget it all. Not memorialise it. The one thing I have let them do is take my painting, the one that marked the beginning of my final escape attempt. Apparently they're putting it in a gallery with a small passage of context underneath it. I might go and see it one day. Once I've had a chance to come to terms with everything.

I take a deep, steadying breath and disentangle myself from Mum's arms. Reaching into the pram, I lift you out.

'There's someone I want you to meet.'

I pass the tiny bundle into Mum's waiting arms. She gasps, fresh tears spilling down her cheeks as she gazes at her grandchild for the first time.

'Oh, Lauren,' she breathes. 'She's beautiful. Absolutely perfect.'

Dad peers over Mum's shoulder, his face alight with wonder and joy. He brushes his knuckle gently over your head.

'What's her name?' he asks huskily.

'Robin,' I reply, a tide of emotions rising within me. 'Her name is Robin.'

Mum kisses your head. You stir, blinking sleepily as you take in your grandparents' tear-streaked faces.

'Hello, sweet girl,' Mum coos. 'We're your nanny and grandad. We love you so much already.'

Watching my parents cradle you, their eyes shining with love, I feel the broken pieces of my world begin to knit back together. My family surrounds me, sheltering me with their strength. And in your eyes, I see the dawn breaking over all our tomorrows.

* * *

The cold air stings my cheeks as we leave the police station. I clutch you close. Dad pushes the pram behind me. We say goodbye, promising to see each other soon. Part of me never wants to leave them again but I know I need to stand on my own two feet. There will be hard days ahead. Days when the memories threaten to pull me under. When doubt and fear cloud my mind. But I will face them with courage, drawing daily strength from the precious soul who depends on me.

As I reach the bottom of the steps, Amy pulls up in her car. I raise my eyebrows.

'I thought we were meeting for coffee later?'

'Can I give you a ride?'

I look back at my parents and they nod, smiling.

'We'll see you soon,' Mum says.

I go to get in the car but stop, rush back to her, hug her one more time. She holds me close and I can't believe we went all this time not being able to embrace like this. Eventually we part. I open the back door of Amy's car. The car seat Amy's parents purchased for you is already installed. They knew we were going to be in each other's lives, Amy and me, and they've gone all in, showering you with more gifts than I know what to do with. I buckle you in and both Mum and Dad lean in for one more kiss on the head.

I slide into the passenger seat beside Amy. I haven't managed to get behind a wheel again since our ordeal but she got back to it straight away. I suppose she was away from it for much less time. I'll get there.

I wave to my parents as we pull away and Amy squeezes my hand tightly.

'How are you doing?'

'Better,' I reply honestly. I glance round to the back seat. Amy's put a mirror up so that I can see you even with you turned to face the back.

When I turn back around I notice that Amy's eyes are glistening.

'She really is beautiful, Lauren.'

I know Amy sees the same hope I do reflected in your tiny face. The promise of light piercing the darkness. New beginnings rising from the ashes. The road unfurls before us. The future, once shrouded in fear, now shimmers with possibility.

Acknowledgements

Someone once told me that writing books gets easier the more you do it.

They lied.

So, I suppose, I should thank that person. Because if they had told me the truth – that every book you write, whether it's your debut or your fourth or even your fourteenth, has the ability to turn you into a jittery, coffee-infused, insecure mess in the corner of the room – I might not have chosen this career path.

That being said, I have chosen it, and I have a few people I'd like to thank for helping me to keep going, despite aforementioned mess.

My agent. My wonderful, wonderful agent Emily Glenister. I can't quite express the relief that comes from knowing you're just on the other end of a phone call when I need you. You're a beautiful person inside and out, and you share my love of Nashville which automatically makes you one of my favourite people.

I can't not mention the incredible team at Embla Books. My editor, Martina Arzu, came into this book with such infectious enthusiasm, and together with Emily Thomas you helped me to turn a collection of incoherent ideas into a book that I'm actually pretty proud of. Let's not forget my fantastic copy-editors Emma Wilson, Sandra Ferguson and Stephanie Carey, who not only dealt with my endless timeline mishaps (sorry!) but also pointed out when I had managed to change a main character's name halfway through the novel. Of course, there are so many other people on the Embla team who work tirelessly to bring these books to fruition, and I can't thank you all enough. Miracle workers, the lot of you.

A special shout-out to Crawley Waterstones. I don't know if anyone realises this, but authors get bloody terrified walking into a bookshop and asking if they'll stock their book. The team at Crawley Waterstones are so incredibly supportive to local authors and they all deserve a raise.

To the fantastic, wonderful people I work with at Jericho Writers. I still can't quite believe I get to not only write books for a living, but that I also get to help other people write books for a living. The fact that I can go into my one-to-one with my boss and spend half an hour chatting about the pains of developmental edits means that, at the end of a long week, I'm left with some semblance of sanity. Not a lot, but enough to get me by.

To my family. I always worry I'm going to annoy you by listing you in a particular order, and I know you'll wind me up whichever way I do it, so we'll go for a brain dump: My husband Sam (I don't actually hate men, despite what this book might lead you to think), my daughters Élise and Evie, Mum, Dad, Debs, Isaac, Molly, Grandad, Colette, Jonathan, Grace, Thalia, Elijah – also a special mention for my Grandma and dearly departed Grandad. I'm so glad I got to hold your hand one last time.

To Jasmine, Shelly, Ali, Pippa and Harry. It doesn't matter how much time goes between us seeing each other, it always feels like yesterday. Who says you don't get to keep the friends you had at school, eh?

To Sophie Flynn, Anna Burtt, Lauren North, Natali Simmonds, William Shaw, Jo Jakeman, Sarah Bonner, Eve Ainsworth, Philippa East, Nikki Smith, Talia Samuels and all the other authors I'm lucky enough to now call friends. You're all incredible.

And, my dear reader, to you. If this is the first of my books you've read, I promise you I'm not this dark and twisted in real life. If you've been with me since the start, just know you mean the absolute world to me. DM me, tweet me, come and say hi at events. I'll buy you a hot chocolate with extra marshmallows to say thank you.

About the Author

Becca Day lives in the middle of the woods in Surrey with her husband, daughters and cocker spaniel. She studied acting at Guildford College and went on to start her own Murder Mystery theatre troupe. It was this move that inspired her love of crime fiction, and when she sold the company she threw herself head first into crime writing. Aside from penning novels, she is also Head of Membership & Marketing for leading literary consultancy and writing community Jericho Writers, as well as director of the London Festival of Writing.

About Embla Books

Embla Books is a digital-first publisher of standout commercial adult fiction. Passionate about storytelling, the team at Embla publish books that will make you 'laugh, love, look over your shoulder and lose sleep'. Launched by Bonnier Books UK in 2021, the imprint is named after the first woman from the creation myth in Norse mythology, who was carved by the gods from a tree trunk found on the seashore – an image of the kind of creative work and crafting that writers do, and a symbol of how stories shape our lives.

Find out about some of our other books and stay in touch:

X, Facebook, Instagram: @emblabooks
Newsletter: https://bit.ly/emblanewsletter